ONLY THE MOON

A Short Story Collection

RAYMOND S FLEX

CONTENTS

WHILE YOU WERE SLEEPING

I

CHARLES FELT the welling of phlegm at the back of his throat. Those tickling sensations that he knew would bring on a cough at any moment. But he could hold it off. Just for another scratch of the quill.

Another word.

Another letter.

Another . . .

But it proved too much to bear.

He grasped for the pocket of his arch-shouldered, charcoal jacket and slipped out his handkerchief. He held the raggedy material up to cover his nose and mouth. He coughed until his chest ached, until he felt the blood bubbling up to his brain.

Removing him of sense.

And battering at his temples.

For a long moment, he sat, staring at the page. At those scribblings there. Those loopy letters, the uneven lines, and the inconclusive phrases.

Marionettes did little to stir the mind. Of that there, really, was not much doubt. What with them being made of wood. And of string. And of . . . whatever else.

He glanced up. Reclined in his round-backed, wooded chair. Rested his arm a moment. Tried to guard against the throbbing pulse at his throat. It jabbed so heavily. His dried-up sinuses left him with the taste of blood on the tongue.

When he breathed in, he only caught dust, drifting up into the stifling air of the muggy early-summer evening. He observed those grey, overcast skies outside. The ones which threatened to break out in storm at the drop of a pin, but which held off for the time being.

And it was then, feeling like he had nothing inside of him, that he was a mere husk to be whipped up and blown about the lightest of breezes, he was certain that someone was watching him.

He spun about in his chair, gazed off across the drawing room: past the overstuffed fainting couch—his father's acquisition earlier that summer—over the walnut floors—buffed to within an inch of their lives—and out to the doorway, where he caught sight of the dainty figure.

His cousin.

Lucinda.

He took in her darkened features, features which seemed appropriate given the weather which loomed about today, and which he would've thought she'd blend in with quite easily.

She wore a fair, white summer dress which reached down to the balls of her delicate ankles, and which seemed a shade or two lighter than her skin tone.

And several more tones lighter than her sable hair.

She smiled at him as she leaned up against the doorway, absent-mindedly toying with the frame, her dirtied fingernails ebbing in and out of the wood.

"How does it go, brother?" she said.

She often called him 'brother' throughout the day—a sort of a joke ever since she had been staying at the family home; ever since she had arrived a little earlier in the summer.

Come to stay here while her mother—Charles's aunt—recovered from a grave sickness.

Charles had a good knowledge of sickness, and how it had left him not more than a year before. And so she had his sympathy. She could call him 'brother' if she wished.

Charles turned back to the paper before him, to those scribblings there. For the marionette show that he had planned. And which, though he wouldn't admit aloud, had him thoroughly beaten for the time being.

Only did he realise he had lost himself in the scrawled black marks when he felt the warm breath of Lucinda up against his arm.

He slipped her a sidelong glance, a smile peeling back his lips.

Though he felt that he was no longer a child, now that he had passed his eighteenth birthday, he couldn't help that deeply held sympathy of his . . . the one which gripped him so far into his soul that he wondered if he'd *ever* be able to let go of it completely.

"Haven't you anyone to play with?" Charles said.

Lucinda shook her head. And then glanced over the page.

Almost as soon as she had arrived to the house, Charles had noticed that she could barely read. And he wondered what other matters her sickly mother had neglected to see to.

Lucinda screwed up her eyes as she attempted to decipher the page lying there, on the desk. When she gave up, she met his eyes with her own and said, "What does it say?"

Charles smiled wider. "Well, it is a story—not finished yet," he added quickly, almost defensively, as if his little cousin—surely no older than nine or ten—might wish to critique him.

He cleared his throat, realised that he still held his handkerchief bundled in his fist, and then he replaced it in the pocket of his jacket.

It was funny how, when he was around others, he didn't have so many urges to break out in coughing fits. Perhaps it had something to do with speaking.

Maybe he should try speaking along as he wrote.

That might solve his issue . . . if his father didn't come to think that he was a madman, muttering to himself in darkened rooms.

Charles did his best to explain the story of the marionettes: the baker, and his wife, and their children, to describe the comedy he had devised and how it should come across to the puppeteer.

Lucinda listened with a pout, her head cocked to one side.

He wished to explain further.

To understand if *really* she fathomed his meaning.

It was only as he caught sight of the clock, saw that twenty minutes had passed, that he realised Lucinda was staring hard at him. And he took the cue to stop.

Lucinda drew that quick breath of hers, hardly billowing her cheeks to do so, and she said, "Uncle says that supper is ready."

Charles stood up smartly.

Realised that he'd frittered away time.

That his father would be waiting.

Charles examined the looking glass on the other side of the drawing room, smoothed the creases out of his jacket, and then set off at once, hearing the *pitter-patter* of Lucinda's bare feet following at his heels like a faithful dog.

Yes, just like his own faithful little mongrel.

Following him about *everywhere* he went.

2

C HARLES ONLY REALISED it had gone dark outside when he proceeded on towards the dining room and saw the candlelight glare creeping out around the doorframe. He paused for a couple of moments, several paces before the doorway, as he always did before a meeting with his father.

Just a moment to compose himself.

To keep himself from simmering over, as these meetings, no matter how innocuous, were wont to do.

When he looked about himself, he saw that Lucinda had gone.

That she had simply wandered off.

He cleared his throat, checked his handkerchief, and then rounded the doorway and entered the dining room.

His father sat at the head of the polished, ten-seat oak dining table, as always. He wore his napkin burrowed into his upturned collar and he was already slicing up his trout:

His favourite dish.

His small, circular glasses sat perched almost on the nib of his nose and he did not look up when Charles took his place beside him.

These days had been difficult.

Just himself and his father about the house.

His mother on a visit.

Sometimes Charles wondered if he really was his father's son, or if there might be some unsayable scandal in the family.

Charles took his place opposite his father. When he sat, there were a good few places between the two of them, not to mention the flickering candles.

Charles gazed down at his plate of trout.

He couldn't stand fish.

Couldn't get past the smell of it . . . that slick, slimy way that it seemed to weave a rotten stench in with the butter . . . and he could hardly get himself started on the thought of the dried-out texture.

That, perhaps, was the worst part.

But, like a veteran soldier, he took up his silver cutlery and stared down at his trout lying there, on his plate. A few boiled potatoes off to one side. A slab of already melted butter perched on top.

The only sound which broke the silence between himself and his father was the gentle *clink-clink* of his father's cutlery on his porcelain plate.

Charles drew in a thick breath, trying to ward off that tickling sensation at the back of his throat, and he set about the loathsome task of slicing up his trout.

He'd just about inserted the prongs of his fork into the poor, *dead* animal's neck when his father spoke up. "Didn't hear the dinner bell, then?" his father said.

Charles glanced across the table to his father. Saw that his father remained concentrated on the plate before him. A neutral expression fixed on his face.

"No, Father," Charles said, speaking truthfully.

His father flashed his severe eyebrows a moment and, still facing down into his plate, he munched pensively on his fish. "I shall have to ask Mr Gibbs to find a larger one."

Charles didn't rise to the bait. He knew that it would only mean trouble . . . and then they would get into *that* old discussion all over again, that discussion of religion . . . and it was worth his best efforts to keep himself from tumbling down *that* rabbit hole.

Charles managed to raise a half smile and then he picked on through his dinner, taking care not to make too much of a sound, not to make some sort of a clumsy error . . . not to allow either his knife or fork to land on his plate with a stomach-jangling *clang!*

Gladly, for Charles, the rest of dinner passed in silence, and it was only when Mr Gibbs brought in his father's pipe and tobacco, that Charles could really allow himself to relax just a little.

Soon he would be out of this dining room.

Back to his desk.

Continuing to work at that *damn* marionette play.

Just like always, Mr Gibbs offered Charles a pipe and, like always, he refused.

When Charles looked up, he saw his father giving him that same disapproving glare, the one that told him that he was a disappointment.

Weak.

Not even strong enough to smoke a pipe, though his father often claimed it would do wonders for his cough—give him strength in fact.

But Charles was quite happy without a pipe. For the time being, anyway. He wished to put off adulthood just as long as might be humanly possible.

Charles was on the cusp of asking permission from his father to leave the table when, with a puff of bluish smoke over the flickering candlelight, his father spoke to him.

"How is that diversion of yours going?" his father said.

Though Charles managed to keep his expression neutral—years of patiently-won practice had gifted him *that* ability—he did feel just about every muscle in his body lock up. All his nerves get all twitchy. His heart skitter at his tonsils.

Charles cleared his throat. Resisted the urge to reach for his handkerchief.

His father always disapproved of Charles coughing in his company.

As if it was a show of weakness.

An *insult* to his parenthood.

"Oh," Charles said, attempting to keep his voice unaffected, and clinical, "it is going just fine, Father."

His father puffed another couple of times on his pipe. Flashed a glance over the tops of his glasses, and then said, "Your mother should be arriving back home tomorrow."

Charles had been waiting for this moment for the longest time . . . been desperately *wishing* for his mother to return, and so relinquish the pressure that, no doubt, both he and his father felt.

It sounded almost too good to be true.

Charles waited out another few beats of his heart, trying to ascertain whether or not his father might have something else to add, and seeing that, apparently, he didn't, Charles took the opportunity to lever himself up out of his chair and make for the door.

In the doorway, Charles put on a smile. Did his best to pin it to his cheeks. "Sleep well, Father," he said, and then he took a step.

A step closer to his desk.

To his work.

To the play.

But, right at the last moment, his father called him back.

Charles glanced back to the head of the table, to his father sitting there, the pipe prodded between his thick, violet lips, his left palm supporting the bowl. "You, uh," his father began, "you haven't been seeing any more of these . . . these *visions?*"

Charles felt his heart clench tight. His gut gave a rumble despite him filling it with trout not ten minutes earlier . . . or perhaps it was *because* he'd filled it with trout.

He knew what his father was talking about.

Knew that he was talking about Lucinda.

His father didn't understand, not really . . . of course he didn't . . . how could he?

The way that his father saw things, there was lightness and

darkness, and this fell very much to the devil's side, and it was an unfixable fault.

Though Charles knew that he would hurt his father, he also knew that there was no other option. He gave a dry-throated, "Yes," and then waited for his father's response.

His father seemed to lose himself to a spot in mid-air, right before his nose, and then, with an almost imperceptible nod, he appeared to dismiss Charles.

And Charles took his chance.

3

CHARLES SAT ALONE. Only a flickering candle for company. He could sense her behind him. Could sense *Lucinda* behind him. She was here with him now, just as she had been for the whole of the summer. Following him about. Keeping him company.

Was it true that she could be a mere fantasy?

. . . Was there really anything much wrong with *that?*

Though he knew that his father didn't account for dreaming —*refused* to abide by it—Charles knew that he was very different. He might consider himself more alike to his mother if only he had known her a little better, if only his father's monotone didn't thrust her voice downwards; bury it deeply enough to make it unintelligible.

Charles scratched away at the page. Not really knowing. Not really having a purpose in mind. Except for the 'diversion' . . . as his father had put it.

He preferred the unreal to the real, he found he could control it much better, enjoyed the feel of his hands, just like those of the puppeteers, on the strings, dragging the tiny, wooden figures about, making them dance out to their own whim.

The grandfather clock chiming midnight, over in the corner of the drawing room, almost succeeded in giving Charles a heart attack. He straightened up in his chair. He rubbed his aching eyes. And he glanced back, back to Lucinda as she watched him from the fainting couch.

She wore the same white summer dress, and her feet didn't quite touch the floor, so she swung them back and forth gently bringing them to knock up against the base of the couch, with a gentle *thump, thump . . . thump, thump . . .*

Charles could feel his mind ebbing away from him. Could feel the tug of unconsciousness at the pits of his eyes, and he knew that he would soon have to give in.

But he wished to finish.

He *had* to finish the play.

He had promised himself that it would be done when his mother returned, so that he might show her, show her that he really wasn't like his father at all, that he had something *different* inside of him . . . or perhaps it would show her the opposite, that he, really, was more like his father than he could ever imagine.

With a heavy heart, Charles raised himself up out of his chair, made his way over to the fainting couch.

Lucinda shovelled herself out of his way, propped herself up against one of the arms.

First Charles allowed his arm to reach the back of the couch, to flex out there, and then he brought his feet up onto the couch too. Onto the material. And he allowed himself a long, *frustrated* sigh . . . he waited out the ticks of his heart, and felt the irresistible urge to close his eyelids, just for a moment, just for a matter of seconds, just to rest, and to . . .

4

S UNLIGHT REDDENED the backs of Charles's eyelids. His
limbs felt unwieldy. Heavy. And his heart was like a stone
within his chest. He could taste the stale fish still on his tongue.
And he could smell the sickening odour of the polish on the floors
surrounding him.

One of the house staff had been in here, this *morning*, to take
care of the cleaning in anticipation for the arrival of Charles's
mother later that day.

When Charles glanced down at himself, he noted the blanket
which was drawn up to his chest, knew that it must've been Mr
Gibbs who'd tucked him in, hadn't seen reason to disturb him.

But it was only when he heard Lucinda's light voice near his left
ear, felt the warmth of her breath, that he really knew he
was awake.

Charles startled just a little. He straightened on the fainting
couch. Propped himself up into a sitting position. He took in
Lucinda: her black hair shimmering lightly in the morning sunlight.
He blinked the sleep from his eyes. Dug out the grains of sand in
the corners of his eyes, those little reminders of the night before.

Outside now he heard a distant *clickety-clack*.

The wheels . . . wheels of a carriage . . . his *mother's* carriage.

On instinct, Charles glanced off over to the desk, to his work,
lying there.

Face up.

Those scrawlings . . . the scribbled-out letters, and the . . . *dear
God!* . . . he hadn't thought to finish his work . . . he had merely, well,
he had . . . *fallen* asleep here, just gone and drifted off.

He looked back to Lucinda, saw that she wore a faint smile on
her pale-pink lips, and that she had words on her tongue.

"I finished it," she said, "while you were sleeping."

Charles couldn't quite comprehend what Lucinda told him. For a few seconds it was impossible—a total impossibility.

He gazed over at the desk.

To the pages there.

Written out in *his* hand.

He rocked himself up off the fainting couch, padded on over to his desk, still wearing his shoes from the night before.

He leafed through the pages.

. . . Yes, several of them . . . many—*many*—more than he had written the night before . . . or at least that he could *remember* having written the night before.

He looked about him.

Looked for Lucinda.

But she wasn't there.

She was gone from his side.

And, in the distance of the waking house, he heard the *clickety-clack* of the carriage wheels popping in and out of the cobblestones of the street outside; the *clopping* of hooves and he knew she was here, that his mother would be back home shortly.

As if in confirmation of this, he heard the smart *slap* of shoes growing louder down the corridor, coming towards the drawing room. And Charles was just in time to see Mr Gibbs there, flaw-lessly presented, like always, and wearing that pert, half-smile of his.

"Your mother, Master Dodgson, she has arrived."

Though Charles felt a rippling numbness all over, he managed to get the words out. "Thank you . . . thank you, Mr Gibbs."

Mr Gibbs left him.

Charles turned his attention back to those pages. To the pages in his hand. To the many—*many*—pages there. All ready for him to show to his mother.

To show her his imagination.

His *inspiration*.

His dreams.

He looked about, tried to seek out Lucinda—*to thank her!*—but she was nowhere to be seen. She had left him for the time being.

He was all alone now . . . just as he had been while he'd slept.

KINGDOMS

BENEDETTA COULD FEEL nothing but space. Opening out before her. An *ungodly* chill up against her swan-feather smooth skin. Her heart throbbed slow and regular, almost as if it hadn't got around to realising how much trouble she might be in.

Trouble?

Benedetta flexed her mind a little further.

Yes, trouble.

When she breathed in now, she could no longer feel the constant pressure of the bodice up against her bust. She had to admit that that was something of a mercy. She only ever got that sort of pleasure at the end of each day when she could take her bodice off—alone in her room, at the top of the tower, the door well and truly locked and the curtains drawn down over the single, large window which looked out over the Royal grounds.

Her *father's* grounds.

But she wasn't there right now.

She was somewhere else.

Only when Benedetta thought to open her eyes, did she realise that they were *already* open. But there was only darkness. Nothing but darkness. Closing in all around. She might've had reason to feel somewhat taken aback, but the fact of the matter was that she had a sure, firm floor beneath her feet.

Cobblestones?

Boulders?

Something hard.

Something unmoving.

She held herself still in the darkness, doing her best to make out some sort of a shape. Something which she might recognise. And yet . . . and yet . . . her mind seemed to just get away from her. It seemed to play tricks with all her senses.

Almost, at the back of her head, she could smell those buttery odours of the turkey basting which her father's chefs had been putting the finishing touches to down in the castle kitchens. She could still taste the leaf of mint she had been sucking on, using to stay awake, to stop her drifting away before the night's ball.

The ball which she had been supposed to attend.

But which was gone now.

Now that she was here.

In the darkness.

She focussed in hard on her surroundings, hoping to hear some-thing—*anything* at all—but there wasn't even silence, which was to say, those sounds which everybody would term 'silence': the half-distant *creaking* of floorboards, or the *whine* of unoiled hinges, the stirring of horses in their stables, and the muffled barks of the huntsman's dogs which ran wild about the castle grounds.

No, there was no silence.

There was, quite simply, nothing at all.

Benedetta might've stood there for hours. It might've been days.

Weeks?

Years?

. . . All frames of reference left her. She was rendered disorien-tated, unable to fix her attention onto anything at all. Not even the past. The past . . . her memory, even, appeared to be slipping away from her mind's eye.

Gone forever.

As if it never even existed.

And it was then, right when she felt closest to her wit's end, that she heard the voice.

A feminine voice.

Inside her mind.

— *Is there somebody there?*

Benedetta felt her chest tighten. Her breath came in short bursts . . . it was almost like her handmaiden had managed to get her into her bodice again. She recalled all those stories, back in the castle, of hearing voices within your own head. All those links to craziness. All those madmen which her father would have sent to the city dungeons. She had never believed that *she*—of all people, and so finely bred—would hear those same voices within her own mind.

But there it was.

Should she reply?

Before she got a chance, another voice—*distinct*—sparked up within her mind.

Another female voice.

— *Yes, I'm here.*

All of a sudden, Benedetta felt like she was somehow eavesdropping on a conversation she had no intention of listening into . . . and, anyway, just where *were* those voices coming from? She couldn't see anybody surrounding her. Nobody before her eyes.

Where else *could* they come from *but* from within her own mind?

— *Are we . . . in heaven?*

— *I'm not sure.*

Benedetta's mind felt like it was a tightly squeezed sponge.

More than anything she wanted to know the answer to those questions . . . and she supposed that if she just stood back here and listened, then she might have her answer.

The conversation went on.

This time with a third voice joining.

— *It's awfully barren here, isn't it?*

And then a fourth:

— Not quite what I'd been led to believe.

There was a long pause within Benedetta's mind, which was quite weird when she got a chance to think about it. She was used to *not* thinking at all. That was what her handmaiden was always scolding her for. There must've been dozens of times when Mrs Ravanelli had happened upon Benedetta gazing pensively out of some turret window. And Mrs Ravanelli would scold Benedetta until she would turn her focus onto some more 'relevant' detail, which, according to Mrs Ravanelli, normally encompassed picking out a dress for the evening's ball, or going down to the kitchen to taste the basting for the turkey.

Tasks that required no thought.

Only *feeling*.

She tuned back into her surroundings.

The out-of-body conversation happening about her.

The first voice was speaking again.

And she was beginning to be able to separate their identities in her mind. But not without a little help from the potted introductions each member of the conversation was pitching in Benedetta's —otherwise silent—mind.

— Well, I am The Princess Gwen of Gwynock, daughter of the great King Glyn, the ruler and master of all rolling, green hills.

— And I Maid Adélaïde, daughter of Lord Eric, the tamer of snow-capped mountains, and frozen valleys of Tallilee.

— I am Lady Faiga of Saxonburg, daughter of Earl Heinrich, tormentor of the odious peasant rebels, and the vanquisher of all evil.

— As for myself? I am Princess Juana, daughter of King Oscar, warrior, sea-farer and bringer of good fortunes to the whole of the glorious kingdom of Ernetza.

There was a longer pause from within Benedetta's mind and she couldn't help wondering if they were all waiting for her. If they actually realised she was here. She wondered if she might've gone blind, and that she was the only one among the other *noble* ladies who was unable to see . . . but then she reminded herself that they had all made comments along the lines of being unable to see the air before their eyes. Was something parting before Benedetta? Or was it just her imagination?

Yes, most likely it *was* just her imagination.

The thick veil of white mist showed no sign of thinning.

When the women spoke again into her mind, she found she could now separate their identities:

Princess Gwen of Gwynock: *Forgive me if this might sound somewhat odd, but I find that I am able to sense . . . someone else . . . a presence?*

Lady Faiga of Saxonburg: *Yes, another here. Among us.*

Princess Juana: *I sense this also.*

Maid Adélaïde: *Won't they speak? Do they speak?*

Benedetta felt a strange stirring at the base of her stomach. Her heart throbbed in her throat. She did feel something of an intruder here, and yet, at the same time, she couldn't help but feel that there was no way out. That it wasn't a simple matter of getting up and leaving this conversation behind. Wherever she was now . . . whatever this *white* space was which surrounded her . . . she was very much stuck here. So she decided to try herself out with this conversation going off in her mind:

Queen Benedetta: *Uh, I am the Honourable, and Noble, Queen of Perezia.*

There was something approaching a gaping sigh within Benedetta's mind.

She wondered if somebody else was going to put something in.

In the silence, she had a chance to think about what it was the others had said. And—*damn her wandering mind!*—she had been unable to stop herself from scanning all those titles the other women had reeled through. Processing them on a subconscious level. Piling up the pyramid of hierarchy in her mind. The first to speak once Benedetta had spoken was Princess Gwen:

Princess Gwen: *Your Majesty, I truly had no idea, I . . .*

Maid Adélaïde: *Please, Your Majesty accept my most humble apologies, if I had only known I would have . . .*

Princess Juana: *And I too beg your forgiveness, because it is such a grave sin not to acknowledge those crowned by god, even in this place, in this . . . this . . .*

Lady Faiga: *My apologies, I pray you shall accept, Your Majesty, and should we pass from this world onto the next, you may depend on me as your faithful servant.*

Benedetta was somewhat taken aback. Of course, what the others all said was true enough, and in her early days as queen, she had started to get used to all of this odd, *awed* behaviour of those of lower standing. But here, now that they were *here*—in this place—it seemed somewhat odd to have the same reverence surround her.

Princess Gwen: *Your Highness?*

Queen Benedetta: *Yes?*

Princess Gwen: *Would Your Majesty wish to speculate as to what this place we now occupy might represent? What it might mean that we five find ourselves here?*

Benedetta thought on this for a few moments. She knew there had to be *some* explanation. And yet she really couldn't quite bring her mind to give her any sort of satisfactory explanation.

Heaven?

Hell?

. . . Somewhere else?

Certainly, she had no recollection of dying . . . but there, that might be a decent enough start, for her to think just what she had been doing.

What was her *last* memory?

What was the *final* thing she remembered?

She thought hard on this.

From her best bet, she could recall taking a stroll through the castle courtyards. She remembered how she had been a touch tired, and hardly stirred by the coffee which she had taken that morning at breakfast. She had spent a long night fending off her husband—the *King's*—unwarranted advances into her own quarters. She had just finished up reading through the last volume of a quite tiresome history of Perezia. She had believed, somewhat naively, that since she had married into the kingdom, she should learn to understand something of its past.

But the history had been just like all the others.

One 'glorious' battle followed the next, just another notch on the bedpost for Good as it triumphed over Evil. And there was far too much mention of noble deeds in combat, the conquering of foreign maidens—she had learned *that one* first hand—and the general utilisation, or 'stirring of affection within', the peasant classes for her tastes as they accepted their 'true' and 'just' rulers. Of course, as her mother had always instructed her, in those late-night chats when all the men had drunk themselves into a stupor, and the castle staff buzzed about them clearing up for breakfast, Benedetta had made sure to complete her responsibility as a newly-wed queen, consummating the marriage. But that first experience had left little appetite for a second round.

Hence Benedetta doing her best to evade her husband at every opportunity.

And, all things considered, she had been giving the whole effort a good shake until *that* fateful night. In the end, she had sort of lodged the *Glorious and Noble History of Perezia* in between her and the king's genitals, where it had acted as a more-than-adequate makeshift chastity belt.

That morning—following the night before—she had been strolling through the courtyard. That was right. That was what she'd been doing. She had been minding her own business, in her flowing, turquoise morning robe, her pointy hat and veil perched on top of her sleek, sable hair, her mind on anything else other than the kingdom, or the king, or the real world.

And that had been when she'd seen him.

Tending to the horses.

Had he . . . yes, he must've been a sort of stable boy . . . perhaps a few years her junior, and with blond hair which gleamed like golden thread, and cheeks slightly reddened by the morning sun. He had had bristling muscles—so unlike the king's frumpy, sagging body. When he finished tending to the horses' hooves, he stood straight-backed and upright, and dabbed at the slight layer of sweat which had formed on his forehead with the sleeve of his tunic.

That was it . . . the *last* memory . . . the *final* memory which she had.

And then she had ended up here.

Thinking quickly now, she turned her mind to the other ladies which occupied this same plane—whichever *plane* that happened to be—and she put a theory to them.

2

E ACH LADY had her own story.

And each, in its own way, dealt with some sort of infraction.

Some sort of a betrayal of training.

Of all the hard work put in over the many—*many*—years.

By tutors, and mothers, and grandmothers.

All those lessons which had been so deeply ingrained into Benedetta that she almost fancied they flowed through her veins as easily as blood.

She had had her 'fling' with the stable boy, or whatever it had meant by her simply *looking* . . . at the same time, Princess Gwen had arranged a midnight meeting with a rather fetching member of her father's barracks. For Lady Faiga it had been a woodsman. Maid Adélaïde had dared cast a sordid look at the head oarsman of her father's boat. Princess Juana had come a cropper when she'd taken an early-morning visit down to the kitchen, only to find one of the younger porters washing himself in a wooden tub.

Soapy suds *everywhere*.

Yes, it seemed that Benedetta was getting to the bottom of this whole situation.

If not seeing the *how?* then at least making inroads into the *why?*

She wondered if this sort of level of intuition might have something to do with her newly gained powers of queendom . . . and she, for one, embraced this chance since, up till now, her powers of queendom had only really extended to giving advice on frivolous matters about the castle or resisting unsolicited advances from her husband, the king.

Queen Benedetta, now feeling somewhat humbled by the attention of her lower-ranked sisters, decided that it was time for her to take charge:

Queen Benedetta: *The question as I see it now is: How do we go back?*

Princess Gwen: *If you will excuse my imprudence, Your Majesty, but should the question not be more along the lines of: Do we wish to go back?*

Queen Benedetta had to admit that she quite liked these voices in her head.

Could voices in her head really be all that bad?

3

WITH ONE PIECE OF THE PUZZLE all slotted into place, Queen Benedetta led the other ladies' attempts to find their way out of this place, off out of this 'kingdom', for want of a better word.

They'd all attempted to shuffle through the white mists, to somehow come across one another, see if they couldn't find a way of interacting on a physical level, but, after much trying, it seemed that it was quite simply a nonstarter. Taking steps in any direction, for any of the ladies, was simply a matter of striding along the —*thankfully firm*—ground and into *yet more* white, impenetrable mists. Not so much as the volume of the voices within Benedetta's mind shifted when she took a step here, there, or—*really* —anywhere.

The only reason she managed to make any progress at all was really the result of an accident . . . albeit a happy one.

As she stepped into the void, she couldn't help her mind getting away from her. Just for a second.

But that was all it took.

She found herself, for some reason, imagining her old bedroom, back at her father's castle. In her mind's eye, she had freeze-framed the room to when she'd been about fifteen or sixteen years old. She had her four-poster bed, the silky, semi-transparent curtains, and the scent of honeysuckle floating on in through the window.

Just like she remembered.

And it was just like that when she realised that the world was building itself about her. That whatever she thought inside of her mind came into being before her eyes.

When she reached out now, she felt her soft fingertips coming into contact with cool stone. She felt its smooth shape up against her skin.

And as she breathed in, she caught a heavier scent of the honeysuckle. She had to admit that she was quite glad for this ability . . . however she had managed to make it come about. She spoke to the other girls within her mind, but, for some reason, could now not make any sort of contact. As she brought her bedroom out from her imagination: the large, panoramic stone pillars, and the dainty window boxes she had always admired, she couldn't help but forget all about the girls.

They'd only just met, after all.

And here Benedetta was building her own world!

Soon enough, the whole of her bedroom, as she'd seen it within her imagination, was spread out before her. The room was even complete with the view out the window, of the rolling green hills.

The chattering of birdsong drifted in through the window too.

A little further in the distance, almost lost in the mauve haze of the afternoon, she could just about make out the snow-capped mountains.

When she glanced down to the rug which lay at the foot of the bed, she saw that her puppy Dario was there. All curled up in a ball of black, curly hair. It was the dog who her father claimed had run away, but which Benedetta secretly believed had been stomped by a horse, or something.

Her father had always gone out of his way not to upset her.

Except when it came to marriage, that was.

When Benedetta took a step forward, she noticed the tear snaking its path down her cheek. It felt warm, and smelled a little salty. She reached up and wiped it away.

Only then did she realise she was smiling.

From ear to ear.

She took another few steps forward and then crouched down to Dario. She roused him with a gentle stroke along his puppy spine. Dario glanced up at her, and then, with a wag of his fledgling tail, and his pink tongue lolling out from between his puppy lips, he launched himself at her.

She took him in her arms, and cuddled him to her chest.

Now the tears were rolling down her cheeks and there was—seemingly—nothing she could do to stop them.

She only raised her head back up to the 'real' world when she heard somebody calling out her name, or, well, calling out her name *and* her title.

"Queen Benedetta?"

She turned on her heel. She looked to the sturdy, oaken door of her bedroom, almost expecting it to already be thrown open. But it remained in its place. Nobody had thought to bustle on in.

Slowly, and hoping that her tears might dry in the meantime, she approached the door, still with Dario clasped firmly to her chest. She opened up and peered out into the stone corridor. It was just as she remembered it being from her childhood days: the tapestries hanging down, the suit of armour at the end of the corridor—sunlight glinting off its metal.

Benedetta heard her name called again.

Once more.

The voice seemed to be getting louder.

She took only a couple of steps before she came face to face with a girl she had never seen before.

The girl wore an emerald green gown with a neat, box-shaped hat perched on her head. The veil—*also green*—had been thrown back over her shoulder, and she was grinning all over, her peachy, clean skin glimmering in the afternoon sun. The girl seemed to remember herself. She dialled her smile down a couple of notches and then curtseyed. Benedetta gave her a nod of acknowledgement, and then the girl said, "Queen Benedetta, it's just like I imagined it —just like I thought in my mind!"

"What?" Benedetta said, seeing the girl bounce about before her.

The girl couldn't have been much older than sixteen, or seventeen.

And there was something familiar about her voice.

Familiar from *before* . . .

But she had no chance of tracing her mind back before the girl seized hold of her hand and dragged her along the corridor.

Benedetta kept her other hand to squeeze Dario to her breast.

Dario, despite all this drama, had drifted back off to sleep in her arms.

As the girl dragged her around the corner of the corridor, Benedetta suddenly found herself confronted with an entirely different scene. The stone was replaced with wooden panelling. And the day outside—*even*—was shifted from the warm, afternoon, summer's day which she had so lovingly created within her mind.

Fireplaces crackled with enormous flames.

She could feel the warmth coming in waves.

Bringing her out in a flush.

She turned her attention back to the girl.

Realised who she was.

She squared her voice with the one she'd heard in her head back in the void.

Princess Gwen of Gwynock.

That was who she was.

Princess Gwen continued to grin to herself, showing off her bright-white teeth—teeth which reminded Benedetta of her own youth . . . although, at twenty, Benedetta supposed that she shouldn't think of herself as an old maid just yet.

"Isn't it wonderful?" Princess Gwen asked.

Benedetta realised that she was smiling too. She glanced about her, deciding that this must represent something like what Princess Gwen had imagined within her own mind, back in the void.

And now it had come true.

But Benedetta had questions.

So many questions.

As she turned to Gwen, she couldn't help herself saying, "I don't understand how it's possible—how we have ended up in the same castle."

Gwen hunched her shoulders. Her grip on Benedetta's hand seized tighter still. "*He* can explain," she said, turning away, leading her onward through her own imaginings, "this way!"

Benedetta found herself being tugged along.

Across the plush, wooden floorboards, and toward the darkened archway ahead.

As they passed through the archway, Benedetta found herself saying, "The others—uh, the other girls?"

"This way! This way!"

And, sure enough, Benedetta found Princess Juana, Lady Faiga and Maid Adélaïde; each of them with their own rendering of their memories—their own personal wing of a castle, if Benedetta thought of it that way. It seemed that the other girls were just as bemused as Benedetta was, and they were all swept along in Gwen's wake as she was—*apparently*—taking them to go see 'he' who would explain.

Gwen let go of Benedetta's hand when they reached a spiral staircase so that she might be able to hitch up her skirt. And then —just like that—all five of them climbed the stairs.

4

ROUND AND ROUND THEY WENT. And all the time Dario remained asleep in Benedetta's arms. Apparently he was untouched by the ever-increasing nausea that was taking hold of her own gut. Benedetta had never been the greatest when it came to clambering up things in a spiralling motion. She had never had a head for heights, either, which was most unfortunate seeing as, every time she glanced out the window, she was greeted with a *very long way down indeed* to the ground.

But Benedetta told herself to trust in Gwen.

She'd already gone *this* far.

And she would rather like some kind of assurance as to just what'd gone on here.

Not before time, they reached the upper platform of the tower, and Benedetta found herself more or less on solid ground. 'More or less' because there were still a whole bunch of windows looking down from the—*not inconsiderable*—height.

Gwen, though, seemed untouched by the altitude. She led them all up to the heavy wooden door.

Benedetta couldn't help noticing how there were several chunks of wood missing about the door, as if some rodent had been gnawing away at the edges, and she couldn't help wondering that it must kick up a hell of a draught there. She also caught herself wondering how in *her* castle such conditions would not be allowed to prevail . . . but then she reminded herself that this wasn't *just* her castle . . . all these other girls shared it with her.

Gwen rapped her knuckles twice against the door, and there was a muffled answer from within. Although Benedetta couldn't quite tell whether or not it was in the affirmative, Gwen seemed encouraged enough to plough onward. And, before long, the five girls all stood within the room at the top of the tower. All of them standing about a withered, bearded, grey-haired man of—*surely*—eighty or more who was scrawling away at a seemingly never-ending piece of parchment with a quill and a pot of black ink.

He made no reaction to the girls standing in the room with him, and Benedetta couldn't shake the feeling that they might be imposing. But she held herself still, allowing herself to be a mere observer as Gwen trod over to the man and tapped him lightly on the shoulder. "Um," Gwen said, "Excuse me?"

The man flinched. He raised his arms as if one of them might wish to strike him on his birdlike, fragile scalp. His quick, light-blue eyes danced about their sockets, taking in the whole scene. And, only then, did he seem to collect himself together.

To get over whatever fear it was which possessed him.

"*Ah,*" the man said, "yes."

He sounded somewhat distracted. He briefly turned his attention back to the parchment, made a couple of scratches, and then dropped the quill into the pot of ink.

Gwen glanced to Benedetta, but Benedetta could tell that her words were meant to be heard by all five of them. "I caught him in my room, when I arrived here. He was painting the twirls onto my bed with this slick, silver paint. Just how I imagined them. He told me to come and find him here, in the tower, when I was ready. When all of us were ready."

The crotchety man—who Benedetta now saw wore beige rags, and nothing on his feet—rolled up the parchment he'd been working on till a moment ago and slotted it into a whole shelf chocked full of folios and quartos. Then, and only then, he bunched his fingers into fists and pressed them to his hips. He looked over the five women, lips pressed together, and, from what Benedetta noted, a very *particular* shade of mauve. "So, you're the troublemakers?"

" 'Troublemakers' ?" Benedetta put in, feeling that she was the spokeswoman of the group—no matter that Gwen had been the one to bring them before the man.

"Hmm," the man said, squeezing his eyes shut as if he was appraising a series of finely cut diamonds, *"Troublemakers."*

With that final remark, the man busied himself about his shelves. He got down on his hands and knees and then—from some position down on the shelf where Benedetta couldn't see—he produced an enormous tome. When he snatched it up, she was convinced the man would wilt beneath its weight. But, somehow, against all odds, he clung onto it, lugged it across the room and then let it slip through his fingers where it landed with a loud *thump!* on his tiny, slanted desk.

Before anybody could make another sound, the man started into flipping through pages. He held a finger in the air as if to ward off any attempt at conversation. He continued to flip through the book, apparently wrapped up in his scanning before he came to a halt.

Brought his finger down with a wild stab.

"There!" he said, turning back around to look at the women, his eyes ablaze with either rage or joy—Benedetta couldn't tell which.

She tried to steal a glance over the man's shoulder, but what she could make out of the text was in a language which she couldn't identify, let alone understand. " 'There' what?"

The man's eyes, again, moved over them swiftly. "Women," he said, as if this should help out understanding, "You're all *bad* women."

When his eyes left her, she couldn't help but feel her mouth turning up at the corners. A smile threatening to break out on her lips. When she glanced about the other women, she realised that they were close to grinning too . . . whenever the man wasn't looking right at them.

The man shook his head, and turned back to the book. "Had to take you all out—had to toss you all *away*." He slipped into mumbling something incomprehensible.

"I'm sorry?" Benedetta said.

The man continued to mouth along something from one of the lines of his book, and then he looked back at her irritably. "I *said*, that some people just don't know how to do what they're told."

She was a little taken aback by this comment. "What do you mean?"

He threw up his hands. "I *created* you, don't you understand that?" He breathed in deeply and then sighed out—all over the book. "But you started thinking for yourself, all those little '*forays*' "—he made bunny ears as he said this—"all those little fantasies." He shook his head and looked back at the book, a touch dejectedly. "Going off on your *own*."

She blinked a few times and then looked about the other girls. Like her, they were stumped by this all. She turned her attention back to the man. "What do you mean you created us?"

The man scratched his scalp and continued to peel back the pages. "I'm a writer mage. Can magic tales together, can't I?"

"Obviously."

He continued, "Only thing is that I sometimes have trouble keeping my creations under control." This time he glanced back at them, his glower now fading, and becoming somewhat defeated. "Like now."

"Sorry."

The man waved his hand as if it was nothing. "Fine, fine."

There was a long silence and then he turned around, looked the five girls over, and then said, with a touch of impatience, "Anything else I can be doing for you?"

No reply.

Benedetta again decided to speak up. "So, this is where we are now? We're here, in this castle, in these places that we've made ourselves?"

"Uh huh," he said, now back to his book, reaching for his quill to alter something within the text.

"Forever?"

He glanced back at her over his shoulder. He narrowed his eyes a touch. "For as long as you can imagine."

That sounded long enough to her so she took this as her cue to lead the other girls back down the spiral staircase, to ground level, where she felt much more at home.

For a little while the girls just all stood at the bottom of the steps.

All of them speechless.

"So," Benedetta said, feeling a hop of jubilation in her voice, "guess that it's all up to us now, then? We can do whatever we wish here—imagine whatever we wish here?"

"Seems like it," Gwen said.

There was a whole lot of glances exchanged.

Not to mention more silence.

And then, as if they'd reached a mutual agreement ahead of time, they all spontaneously broke away, heading to their own part of the castle. The parts of the castle that they'd created with their own imagination.

As Benedetta lay back on the four-poster bed she'd created, she couldn't help but feel a stirring at the base of her chest. Some sort of a warmth. Something which accompanied *thoughts* . . . all those *thoughts* . . . all those *repressed* thoughts from throughout her life.

And now—*now*—she could make them all take form.

She could really have some fun.

CRUMBLE

I N THE END Helen supposed it didn't really matter all that
much. Their marriage was over and that was all there was to it.
She walked along the street, taking in the neatly trimmed bushes,
the even more neatly trimmed lawns and she thought about how
she and Dwayne might well have lived in a suburb such as this one.

One day, though, that dream was gone.

Her steel-capped boots weighed down every step she took as
she listened to the faint stomp of her heel, the rustle of keys in her
pocket, and tried her best to put her personal issues behind her.

She had a long hard day ahead and it was best to keep her mind
free of distractions.

As she drew closer to the large temporary wooden gate up
ahead, with its peeling white paint and bright safety signs pinned up
on it, she turned her mind to another day among the cement dust,
the constant drilling and the inevitable inane chatter around mid-
morning coffee time.

Tonight, just like every night, she'd spend about half an hour
getting the bitter tastes of the construction site out of her mouth,
using her toothbrush and lashings of toothpaste to get clean. But
did it make sense any more, this daily drudge, now knowing that
when she got back home Dwayne would've cleared his stuff out of
their boxy one-bedroom apartment?

Already smelling that cement dust on the air, the grinding
mixer, she stopped walking, peered up at those great big wooden
gates, and decided today was going to be different.

Today would be the start of a new life for her.

Dwayne was the past now and, although she wished him well,
she knew she needed to make some big changes in her life.

She sat down on the curb and yanked off her steel-capped boots, one after the other, then set them down and walked on, away from the gates, wearing only her socks.

The pavement felt rough against the soles of her blistered feet. She could feel the fabric of her socks getting all stretched to the point where it might rip at any moment.

But what did she care? Her mind was made up.

Now she would be off to start a new life, just like Dwayne was off to start a life of his own.

With whoever that might be.

As she got to the end of the road, to the intersection, she looked off to her left and then to her right. Then she remembered what she'd stuffed into her pocket that morning. That, just as she'd headed on out from the house, she pocketed that snow globe of Dwayne's, the one with the snowman and the skiing lodge.

She dipped her hand into the pocket of her jacket, removed the snow globe from inside, and inspected it again. There was a blizzard going on just from the force of her having taken it out, and the snow globe seemed a little weird—out of context—on this bright summer morning with the sun beaming down through the leaves.

She really had no idea why she'd taken the globe, maybe at the back of her mind she'd had a vague longing to do Dwayne some harm—to frustrate him in some way.

But taking the snow globe, what did it actually mean to him? Had he *ever* revealed whatever lingering sentimental importance it had to him, or had she picked up on one subconsciously?

She could, after all, recall a few occasions where she'd asked him if she should take it down the tip with her—whether she should toss it out, and he'd always tell her no, he 'liked having it around.'

And that'd been enough to save the snow globe from the bin.

But now, staring into that snowstorm, looking at the ski lodge with the windows painted-up with yellow—supposed to represent a fire burning away inside—she supposed, it took on far more significance. If only because, by the end of the day, it would be all that would remain of Dwayne.

Because he was otherwise gone from her life.

When she returned to their one-bedroom apartment he wouldn't be there.

Helen thought about pocketing the snow globe again, and then heading on off along the street to wherever it was that she was meant to be headed now, but instead she stood there, clutching the snow globe in her fist, watching those gentle flakes dance about behind the glass in whatever gooey liquid it was the manufacturers used.

And then, because there was no one around to judge her, and because she had no direction to go, she gave the snow globe a hard shake. And kept shaking it. She didn't stop. Continued to shake it for well over a minute, just standing there on the roadside.

As she continued to shake it, she caught a sensation of pins and needles up against her skin, kind of a ticklish feeling.

At first she was certain that it was cramp, but then, when she stopped shaking the snow globe, allowed the snow to settle within it, and she flexed her fingers to try and get shot of the cramp, the feeling didn't go away.

She stared at her fingers, unable to quite comprehend what was going on with them, just what it was that she was feeling right now.

It started to happen slowly, so gradually in fact that she almost didn't notice until the whole world seemed to be caving in on her.

The trees which lined the street bending inwards.

The street beneath her feet bending *upwards*.

And the sky falling down onto her head.

She must've thought about screaming but if she did try to make a sound, it died right away in her throat, and she felt herself being whisked away quickly.

And nothing she could do would stop her.

2

THE WORLD turned into a blur of white. It was blinding for her. The brightness of it streamed into her eyes even though she had them clasped shut, as if someone was shining a torch directly onto the backs of her eyelids. A hard chill hit her cheeks —*bit* at them.

She seemed to be catching the cold on her insides too, and on her tongue she had the vague taste of vanilla ice cream. When she breathed in it smelled of butter, all sickly sweet, just the way she *hated* it.

The only sense that wasn't being assaulted was her hearing, she couldn't hear anything apart from the gentle *rustle* of . . . what exactly?

Then it occurred to her, even before she thought to open her eyes, that it was the sound of snowflakes quietly drifting down.

When she did open her eyes, she found herself sitting in a chilly snow dune. Crisp, virginal-white snow surrounded her, and when she looked off into the distance, into the gloom that seemed to surround her, curl about her, like a fog, she realised just where she was.

She glanced over her shoulder to confirm what she already knew in the pit of her stomach.

There was the ski lodge. Its rigid, cosy wooden log cabin, and sitting—or should that have been *standing?*—beside it was the snowman.

She was *inside* the snow globe.

All at once she felt her temples pounding with blood. Her heart raced so fast that she wouldn't have had a chance to count its beats even if she'd had the inclination.

When she looked up, she saw the snowflakes continuing to fall down on her, and felt their light, chilly touch as they brushed up against her cheeks.

For a long while she just sat there, in the snow dune.

And waited.

What she waited for she really had no idea.

Maybe she was waiting for a paramedic to bring her around with a soothing voice filled with concern. Or perhaps she was waiting for a car horn to blast her awake, from where she'd tumbled into the road and hit her head against the hard asphalt.

But none of these things happened.

She just stayed right where she was in this impossibly quiet, tranquil spot, the snow still tumbling down on her and the ski lodge very much still standing there with the snowman beside it.

When she tried to peer off into the gloom that surrounded the little clearing she was certain that she could see a vague curvature to the area beyond, though she really couldn't say with any degree of certainty.

Was she . . . *trapped* here?

Helen scrabbled to her feet, noticing that she was still only wearing her socks. It was then that the impossible chill caught up with her, that she felt that juddering sensation of shock pass up her spine. Her feet were soaked, totally wet through from where she'd been sitting in the snow dune.

Her teeth began to chatter, and skittering sensations ran through her blood—sensations that she knew to recognise as an Extremely Bad Thing Waiting to Happen.

It didn't take a doctor's mind to inform her that she'd be much better out of this snow as soon as she could possibly manage it, and that meant she should head for the lodge.

She stumbled on through the snow, the freezing cold of the stuff running her right through to the bone and twisting up her gut. She fixed her stare onto the front door of the lodge and to the brass plate that she could see nailed-up there. As she drew closer to it, got within five or six paces, she could read the name on the plate:

Berrens Lodge.

Berrens?

That was Dwayne's last name.

She had enough time to think through how odd that was before the chill caught her again and she found herself reaching for the knocker—a brass gargoyle-type-thing with a hoop sticking out from its fanged jaws.

When she brought it down, the sound was thick and woody, and seemed to echo about her as if it had been as powerful as a gunshot.

It sent another tingle up her spine.

She waited.

Listened for any sound within the lodge.

Nothing.

Nothing she could *hear* anyway.

She stood there another moment and then realised just how stupid she was being.

This couldn't *really* be happening after all.

Just like she'd thought, this was just a hallucination, she'd bumped her head and blacked out, or something . . . or something.

In any case, given the circumstances, and just how iced-up her feet were feeling, she felt that she could forgo her manners just this once, and so she reached for the brass doorknob, turned it, and then pushed the door back into the lodge.

3

ALMOST STRAIGHTAWAY, a waft of hot air hit her. She was struck by the reassuring, homely smell of wood burning and a sugary scent on the air. It was only then that she realised just how hungry she was, and it seemed her mouth only just beat her to the punch, beginning to salivate all over the place. She listened hard for any sound within the lodge, but all she could hear was the light crackle of firewood burning away in an as-yet-unseen stove.

The hall before her was simple.

Just a boxy little area that she guessed acted as the porch of the lodge.

The light that spilled in from underneath the interior door shed a little light.

Not that there was all that much to see.

A flat, and extremely solid, wooden wall stood before her. She saw that there was a single, bent and rusted nail sticking out of it, and a rectangular shape where the dust hadn't settled onto the wood, where she guessed a picture frame had hung before.

She took a step forwards, and in that moment a sudden wind caught the door and brought it shut with a heavy *slam* behind her.

The shock of the sound in such a quiet place sent another tremor through her blood, jangled her muscles.

She listened for the inevitable reprimand from within the lodge.

But she heard nothing.

Odd.

If someone had walked into her apartment in the middle of a blizzard-strewn day, and then had the temerity to *slam* the door on their way in, why they'd be right out on their ear. Though, to be fair to herself, she probably wouldn't have left the door unlocked in the first place. Their . . . no, *her*—she'd already forgotten that Dwayne was leaving—*her* neighbourhood wasn't exactly the safest of places.

Certainly not somewhere to leave your door unlocked, in any case.

Still hearing no voice from within the lodge, she decided that it was up to her to announce her presence. Which she duly did, calling out, "Hello?" into the apparently empty lodge.

Nicely warmed, if devoid of life.

The wooden logs that formed the walls of the lodge seemed to absorb her voice.

So she tried again.

"Hello?"

No reply this time either.

She took another step forwards onto the bare wooden floorboards of the lodge. She saw the door ahead of her. The interior door. She reached out for the doorknob, waited a beat, and then gave it a turn.

The mechanism was well-oiled or, at least, it didn't stick as she turned it. The hinges, too, seemed to be in a good way, as she pushed the door into the lodge, the heat wafting out even warmer now, sending a hot flush pounding through her cheeks.

She emerged into a living room: a beaten-up, yet incredibly comfortable-looking, sun-faded brown sofa, with a pair of matching high-backed armchairs, standing at either side of the sofa like a pair of faithful sentries.

She turned around and saw the furnace, the source of all the heat. It was a simple steel chamber with a heat-retardant window which allowed her to see the flames licking at the glass within.

Up on the mantelpiece which ran along the frame of the fireplace, she saw a snow globe, very much like the one she'd shaken up, the one that had brought her here.

She didn't get too close.

She figured that, already, she'd had more than enough of snow globes for today.

A simple, rounded sheepskin rug sprawled out over the wooden floorboards before the stove and between the sofa and armchairs.

For a few seconds she just stood still, allowing the heat to pile up against her face, to warm up her completely chilled blood. She could feel the warmth bringing her back to life. She remembered reading, back in school, about how cold-blooded animals were sort of solar-powered, that they had to lie about in the sun for a long while to generate energy.

Sometimes she wondered whether she might be cold blooded, what with the effect the sun had on her. The few times she'd gone off with Dwayne to Spain for a few weeks' holiday she'd always come back tanned and gleaming—and all the guys at the building site would tell her how she was 'glowing' after the holiday.

She could quite easily have stood about there all day, just absorbing the heat from the stove, but she knew that this wasn't her home and what she was doing . . . whatever *this* was . . . it was an intrusion on someone's privacy.

And so she glanced about the living room, saw the set of stairs leading upwards, and then looked over to the only other doorway which led out of the room, and which seemed to be the source of the main light within the lodge:

A slick, bright-yellow light.

As she took another few steps towards the doorway, she caught a familiar smell, a smell of apple crumble, what had *always* been her favourite desert. And she couldn't help wondering to herself whether there might be custard too . . . even though the whole possibility of her getting the chance to try some of it was less than remote, since she was an intruder after all.

The best she could hope for, when she finally *did* run into the people who owned this lodge, was that they wouldn't attack her with some blunt object. If she was really pushing her luck, they might be kind enough to give her directions on how to get out of this . . . well, there was no other way to put it really . . . *snow globe*.

So, taking a deep breath, Helen crossed the threshold.

4

A S SHE'D HALF SUSPECTED, the doorway turned out to lead into a kitchen.

One of those beautiful, wood-panelled kitchens, the type that she never saw any longer—it seemed all the rage these days to tile kitchens . . . perhaps that was more hygienic, easier to clean:

More practical.

The smell of the apple crumble grew stronger and now when she breathed it in it was so potent that she could almost taste it on her tongue, could almost feel the near-scorching temperature of it up against the inside of her mouth.

A navy-blue AGA oven occupied most of one wall of the kitchen—the wall opposite where she stood. Since the hobs were devoid of anything at all, she supposed that the apple crumble was baking inside one of the half-a-dozen hatches, the oven doors.

Just the sight of it sent a tingle through her blood, a kind of *cosy* feeling.

Almost like she belonged here.

. . . *Oh God*, what was she going on about now? She just *knew* this was all some sort of a delusion, and most likely the type brought on by a swift blackout followed by a head injury . . . but if that was true, then why didn't she wake up?

Over in the corner of the kitchen, she could see a rustic wooden table with four chairs all drawn up around it.

Each of the chairs had a cushion, all with that same sun-faded, brown fabric which matched the fabric of the sofa-and-armchair set in the living room she'd just passed through.

"Can I help you, dearie?"

When that throaty, hoarse voice sounded over her shoulder, she near enough had a heart attack.

Helen spun around and looked over to the person who had spoken—an elderly woman with wispy white hair, wearing a light-pink housedress with a plain, white apron drawn down over her front. She clutched her hands at the ribbon of her apron, and had leathered, wrinkly skin. When Helen sucked up the courage to meet her eyes, she saw that they were a bright, sharp green colour.

She had seen those eyes many times before.

Those were the eyes she had woken up to every morning.

Dwayne's eyes.

Helen felt something catch in her throat, a lump that prevented her from being able to get so much as a word out. She felt . . .well, really, she couldn't say *how* she felt. Standing here with this kindly old woman looking at her, waiting for an explanation on just what she was doing here—breaking and entering into her lodge.

Before Helen could get the words straight on her tongue, the old woman smiled a deep smile that brought out trenches of wrinkles from her cheeks, and around her mouth. She stepped lightly despite her rounded, square-shouldered shape, and headed towards the AGA oven. While she walked, her open-backed, fluffy brown slippers made neat little *slaps* against the wooden floorboards.

"Should be almost ready now," the old woman said, her back to Helen.

Helen eyed up her options, thought about the doorway behind her. She could find her way back to the front door of the lodge blindfolded if she had to. Working on construction sites her entire life had given her the ability to find her way about buildings as if they were as familiar as her own body. They had patterns to them. Patterns that she'd absorbed subconsciously.

And deeply.

But, at the same time, she saw no need to run.

Why should she run?

Because this old woman didn't seem surprised to see her here?

A perfect stranger?

Though Helen knew it was just about the most stupid thing she'd ever done, she actually reached down and pinched the loose flesh on the back of her hand. She felt it.

But was that any proof that this *wasn't* some sort of a delusion?

Because what else *could* it be?

She'd had a stressful day, and she knew that her mind was just putting things together—the snow globe, it'd transported her here to this scene . . . the old woman's eyes: her subconscious had given her that from the many images of Dwayne that she held within her mind . . . the name of the lodge itself: *Berrens Lodge* . . . well, she'd just taken that from Dwayne's last name, that was all . . . the apple crumble? . . . It was no secret to her own mind that it was her favourite food.

That crumble was her very favourite dish.

She watched on as the old woman crouched down and opened one of the AGA oven doors. She used her apron to shield her hands from the heat, and stuck her arms into the oven, drawing out a high-sided baking tray which she then laid to rest on top of the AGA hobs.

Semi-transparent baking paper lay on the top of the apple crumble, and the old woman picked out a wooden spoon from a ceramic pot beside the stove. She peeled off the layer of baking paper that rested on top and then dug the spoon into the crumble itself.

She half turned, looked to Helen, and then said, "I thought you might be hungry, and Dwayne told me this was your favourite, is that right?"

Though Helen still felt the lump in her throat, her well-ingrained manners: the result of a loving childhood, got the better of her, and she said, "Yes, it *is* my favourite."

The old woman went over to the wood-panelled cabinets, fished about inside them and, with a light *clink* of porcelain—two deep bowls, cutlery: a pair of dessert spoons—she served the crumble with the wooden spoon, dished it out into the bowls. Steam clawed up into the air with little spiralling puffs and the smell of crumble got richer still.

The crumble served, the old woman made her way over to the table off in the corner of the kitchen, and went about setting the table.

A creeping numbness seemed to be taking hold of every nerve in Helen's body, and a shudder passed over the surface of her skin, as if her body had neglected to notice that she now stood within a very nicely warmed lodge and there was the prospect of apple crumble to come.

The old woman wiped her hands on the sides of her apron, and then sat down in one of the wooden chairs, propped her elbows down on the table, and faced forwards, seeming to stare into space, to stare at the chair opposite her, as if inviting Helen to sit down.

Helen stayed where she was. Though she would have loved this scene, if it had been in fact happening—could she have come up with something *more* comforting?—it was the knowledge that really whatever was happening to her in the *real* world must've been just . . . just horrendous.

She kept her mind focussed, determined to break through her own illusion, to show her subconscious that this simply *wasn't* happening.

That was the trick surely.

Because how can you keep dreaming once you no longer believe the dream?

And so, with resolved spirit, she looked to the old woman, still appearing to her in profile since she continued to stare at the chair opposite her, and Helen said, "Where am I?"

The old woman continued to face forwards, apparently undis-turbed by whatever matter it was that Helen was raising with her.

When the old woman *still* didn't respond, Helen could feel herself growing more and more confident that this was a delusion, and that *none* of this was actually happening.

She waited for the stomach-churning moment as she was whipped away from the scene—as she returned to real-world consciousness, and to whatever had really happened to her.

But, just when she was confident that she could feel the world breaking apart around her, the old woman let loose a vague sigh, and said, "Please, dearie, sit down. It'll all be much clearer in a few moments."

Helen felt her chest tighten. She waited another beat, waited for the world to break apart.

But, if anything, it grew richer, thicker.

And the smell of the apple crumble got stronger still.

Decided that there was nothing she could do for the time being, Helen headed over to the kitchen table.

And took her seat on the chair opposite the old woman.

5

HELEN STARED DOWN at the crumble before her. She took in the golden-brown crust, and then the oozing green goodness of the steaming apple insides as it seeped about the base of her bowl. She took up her dessert spoon, gleaming from an —*apparently*—recent polish.

She looked across the table, to the old woman, and she waited.

Already the old woman was eating her apple crumble, spooning a portion up to her lips, pausing to blow on it, sending the steam rolling off.

Helen watched the old woman as her lips parted and laid the crumble down on her tongue. As she chewed, the old woman closed her eyes and made a light, almost indiscernible, "*Hmm*," as if she was giving herself the greatest of pleasures.

Helen looked over her own serving of apple crumble. Glanced about herself as if she might be able to detect a tear in this world that had devised itself around her, but, finding none, she scooped out a portion, brought it up to her nose, breathing in the smell of it, and then parted her lips and took it into her mouth.

The flavour was like nothing else she had ever tasted. It was all at once sickly sweet, and yet with a slightly sour note to it . . . that sour note you got from cooking apples picked just a week or so before ripeness . . . that little *kick* it gave to the flavour.

Before, the moment she'd come on in out of the snow, and into the lodge, she'd thought she'd known the definition of true warmth, and it was only now that she realised she had been wrong.

As she chewed on her crumble she was almost certain she could hear the sugar crackling in her mouth as it met with her grateful saliva. And she couldn't think of anything else other than the fact that she couldn't recall ever before having felt so close to perfection, so close to feeling all warm on the inside as she did on the outside.

After the first bite, Helen wasn't sure whether she could take another.

The experience had just been so . . . so *intense*.

Difficult for her to fathom really.

When she looked across the table, she saw the old woman had laid her own spoon down in her bowl of crumble, had left it there, and was looking Helen over with her sharp green eyes. "So," she said, "*you're* the one that Dwayne's always talking about."

"What?" Helen said, setting her own spoon down in her bowl, and only now beginning to realise that the feeling of the crumble was fading a touch.

She would've been hard pressed to think that she would ever be able to speak again after that mouthful of *by far* the most perfect apple crumble she'd ever tasted.

The old woman nodded, and when she did so the loose, leathery skin that clung to her neck like a turkey's bib shook a little. "Yes, he's *always* talking about you."

Helen felt her gut churn a touch, and she realised that she was starving. That she simply had to keep on eating the crumble, that was the only way for her to manage the hunger pangs she felt. "What do you mean?" Helen said.

The old woman let loose a sigh, looked across the kitchen, and only when Helen met her stare did she realise there was a man standing there.

He was skinny.

Lanky.

Taller than Helen, though that wasn't saying much since Helen's nickname on the construction site was 'Titch.'

He wore a tatty brown waistcoat with a light-cream, grampa shirt underneath, two of its buttons undone. He had a bushy beard and held his hands on his hips, his bony fingers jutting upwards and out as if a spider clung to him awkwardly.

Helen felt her blood fizzling, and her heart seemed to dip in her chest.

It was like it bobbed right down to the base of her stomach.

The man looked over Helen for a moment, then back to the old woman, finally his gaze settled on the stove, on the apple crumble there. "What's this all about, then?" he said.

The old woman's expression seemed to stiffen just a little, that easy smile of hers seemed to falter for a moment. "It was a surprise," she said, "we've got company unless you hadn't noticed, and it's *her* favourite."

"This mean dinner's late, then?"

The old woman sighed, then nodded, again shaking that loose skin beneath her jaw vigorously. "Yes, it means that it'll be a bit later." Then she arched her back, looked over at the man with those sharp green eyes of hers . . . with *Dwayne's* eyes . . . and said, "Now why don't you grab a bowl and come sit with us, eh? This is her— this's the one he's always been talking about."

From where he stood, over at the door to the kitchen, the old man squinted, still holding his bony fingers to the waist of his trousers as if he had to look through a very thick fog to get any sort of a proper glance at Helen.

Helen felt her chest tighten. This, really, was all getting a little too weird now—now was the time for her to make her excuses, her apologies, and to leave this old couple to it.

She was sure they'd know how she could get out of this place.

Or how she could wake herself up.

The old man set about serving himself crumble at the stove.

Helen stared down into her own bowl, to the delicious dessert that still remained there, almost imploring her to take just another bite.

But she resisted.

Most likely this wasn't real anyway.

She looked up, over her bowl to the old woman, now taking another bite of her own crumble, and she said, "Er, look, I really appreciate this, this . . . *crumble* here, but I really do need to get going, you see . . ." she thought for a second how she might explain it, but couldn't find any way to do so, instead she settled for, ". . . I need to get *home*."

The old woman took her time, continuing to chew on her mouthful of crumble, apparently thinking this over, thinking over just what Helen had said to her.

Before she could reply, the old man joined them, pulling up a chair alongside the old woman—the woman Helen supposed was his wife.

The two of them sat on the other side of the table, both of them using their spoons to paw through their crumble, bringing yet more steam wafting upwards.

When the old woman finished her current mouthful, swallowed it down, she caught Helen in those green eyes of hers and said, "He hasn't told you about the snow globe, has he?"

Helen felt her heart skip a beat. "Told me *what* about his snow globe?"

The old woman laid her spoon down in the bowl, slipped the old man a sidelong glance . . . but the old man didn't seem all that interested in whatever it was that the old woman was getting at, his bushy beard almost brushing up against the crust of his apple crumble.

The old woman looked to Helen again. "Does he even know you're here?"

6

THOUGH HELEN got the feeling that she would know the answer to the question she was about to ask, she went ahead and asked it anyway. "Does *who* know that I'm here?"

The old woman kept Helen's gaze held with her own. "Dwayne."

Helen felt her throat dry up. But she managed to get out a reply, "Where am I? What *is* this?"

"You mean," the old woman said, again glancing to the old man . . . and again getting nothing in the way of a response, "he never told you about us?"

Though this was a delusion, a dream—*whatever*—she was certain that she could feel a tightness about her skull, that tell-tale sign that she had a migraine coming on. It was just like whenever the boys at work would whip out the pneumatic drills—it was that sort of anticipation.

Helen shook her head.

The old woman nudged the old man in the ribs, and this did manage to get him to stop eating, and to look up at Helen with his mouth full of crumble, still chewing away.

There was total silence in the kitchen, the only sound which Helen could hear was the gentle *crackle* of the logs in the stove in the living room.

All of a sudden, Helen felt like she was too hot, like she was sweating all over, and that if she stayed here for a moment longer she would just melt.

But, at the same time, she could feel the two of them—the old woman and man—pinning her to the back of her chair with their stares.

"Dearie," the old woman said, "I'm . . . *we're* Dwayne's parents."

Helen felt her blood run cool, the air seemed freezing cold all of a sudden. She could feel her muscles all seizing up and her stomach crunching in on itself.

Before she could get her thoughts straight, she found herself shaking her head, and saying, "No, no, that can't be it, I mean . . . I mean, Dwayne's parents, they're . . . they're *dead*."

Helen couldn't so much as twitch an eyelid. Her eyes remained glued on the old couple, both of them fixing her with somewhat sympathetic expressions.

"I . . . uh, is this . . . this a *joke*?"

The old couple kept their places, apparently as glued to the seats of their chairs as she was to hers. She waited for them to exchange glances, for the two of them to break out into smiles . . . and for Dwayne to pop up from somewhere.

But nothing happened.

The old couple, Dwayne's *parents*, kept up their stony-faced expressions.

Helen felt like she was going to break out into a blind panic at any given moment—simply fly right off the handle, rush through the house, and sprint off, bare-footed, through those mounted-up snow dunes and to *hell* with whatever happened to her.

But she couldn't move.

Her body just wouldn't *allow* her to move.

When Helen found her voice again, it was dry and cracked. ". . . Why?"

Dwayne's parents remained focussed on her, and Dwayne's mother spoke. "You see, with Dwayne—*our son*—he found a way to keep us alive, a way for him to keep us with him for always. He managed to keep us here, in this snow globe, so that he might come and visit us whenever he wished to. That was the idea, I suppose."

Helen thought about things. Thought about their marriage, about Dwayne's frequent disappearances. She'd spent years and years trying to work it out—trying to find some *evidence*. For

Christ's sake she'd even gone and hired a private detective, got a pro on Dwayne's case to try and find out just where he would disappear to.

But he would never tell her.

Whenever she confronted him he could go all dewy-eyed, as if he couldn't even see her, as if he was looking right through her, and he'd just stand there, take all the questions she asked him without so much as giving her the courtesy of a reply.

Then she'd get angry, slam a few doors, and go out for a walk to calm down.

And whenever she'd get back he'd be gone again.

Not home till later on at night.

. . . Could this . . . this *delusion* really have some sort of truth to it?

For the time being, Helen saw past the complete and *utter* ridiculousness of this whole thing, and she eyed Dwayne's mother over the table. "Look, if what you say is true, then why didn't he ever tell me—why didn't he *tell* me that he was coming here, to see you?"

Dwayne's mother parted her lips as if to speak. But she held back.

Helen noticed Dwayne's father reach out and take hold of her hand, give it a little squeeze, and then he took over the talking.

"I think," he said, "Dwayne just wanted to keep some things to himself—we all have secrets, after all, I mean, I don't think you can sit there and honestly say that, throughout your marriage, you've always told the truth—told Dwayne every single little detail."

Helen felt her gut twist just a little. That little warming anger at the base of her stomach. Just who the hell did these people think they were?

Dwayne's parents, apparently . . .

"What do *you* know about it?" she said, turning on Dwayne's 'father.'

Dwayne's father met her with a cool stare, and she looked deep into those grey-blue eyes of his, a shade that made Helen think of a murky puddle on an overcast day. "He has confided in us for a long while, he has told us *everything*." He paused for a moment. "And, in turn, we have told him everything else—everything *we* have seen."

Helen screwed up her eyes at him. "Just what do you mean?"

Dwayne's father gave Dwayne's mother a sidelong glance, who gave him an affirmative nod, then he looked back to Helen and said, "We know about the affair."

HELEN FELT LIKE she was sinking. She could hardly comprehend the word that Dwayne's father had just got out. Couldn't comprehend it at all. Oh, she knew *just* what he was talking about, but that, all things considered, really wasn't the part that bothered her most; the part that bothered her most was the *how*—the way *how* Dwayne's father, and apparently his mother too —knew about this.

It had happened about three months ago, after a long day's work she'd come home on a Friday to find—*surprise, surprise!*—that Dwayne wasn't about, that he had gone off to wherever it was that he went off to.

For some reason Helen had reached her conclusion right then, that night, thought that she'd seen through all the crap that'd come before it.

Because there couldn't be any other explanation, right?

. . . The only *possible* explanation was that Dwayne was having an affair.

And she had been so determined *not* to be the victim.

That she would take the initiative.

If she couldn't prove anything then she would have to get her own back in other ways.

The kid along the hall: a blond boy called Danny, about nineteen years old, and only having arrived to their apartment block the month before. He worked down at the local DIY superstore, she'd often run into him while heading off to buy something or other, something that they didn't have to hand on the building site. And she had seen those bulging biceps of his; the ones that she'd seen, when she'd gone and rung his doorbell, had been the long and hard product of exercises on a pull-up bar which hung up in the doorway to his bathroom.

He'd come to the door shirtless, showing off his six pack and those bullet-hard pecs.

And he'd looked confused at first, seeing her there, still dressed in her dusty overalls, in her steel-capped boots, but he hadn't fought it, not when she'd grabbed the end of the dangling belt which had stuck out from the waistband of his jeans.

She'd tugged him all along the exterior landing, to her own apartment, taken him through the hallway, and tossed him down on the bed where he'd looked at her with a gaze halfway between fear and hunger.

Then she'd let him take her.

And she'd enjoyed it too.

All the more because she knew just what Dwayne was up to himself, and that he would never for one moment suspect her.

She'd told Danny to leave soon after, actually led him off to the door, and seen him off along the landing. Danny had glanced back once, over his shoulder, given her a satisfied smirk before bringing his apartment door shut with a dry *thump*.

Then Helen had gone back inside. She remembered the snow globe, standing there on its ledge in the hallway, and she'd had the urge to pick it up and smash it against the wall . . . but she'd resisted.

In the end, she guessed that her taking the snow globe today had been something of an extension of that feeling of frustration she'd had before. She'd realised that the snow globe was something that Dwayne really did care about and she'd determined that she would be the one to take it from him.

Revenge.

Helen blinked a couple of times, and wondered just what sort of a state the research into flashbacks within delusions was at, at the present time.

Or there was always the possibility that this wasn't a delusion at all.

The smell of the apple crumble came back to her, and Helen could feel it almost twisting her gut now, sending a slight nausea weaving through her bloodstream.

Dwayne's father remained straight-faced as he said, "That evening Dwayne had to work late—his boss hijacked him, wouldn't let him leave the office. That evening he wasn't with us, here in the lodge . . . but he did come to visit us later and we thought that he should know everything."

Helen felt her heart draw tight, and she shook her head, feeling like she was on the verge of tears now. "I still don't understand why he didn't just tell me the truth—why he didn't just tell me what was going on." She looked to Dwayne's mother, then back to his father. "He didn't even *try* to explain to me. He never made so much as an effort to explain his frequent disappearances, can't you see that he hurt me just as much as I hurt him?"

Dwayne's father dipped his glance, down at the half-finished crumble in the bowl before him, and then he said, in a much weaker voice, "There's something else you should know."

8

OFF SOMEWHERE IN THE HOUSE—the staircase?—
Helen could hear the light *patter* of footsteps approaching.
When she heard the footsteps in the doorway to the kitchen,
Helen couldn't find the strength to look around.

She was afraid of what she would see.

Of what *other* awful things she might've done.

When she glanced over the table to Dwayne's mother and
father, she saw that the two of them were craning their necks in the
direction of the newest arrival.

Helen tried to put off looking for another few seconds but she
knew, in the end, that she would need to look over.

And so, with her heart rising up to her throat, fluttering against
her tonsils, she looked.

In the doorway stood a little girl, no more than five or six years
old. She was wearing a light-brown nightie, the hem of which
brushed against the tops of her bare feet. She clutched a beaten-up
teddy bear to her chest, which, Helen could see, was missing one of
its button eyes and had stuffing emerging from its stitching.

Her hair was a kind of strawberry blond colour and Helen could
see from the way she was rubbing at her eyes with her fists that
she'd just woken up.

Helen looked to the little girl and then back to Dwayne's father,
searching for some kind of reason to all this.

Dwayne's father smiled warmly at the little girl, and she made
her way slowly, trudging along, making an active effort not to look
at Helen. When she reached Dwayne's father, he pulled her up onto
his lap. Sat her down there on his knee and then he looked over her
head at Helen.

Before he could say anything to her, Helen found herself breaking in. "Is she . . . ?"

Dwayne's father only nodded solemnly.

Helen looked over to Dwayne's mother, unable to put this into any kind of order in her mind. "I . . . I never knew, I didn't . . . he never told me that he'd had a daughter."

Neither Dwayne's mother or father said anything, and the little girl—Dwayne's daughter, *apparently*—just remained propped up on her grandfather's knee.

Helen felt herself swaying in her seat. She looked down at the crumble sitting in its bowl before her and tried to suck up the strength to take another bite. Though she knew it was delicious, it seemed now, no matter how delicious it appeared, that it would only taste of ash in her mouth.

Almost coming apart from herself, Helen rose up from the chair, getting into a standing position. She knew that she had to leave.

That she had to go back to their apartment.

That she had to speak to Dwayne.

This morning it had all seemed so clear to her, all that time he had spent away from her, that disappearing act of his, but now that she knew the truth she felt like it changed everything.

. . . Or did it?

If only he had just *told* her!

Neither Dwayne's mother or father, or Dwayne's dead little girl, followed her as she padded off across the wooden floorboards of the kitchen, as she made her way into the living room, to the stove still crackling away there.

It was only then that she realised she really had no idea how she was going to get away from this . . . this *nightmare*.

As she glanced about the walls, her gaze came to rest on the mantelpiece once more, to the snow globe that stood there.

She took a couple of steps forwards, came closer to it, peered into its glass form.

She could hardly believe what she saw.

There, in the curvature of the glass, she made out the street intersection where she'd pulled out the snow globe and given it a shake . . . was it . . . could it be just this simple?

She listened for any sound behind her, any sign that Dwayne's parents might be watching what she was doing, or that they might be about to stop her.

But why would they?

Why would they want to keep her here?

And so, her heart thrumming in her ears, she reached out for the snow globe, took hold of it in her fist and she gave it a good shake, till she could see the snowflakes floating about on the other side of the glass, obscuring the scene held within.

At first she was sure that nothing at all had happened. That all she'd done was make a fool of herself. But then—*right then*—she felt that same sensation from before.

Felt the world going all blurry about the edges.

Felt herself being swept away.

9

WHEN HELEN REAPPEARED back at the street intersection, outside the snow globe, she felt the sun warming her back, and smelled the fresh, summer breeze. Just looking upwards, into the sky, she could see that it was nearing midday.

And that she had been gone for several hours.

Was this even the same day?

She blinked against her daze, tried to get herself shot of all of those things she could still recall from the lodge: Dwayne's dead parents, his dead *daughter*, and, above all, that sickly sweet apple crumble.

Funny to think of it, but she guessed that she'd be quite happy if she never tasted apple crumble again for as long as she lived.

She squeezed the snow globe tight in her fist and thought long and hard about whether or not she should toss it into a bunch of bushes at the side of the road.

Instead, though, she pocketed it in her jacket.

She moved quickly, only realising that she'd left her boots behind at the entrance to the building site when she took a step and landed her socked foot down on a pebble.

Pain flushed about the sole of her foot, and she suppressed the urge to swear.

She turned back to the building site and hobbled her way along there.

Before long she got to the gate. Her boots had long gone, of course: Health and Safety. And, in any case, she guessed that she'd have to explain her absence to her boss.

So that was what she did, heading on into the temporary cabin where he made his office, explaining to him that she was having 'emotional issues,' and considering that Helen had hardly missed a day's work in her life, he was glad to let her go . . . if not a little perplexed as to why she hadn't just phoned in . . . and even more perplexed when the boots he'd found at the gate that morning, and which he'd left for collection beneath his desk, turned out to belong to her. But Helen just did a lot of smiling and hoped that she'd get away with it.

She made it back to her apartment about twenty minutes later and she scrabbled her way up the steps hoping that she wouldn't be too late—that Dwayne wouldn't have cleared off yet.

But she *was* too late.

As she stood in the open doorway of what had once been their boxy, one-bedroom apartment, she saw that all his clothes were gone, that the photographs that'd once belonged to him had gone, and . . . for some reason this one affected her the most . . . his toothbrush was gone.

She returned to their bedroom-slash-sitting room and threw herself down onto the foldout sofa bed; currently serving as a sofa.

For a long while she lay there facedown, just listening to her heart tick on, not even bothering to think about closing the door to her apartment.

"Hell?"

It was only when she heard the familiar voice that she looked up.

Dwayne.

Standing in the doorway.

Those sharp green eyes of his.

He wore his moleskin jacket over a pair of brand-new blue jeans, and, like always, his square-framed glasses seemed to make the rest of his face somehow more angular.

He had dark bags beneath his eyes, and five-o'-clock shadow.

For a second she felt that old rage return to her—those feelings of betrayal, that woman he was no doubt seeing; the woman who she had somehow mythologised in her mind.

But she allowed herself a breath.

Just a moment to simmer down.

And she fixed him with a stare, risked a smile.

He didn't smile back.

Why would he after all the things she'd said to him?

"I . . . I was looking for my snow globe," he said, "you know that stupid, tacky thing that you wanted to throw out?"

Helen felt her chest tighten. The weight of the snow globe in the pocket of her jacket seemed to become almost too heavy to bear.

But she had to wait this out.

"You couldn't find it?" she said.

He shook his head, broke off eye contact with her.

She could see that his eyes were red around the rims, and she wondered if he'd packed up his stuff then parked his car off somewhere in a layby, had a sob to himself, waiting for her to go out so that he could come home to look for the snow globe again.

"And," she said, "what would you say if . . . I'd taken it?"

He flinched, then blinked several times as if trying to cover it up. He met her eye and then gave a slight shake of the head, the faintest of faint smiles. "It wouldn't matter," he said. "Just like you said it's just junk."

"And what about if I'd found out its secret?"

At this Dwayne did some more blinking, and added a quick adjustment of his glasses over the bridge of his nose to boot.

"Eh?" she said, waiting for him to show *some* sign of opening up to her. "What if your mum and dad"—she felt her throat constrict and a certain iciness enter her blood—"your *daughter* had had a word with me?"

Dwayne's eyes bulged in their sockets. He puffed out his cheeks. "What . . . what are you saying?"

Helen shook her head, smiled faintly.

Slowly she eased herself up off the sofa and made her way over to the doorway. "Oh, Dwayne, don't you see? I thought you were off with another woman, all this time. If only I'd known . . . if only you'd just told me the truth from the start."

Dwayne backed up a little way, onto the landing which ran along the exterior of their apartment, and which led all the way along to Danny's place.

When Dwayne had backed himself all the way up to the railing of the landing he stopped suddenly. Flinched another couple of times. Then busied himself adjusting his glasses once more. "Please," he said, "I . . . I just *want* it, is that too much to . . ."

Helen dug into the pocket of her jacket, whipped out the snow globe and then thrust it into his chest. "There," she said, releasing it, and him only just moving quickly enough to prevent it dropping to the ground and smashing into a thousand pieces, "I've been there —I've been to Berrens Lodge, okay? I know all about it. Just as you know all about me and Danny; your mum and dad told me all about it."

Dwayne clutched the snow globe tightly in his hands, glared at the flurry of snowflakes inside of it, and the brewing storm. He only had time to glance up at her before he disappeared . . . Helen would've liked to have said in a puff of smoke, or something with a little amateur-dramatic flair, but, really, it was only a flash.

One moment he was there.

The next he wasn't.

She watched as the snow globe tottered about on the floor of the landing, flirting with the edge.

Perhaps if she'd wanted to—if she'd *really* wanted to—she

could've stopped it from tumbling over, from falling down the two storeys to the asphalt of the car park beneath.

Or maybe there was something deep within her holding her back.

Telling her that, all things considered, Dwayne would probably be happier living out the rest of his days in Berrens Lodge . . . perhaps it was a small mercy for him to be trapped there forever with the ones he loved and couldn't leave behind.

Or, at least, he couldn't leave them behind for *her*.

So Helen watched as the snow globe broke into a thousand little pieces on the hard asphalt surface and the goo squelched out into a puddle with all those little white, fake snowflakes.

She continued to watch the goo sparkle in the midday sun for another couple of seconds before turning on her heel and heading back into her apartment.

As she brought the door shut behind her, she couldn't help but think that her clothes stank of that sweet, sugary apple crumble.

Good thing she was accustomed to taking forty-minute showers nightly, only this time it wouldn't be to get shot of the dust, and all that other unpleasantness of the building site . . . it'd be so that she could get rid of Dwayne, once and for all, and all the baggage he had carried on his shoulders; weighing down both their lives.

And with which they might both have crumbled.

DREAMWEAVER

G RAHAM SAT IN BED reading while his wife, Lauren, slept beside him.

She thrashed, kicking Graham in his shins. Her face contorted and relaxed. Then, all at once, she sat up straight, opened her eyes and let loose a blood-curdling scream.

Graham flinched, knocking the back of his head into the bedpost and dropping his book. With one hand he rubbed his sore skull, while he reached for his book with the other. "What happened?"

"I just had a horrible dream. I dreamt a hundred gibbering goblins were ripping me apart, pulling my intestines out through my bellybutton."

He put his arm around her. "Don't worry, it's all over now."

"I don't want to go back to sleep."

"Come on, it'll be fine. Your dreams can't hurt you."

"How do you know? You're not inside my head. It's just so real when it's happening."

"Do you want me to call Dr Sheldon?"

"No, no more doctors."

"What then? We can't go on like this."

She pulled away. "What's that supposed to mean?"

"Well, it's okay on weekends, but I need my eight hours during the week and I've only got a small window to get them in."

She turned to face the wall. "My apologies."

"Look, I'm sorry. It's—"

"Maybe you should sleep in the guest room."

"Don't be like that—"

"Or I could go sleep there."

He leant back against the headboard. "How about we try something new?"

"Like what?"

"I'll tell you something to imagine and you drift off to sleep."

"What are you? A hypnotist?"

Perhaps it would be better to sleep in the guestroom. "Do you want me to help you, or not?"

Lying on her back, she shrugged.

"Okay."

Her lips and eyelids relaxed.

"I want you to imagine a river. A long river, stretching to the horizon. The water's deep and dark-blue. It flows gently past. You dip your fingers in and it's cold."

She shuddered.

"Law?"

Her face remained completely still.

"Are you asleep?"

"Keep going," she murmured.

His pulse increased and he smiled. "Now, I want you to step back from the water and lie down in the grass. A breeze blows through your hair. Feel yourself drift away. It carries you off to a placid void. Nothingness."

She twitched and took deep breaths, now fast asleep.

Pleased with his amateur sleep therapy session, Graham pulled the duvet up to his chin and turned out the light.

T HE NEXT MORNING, breakfast tray in hand and mugs of coffee steaming, Graham re-entered the bedroom.

Lauren stirred. When she opened her eyes, it was like someone had come in during the night and polished them up. "I had the greatest night's sleep of my life. Whatever spell you spun worked wonders." She accepted a cup of coffee. "I can't remember the last time I woke up when it was already light. There's none of the drowsiness like when you wake in the dark."

They finished their breakfast in silence.

Downstairs, they discussed his gift, deciding the next step was to try it on someone else, to see whether or not last night had been a fluke.

Graham peered over Lauren's shoulder as she flicked through her address book.

After a lifetime of sleep disorders, she had an enormous array of acquaintances: support groups, sleep problem social networks and insomnia workshops.

Lauren ran her bony index finger along the list, picked out a dozen or so names and made the calls. Of those she contacted, four still had problems and were willing to give Graham a try. Lauren chose the second name on the revised list, Felicity Norris.

3

THAT NIGHT, Graham stood alongside Lauren on the doorstep of Felicity's house.

Felicity answered the door in dressing gown and slippers. She had a large round face and bushy grey hair that hung down over her patchy cheeks. Her beaming smile contrasted with the enormous bags under her eyes.

Felicity hugged his wife. "Lauren! So wonderful to see you, it's been such a long time." She turned to Graham. "And you must be Graham. The dreamweaver."

Graham scratched his arm. "I suppose."

Felicity waved them in. "Don't just stand out there in the cold. Come on inside."

An Aga stove dominated much of the kitchen. Blouses and shirts hung from a clothes line which swooped over their heads. Several cats lay about, stretching and washing.

Graham's nose tingled and he sneezed.

Felicity raised an eyebrow. "Oh dear, you're not allergic to cats, are you?"

He managed a nod before another sneeze erupted.

"Hang on a second." Felicity shooed each cat out and then said, "Please, take a seat."

Graham and Lauren squeezed up together on a bench.

Felicity asked, "Would you like some tea? The water's just boiled."

Steadying himself, Graham snorted back the mucus. "Yes, please. "

With her back to them, Felicity busied herself placing teabags in mugs. "So, Lauren, what does he do to you?"

A film settled over Lauren's eyes. "I don't know. It's like a kind of hypnotherapy. He just tells me about a place, gets me to imagine being there, makes me think about the smells and relax. It worked last night."

"I see," Felicity said. "Still in beta-testing?"

"Something like that," Lauren said.

Felicity poured out the cups and brought them to the table.

Graham was glad to have something warm to drink. It soothed his ticklish throat and relaxed his taut sinuses.

Eyeing them over the rim of her mug, Felicity said, "I have to tell you, I've tried just about everything on offer. As I remember things, Lauren was one of the worst sufferers in our group."

"That's right," Lauren said. "Night terrors."

Felicity continued, "So I imagine anything that works for her will work for me twice as well."

Graham sniffled. "I hope so."

"You're so lucky your husband's stayed with you, Lauren."

A cat wandered in and brushed itself against Felicity's legs.

Seeming to forget Graham's allergies, Felicity picked it up and cuddled it. She continued, rubbing the cat's stomach, "Walter left us three years ago now, didn't he, Snookums?"

The cat purred loud.

Graham felt another sneeze coming on.

Felicity scratched the cat behind its ears. "He'd had enough. I don't blame him, in a way. It's hard enough to find someone who understands and wants to share their life with you, let alone have them put up with your problems."

Lauren clutched Graham's hand and met his eyes. "Yeah," Lauren said, "I've always been lucky, I suppose."

After they'd finished the tea, Felicity led them up to the bedroom.

A strange vision flashed across Graham's mind, like he was about to take part in a bizarre intergenerational orgy, or something.

He erased it quickly, wanting to concentrate on whatever it was he did and get out.

Felicity propped herself up in bed with a couple of pillows. "I have to tell you that I've tried just about everything."

"He's the real thing, I'm sure," Lauren said.

"We'll see," Felicity said and then snuggled down. "I usually sleep with my cats, but I don't want them to bother Graham while he works his magic." She turned to Graham. "When you go out, could you leave the door open? Else, they'll scratch at the wood until I wake up, undoing all your good work." She withdrew a set of keys from her bedside table drawer. "Lock up when you go out. Just push them through the letterbox. I have to say, I'm awfully excited."

Lauren kissed Graham on the cheek. "I'll leave you two to it. Hope it goes well, Flick." She shut the door, leaving them alone.

Not quite knowing how to act in a strange, elderly woman's bedroom, Graham hovered at the entrance.

"Okay then, magic man," Felicity said. "I'm ready when you are."

"Lie back. Make yourself comfortable."

She did as he said, the same grin lining her face.

"I want you to imagine a forest."

"Night or day?"

He grimaced. "Please, just relax. Just think about what I'm saying."

She made a motion as if zipping her mouth shut and lay back.

"So, there's a big forest, dark green. It stretches as far as the eye can se—"

Once more, she opened her eyes.

He gritted his teeth.

She held up her finger. "I'll tell you what I've forgotten. I haven't fed the cats. They'll be up and about if I don't give them something."

"It's okay, I'll do it."

"Oh, thank you. You're so kind."

"Close your eyes. Good. Under your feet is luscious grass, thick and warm between your toes. You can smell it on a gust of wind."

She sighed. Her chest rose and fell evenly. "Don't stop."

He cleared his throat. "You walk closer to the forest and its dark, comforting. The moist wood and pine needles on the trees are familiar and welcoming. Closer and closer. You reach the rim and step—"

She let out an enormous snore.

He tiptoed out the room.

Still marvelling at his apparent gift, he almost forgot to leave the door open. A cat passed through his legs. He pinched his nose to stop himself sneezing.

Lauren sat at the table in the kitchen with a fresh cup of tea steaming in her hands. "How did it go?"

A tingling feeling clambered inside his chest. "She's asleep."

Lauren got up, downed the tea and then set the mug in the sink. "Let's go. I think we're done here."

He walked into an adjoining room. "One second, I have to feed the cats."

She chuckled.

Graham located a tin, examined it in the half-light coming from the kitchen then peeled off the top and tapped the meaty mess into the food bowls.

4

OVER THE NEXT FEW WEEKS, the phone rang itself off the hook. Felicity seemed to have spread the news to anyone who'd listen.

Graham accepted all requests. Some people wanted to pay him, but he declined. It didn't feel honest. Pretty soon, every evening after work, he ventured out to some stranger's house and put them to sleep.

One morning, on his way to the office, Lauren collared him at the door. "Gray? They're taking advantage of you. You've got to charge them."

Graham scratched his head.

"Why not say, from now on, you'll only take payment?"

"Kind of like a prostitute?"

"You're not having sex with them. At least I hope not."

He winked. "Whose idea was this in the first place?"

She rolled her eyes. "All I'm saying is that, if you played your cards right, you could quit your day job."

"I don't know. I'd feel bad taking their money."

"Don't! Take it from a former sufferer, these people spend their entire lives paying money to frauds to fix their problems. They'll spend it anyway. Why not have them pay that money to you, someone who actually does what they claim? What can it hurt?"

He swallowed. "But I don't 'fix' their problem. All I do is put them under for a night."

"Is that what you're worrying about? Please, do you know how much I'd pay for your services, just for one night of peace and quiet? You don't realise how lucky I am to get it for free every night."

"Maybe I should charge you."

She slapped him playfully.

That morning, at the office, Graham placed an advertisement in a local paper. When he got home from work at night, he had over thirty new voice messages. All new clients.

5

MONTHS DRIFTED BY and he was able to quit his job. In many ways it was the perfect life. He would do whatever he wanted all day, adding to his model train set, going for daytrips with his wife and then, at night, he'd head out after dinner and get back just before ten—a mug of hot chocolate and a book ready for him.

Lauren took on the role of manager and agent. He did whatever she said, merely knocking the addresses into his GPS and then driving out.

One evening, returning from putting a local vicar to sleep, Lauren showed him a monthly bank statement. "Look how well you're doing."

Through bleary eyes, Graham read the form. "Jesus. I'm earning more than I did full-time."

"You're earning twice what you did. At this rate we'll pay off the mortgage this decade. To think you wasted so many years of your life scratching about for pennies."

He sank into an armchair and picked up his book.

"Are you okay? You look a little glum."

"I'm all right."

"Do you want more hot chocolate?"

"No, thanks. The sugar gets me wired, makes it difficult to sleep."

She sat on the sofa opposite. "Now, Gray, I've been on the phone with some people today. Publicists. They'd like you to write a book."

He blinked. "I don't know how to write a book."

"Easy, relax. You don't have to write it. Someone comes to interview you and then they go away and write the book on your behalf."

"How much?"

"Five figure advance, plus royalties."

"Okay, I'll do it."

She cuddled up to him. "I knew you'd see sense. There's something else too."

"What?"

"It's a conference. They want you to go along and give a talk."

His book flopped onto the carpet. "Are you crazy?"

"Gray, at least think about it."

"What're they paying?"

"A thousand a day."

He exhaled. "And when does it stop?"

"What do you mean?"

"I don't want to do this anymore. It's sending me around the bend."

She narrowed her eyes. "What're you talking about? It's easy."

"What I'm doing doesn't seem honest. I don't like taking their money."

"We've been through this. I thought you'd reasoned it out."

"Don't you think visiting people's rooms is a strange way to make a living? Selling a book about a subject I have no idea about? Giving talks to God-knows-who?"

"I think you do whatever you can with what you're given."

"Still, I'd like to stop, just a week, maybe. It's been months now without rest."

Her brow creased. "Oh come on, Gray. It's not like you're working twelve hours a day, is it? You just have a simple two, three hours max, one-on-one, and then you're free to enjoy the rest of your day."

"That's easy for you to say."

She threw up her hands. "All right, I'll make the calls. They're not going to be happy. Imagine how you'd feel, if you'd been expecting to sleep and someone said you couldn't. Sounds kind of like torture, don't you think?"

He turned to face her, trying his best to accentuate his blood-shot eyes and the dark bags. The irony of the best sleep therapist of his age was that he'd stopped sleeping himself.

She sighed. "I'll make the calls then."

6

AFTER A FEW NIGHTS of long and deep sleep, Graham was fully-refreshed. He only used his gift on Lauren.

One evening, the phone rang. Graham answered. "Hello?"

"Graham Wainsbridge?"

"Yes?"

"This is Felicity Norris, do you remember?"

His stomach sank. "Of course."

"I know you're running a big operation now, but I was wondering if you might be able to come over and work your magic, just one more time."

"Sorry, Mrs Norris, my wife runs the book—"

"Yes, I realise that, but I was just calling on the off-chance that you might be able to help me out."

"Well, yes. The problem is we have lots of bookings."

Her voice firmed and any trace of the friendliness vanished. "I haven't slept in days, do you have any idea what that's like?"

He did.

"I'll pay double the rate. No, triple!"

He ran a hand through his hair. "Tonight?"

She brightened. "That'd be perfect."

He hung up and sighed.

Lauren walked into the room. "Who was that?"

"Felicity Norris."

Lauren grinned and embraced him. "Oh good, so you're back on the wagon?"

Would he ever put a stop to this? "I guess."

7

WITH THE MONEY from Felicity's session in his jean pocket, he shoved open his door and wiped his feet on the mat. He felt dirty. Why hadn't Lauren listened to his feelings?

He hooked up his coat and trudged upstairs.

Lauren lay in bed, huddled up in blankets, asleep. He waited, counting out the seconds, and then minutes, in his head.

Sure enough, after about twenty minutes, she tossed and turned. She grunted louder and louder until she broke free with a glass-shattering yowl.

He sat on the bed and held the hair back from her face.

Her forehead wrinkled. "Gray? Please, help me. I can't live without you."

"Don't worry, Law, just shut your eyes and I'll send you away."

She smiled and sank back. Her dark hair spread across the pillow.

"I want you to think about a great lake, its water icy-blue. Alongside there's a sailing boat made of fine wood. Step inside. It bobs gently under your weight, sending ripples across impossibly still waters. You push out into the lake."

She breathed profound breaths.

He could stop now, if he wanted. She was asleep. But, if he walked away, was there any guarantee she wouldn't come after him and the money? He needed that to start his new life. "In the middle of the lake you notice a ripple underneath the boat. Soon it transforms into a patch of choppy water."

Her smile transformed into a frown.

His heart beat faster. "The wind picks up and blows the boat about, almost into the water."

Eyelids twitching, she sucked and spat air.

"Water under the boat breaks into a whirlpool and sucks it down. It spirals around and around until . . ."

Her hands clamped the covers.

"It plunges under."

She convulsed over and over. A trickle of blood dribbled down from the corner of her mouth and she was still.

He reached out and felt her pulse. Nothing. He draped the covers over her face then walked downstairs and out the front door.

THE SUBCONSCIENCE

A NGUS DAVIS'S rope hammock swung back and forth.
Back and forth.

It was gloomy down here, beneath the deck of the ship, and he could taste the damp sea salt in the air. He could smell the thickening mank smothering everything, never letting his clothes ever get completely dry.

The boat rolled up over the next wave and then dived downwards just as steeply.

Angus's hammock swung into the side of the boat and his head crashed into the battered wood. Purple stars, the size of pinpricks, scattered his vision. He tried to blink them away, to see out into the darkness.

But it was around midnight now and there would be no light to be found.

All lights had been extinguished by the howling gales. The electrical systems all fried by the mounting waves that curled up over the sides of the ship. A disaster. Just like everything else on this voyage, on this fleapit of a ship. An unmitigated disaster.

But there was really nothing to do till morning.

Till his shift came up.

Gloom enveloped everything.

Stole away all his senses.

He pulled his moth-eaten quilt up to his chin and turned on his side, sticking his fingers through the holes in the netting of his rope hammock and clinging on, waiting for the ship's next lurch.

For some reason, as he clung on for dear life, he recalled a time back at the last port, where he'd sat around with the others.

They'd all had a chilled cherry tart in a café. All of them sitting out on that wooden decking in the sun, the tide lapping at the shore just over their shoulders.

That scene seemed such a long way off now, almost another life. If he could only get a wink of sleep he might be able to think things through more positively tomorrow. If only this storm would just give up its pounding on the ship, just for an hour or so.

That was all he needed.

Just a brief, tiny moment of peace to find some sleep.

Another roller. A real rising swell.

Then the boat dipped.

Long and hard.

And *kept* dipping.

An almighty *crack* of wood sounded all around.

A shudder ran through Angus's blood. He gripped tightly to the ropes of his hammock. He shifted up, into a sitting position.

The gales howled out. Lashed the deck above his head. He glanced upwards. All he could see was darkness. Yet more gloom.

He waited for the ship to right itself.

To climb up the next wave.

But it remained nose downwards.

Heading downwards.

To the bottom of the sea.

Angus's heart ticked about in his mouth. His blood streamed through his veins. His mind drew a blank. His stomach followed the motion of the ship.

Down and down and down.

And all he could think to do was grip the sides of his hammock all the tighter.

And to flush out all thought of what was going on about him.

As he lay there, in the darkness, he listened to the multitude of *creaks* all taking place about the ship. The sounds of water dripping all around him. And his heart kept on beating away.

But he couldn't bring himself to move.

He was simply frozen to the spot.

Paralysed by fear.

Or whatever it was that held him.

It took another gut-wrenching *crack* to thrash him into action.

This time, Angus swung himself off his hammock, landing unsteadily upon his bare feet. He could feel the damp wooden floorboards beneath his soles. And the water—the *sea*—which gushed on, relentless, below.

He squinted into the gloom. Grabbed a hold of a wooden beam. Clung on as the boat tipped from side to side. Completely at the mercy of the waves.

And then he stole his way along the floor, and out of his cabin.

Outside, in the corridor, everything was just as black, and only knowing just where he was going kept Angus from toppling over, from falling flat on his face and knocking half his teeth out.

That and the firm wooden banister which ran the length of the wall, which he grabbed hold of now. And thrust himself along.

Hauling himself—hand over hand—on his way, he headed up to the deck.

When he got about halfway along he noticed the water trickling beneath his feet. Trickling down over his bare skin. It made him pause. Think things through. Wonder whether or not he might be headed upwards or downwards.

Because he had no intention of going down, into the sea.

The smell of the damp wood clung to his nostrils, and the salty air dried out his mouth. And the constant rocking of the boat made his gut shift and quibble.

And just as he brought himself to the ladder which led up onto deck, he heard yet another *crack!* over his shoulder.

This time at least ten times louder than the last.

Without another second's hesitation, he yanked himself up the wooden rungs, and up and out onto the ship's deck.

Moonlight gleamed down, sending shimmering, ethereal light, over the waves. The salt in the air now seemed truly—*totally*—overwhelming. And the *crash* of the waves far too much to bear. The screams, too, the screams carried over the whistling wind and the driving rain.

But they made no impact on Angus. He clung on to the wooden banister. Keeping himself grounded to the deck.

Up above, the rigging whipped free and lashed in random directions. Its ropes sliced through the air, like a cat o' nine tails. Surely strong enough to cut through a man's skin, right to the bone.

It would cut Angus to the bone.

And over there, over on the other side of the deck, he eyed just what he had come for. Just what he needed right now. The object which would save his life. Which could carry him away from this impending disaster.

The lifeboat.

Angus navigated the deck. He ducked when the rigging lashed. And he snatched a hold of something when the ship listed.

And when he watched a mountainous wave swell up at the side of the boat, he bit his lip and grabbed a hold of one of the freely swinging pieces of rigging and allowed it to wrap itself about his forearm.

Cutting off his blood circulation. Sending his heart pounding in his temples.

But keeping him safe too.

Keeping him from being thrown overboard to a watery grave.

Finally, Angus made it to the lifeboat.

It was made of dull, grainy fibreglass. Painted a lurid orange. He had lost count of the times he, or his fellow crewmates, had put out cigarettes on it.

Left those melted craters in its veneer.

As Angus ran his hand over its side, he felt out those little melted holes. Felt his fingertips slipping in and out of them.

He reached the entrance to the lifeboat.

And then, as more of an afterthought than anything else, he glanced back over his shoulder, back over the deck.

Looking for survivors?

Perhaps.

But there was no one.

They were all below deck.

Seeing to the damage.

Making a deal with fate.

And awaiting their certain deaths.

With a final flush of blood through his mind, Angus threw himself through the door of the lifeboat and down into its comforting and—above all else—*safe* base.

Yes, he would be fine here.

If he just saw this out.

Waited for the storm to blow itself out.

All he had to do now was yank on the lever which dangled before his eyes. That would release the lifeboat. Release *him*.

And condemn his crewmates to death.

But hadn't they already made that choice for themselves?

Angus gripped the sodden lever tightly in his fist. He wracked his brains. Something . . . *something* was holding him back. Just not allowing him to yank the lever. Not allowing him to splash down into the sea. Not allowing him to bob away to safety—to the morning light—in his tiny vessel.

His heart beat louder in his ears. And then, on instinct, he glanced to his right. Felt *something* there. And—what did he know? —he was right.

There *was* something there.

Some*one*.

The surprise almost knocked Angus back. Almost caused him to flinch. And to tug on the lever. To set the two of them crashing down into the waves. To set the two of them free.

Who was this?

A man . . . yes, but no one he recognised.

Certainly, no one he recognised.

Though it was tough to see in the gloom, he was certain that the man wore a faded turquoise waistcoat, a spry, and weathered, purple bowtie, and looked about fifty years old or more.

He wasn't dressed for sea, that was for sure.

A pair of wispy white patches of hair clung to the sides of the man's head like puffs of smoke rising from a rapidly extinguished flame.

And the man was smiling.

Yes . . . the man was *smiling*.

A wave caught the ship hard.

The ship bucked to the side.

Angus clung on tight to the lever. To the lever which held the lifeboat fixed to the ship. And then he cast another glance upwards. To gauge just how badly the ship was listing. Its mast now was, by his reckoning, on its way towards the horizontal.

Soon the ship would be dragged down to the depths of the ocean.

Without a trace.

And yet . . . why couldn't Angus let go?

Once more, Angus glared over at the man sitting there. This man who appeared to be more at home in some slummy, night-time diner than on a ship on the high seas. "Who . . . who *are* you?" Angus said.

The man merely smiled. His pearl-white teeth and glassy eyes struck with the sheen of the moonlight. "Forgetting something, are we?"

Angus screwed up his features, still unable to believe just what was taking place here. Was he having visions? Yes, that must be it . . . now, come to think of it, when he would speak with other sailors, from all the ports around the world, he would without exception hear the stories of the nearly drowned.

The ones who had seen him.

Seen the one he was seeing now.

"The Subconscience," Angus said aloud.

It was as if that name had calmed the seas—*calmed* the winds.

Inside of the little wooden lifeboat, the air grew still. And quietness pressed on everything.

The man—the Subconscience—grinned wider still, and then said, "You didn't think you were all alone here, did you?"

"What do you want?"

"I want you to do your duty. To do the right thing."

"'The right thing?'" Angus said, shaking his head, and becoming all too aware of the lever that he only had to give a good tug of to release himself—*and the Subconscience*—from this sinking ship.

The man simply nodded, that grin still spreading his cheeks.

Angus felt his heart pound against his tonsils. And the salt water seemed to seep in through his skin. And into his bloodstream.

Choking him.

Killing him.

He blinked once.

Twice.

Three times.

But the Subconscience was still there.

Angus's grip tightened about the lever. He prepared to give it a yank.

"No!" the Subconscience shouted.

A shudder ran round the collar of Angus's shirt. He looked off at the Subconscience. Shocked at his transformation. No longer that seedy, though reserved, man.

Now a stone gargoyle that spewed fire.

Almost apart from himself, Angus noticed he was letting the lever free. Letting it slip through his fingers. And, before he knew it, he had left it alone completely.

"What?" Angus said, feeling his voice shredded to a nasal whine. "What do you want me to do?"

"The same they always do. I want you to do the best you can."

Angus's vision blurred. Crying. That was right. He was *crying*.

Because he was terrified.

Terrified of dying.

And he wanted nothing more than to set himself free.

But he couldn't.

He just knew he couldn't.

And then, with a swift glance to the Subconscience, he shifted up off his seat and then leaped back up to the door of the lifeboat. He hesitated a second or so. Then butted the handle down with his elbow. Felt the lock give. Release. And he was out onto the deck once more.

The winds ripping over him. Froth from the sea soaking his shirt. And the stench of salt almost too much to bear.

But he prowled onwards.

Back along the deck, retracing his steps.

And back down where he had come.

Down the ladder again.

Into the darkness.

To save their souls.

2

A NGUS felt the sun beating down on him from above. It glistened against his well-tanned skin. Bleached his arm hair blond. And bled the sweat out of him.

He sucked his cocktail up through the tropical, pineapple-coloured straw. He savoured the wash of the gin and the limes. Allowed the mixture to tingle in his mouth before swallowing it down.

When he breathed in, the limes were all he could smell. No trace of that ever-present salty stench. The one which plagued his dreams. That was gone now.

At least for the moment.

He lay back on his deckchair, soaking it all up. Closed his eyes. Felt the chill of the cocktail gripped in his fist. And listened to the playful screams of the children. To their splashes. And the scolding from their mothers.

. . . And, a little further away, the lap of the tide at the beach. As it scooped pebbles up in its curling waves before depositing them back down.

Angus had no way of knowing how long he had spent below deck, on the ship. How long he spent down there freeing his crew-mate. The last one left alive. The last one who hadn't drowned.

And he had carried him.

Out to the lifeboat.

The two of them had sailed to safety.

Been picked up by the Coast Guard.

Arrived back on dry land.

But, just as he had thought, the Subconscience hadn't been there, in the lifeboat, when he had returned.

But he was certain that the Subconscience had been the deciding factor in sending him back.

In forcing him back.

And off to save his crewmate.

Selling his story to a newspaper had been a lucrative move. One which had allowed Angus a little time off from his deck handing. A little time to halt his globe-trotting, and to . . . well . . .

He opened his eyes again, and reached out for his cocktail, wrapped his fingers about the stem of the glass, and then brought the straw back up to his lips.

As he sucked hard on the straw, he caught the eye of a bronzed, bikinied lady on the other side of the pool. Though she wore sunglasses—ones which encompassed almost the entirety of her face—he could make out her eyes lingering over him.

Would he play coy?

Or would he make the first move?

He slurped up the last dregs of his cocktail. Laid the glass back down on the white-plastic table at his elbow.

Now was the time.

Better than any other.

Or so it seemed.

He slipped on his flip flops and listened to the slap of their soles as he made his way about the pool. She saw him coming. Of course she did.

How couldn't she?

Before he knew it, he was standing over her.

Standing in her sun—was that the way to put it?

He watched his shadow linger over her curves. Over her tanned skin. And he took a moment to appreciate the dual lumps filling out the cups of her bikini top. The bikini top, though he wondered why he had taken so much notice, which had a light, flowery design.

Just as he was about to open his mouth, to introduce himself, he heard a *shriek* over his shoulder.

Angus froze up. Every muscle drew tight. His heart beat faster.

When he looked down on the woman in the bikini before him, he saw that she was looking off towards the bar. The shriek had come from the direction of the bar.

Angus spun round.

The bar itself had a sun-faded, straw roof, with bristles as stiff as any self-respecting long-handled brush. About a dozen wooden-topped stools, sprouting up from the concrete floor on steel poles, surrounded it.

Though everyone who'd previously been sitting on those stools was now on their feet, and gawping. Staring at what was going on.

Angus's eyes traced the counter, and then he finally took in the shaded interior of the bar, absorbed what was happening within.

There was no sign of the bartender. He was gone. There was, however, a young girl, hair done up in braids, and with pink, puffed-up armbands, screaming out from within.

Angus's heart beat all the harder. "What . . . what do you think it is?" he found himself saying.

The woman in the bikini at his side made no reply.

Angus felt his heart squeeze and he looked about, desperately panicked. He could see no one *doing* anything about it.

And then a strange thing happened.

His gaze shifted upwards, almost of its own accord, and it reached up to the hotel which stood facing out, to someone peering out from behind one of those netted curtains.

It was the Subconscience.

Of course it was.

This time, though, Angus knew just what he had to do.

Before he could put his thoughts in any logical order, he found himself sprinting along the side of the pool, headed directly for the little beach hut bar.

The wails of the little girl grew louder.

Shriller.

And Angus felt a twinge in his heart.

If anything happened to her he knew it would be all his fault.

He was the one who'd been given the opportunity to do something.

And so now he had to stand up.

As he got closer, the screams reached an almost overpowering volume. But he saw sense. Slipped in through the spring-loaded gate to the bar area, and rushed to the girl's aid.

Apparently she'd got curious, gone fishing about in the stainless steel sink just below the level of the bar. And she'd stuck her hand into the sinkhole.

Now he realised that there was a monotonous *hum* in the air, as if playing some horrific bass accompaniment to the girl's screams.

The waste-disposal unit.

His eyes found the switch. A large red button. Just off to the side of the girl.

He launched himself forwards and jabbed it hard.

The *hum* subsided.

But the girl continued to scream.

Angus told himself to breathe, to take his time. To not do anything rash.

And he found confidence in glancing back up to the façade of the hotel, of seeking out the Subconscience standing up there at the netted curtains.

The Subconscience gave him an almost imperceptible nod.

And Angus knew just what he had to do.

He came around the back of the little girl. Looked over her shoulder.

What had he expected?

A pool of blood perhaps . . . a ragged bunch of sliced up fingers, like mutilated salchichas?

But the sink was clean. Its stainless steel, well, *stainless*.

And so, muttering sweet nothings beneath his breath, he reached out and took hold of the little girl's wrist. It was delicate, and light, and reminded him of when he'd been younger and found a baby bird at the back of his garden.

And how he'd taken it in, put it in a shoebox with some straw till it had got better.

Slowly, and with infinite care, he worked to slip the girl's hand out of the plughole.

At first she resisted. Made all her muscles stiff. But he spoke to her gently some more, and she got round to the idea of loosening up.

And, soon enough, she'd brought her hand back from the sink.

He'd got her free.

She looked up at him for a brief moment. Her tears drying on her cheeks. Catching a few shimmers of sunlight. And then, with a tiny, faint "Thank you," that hardly escaped her lips, she tore off out from the bar area and, Angus saw, towards a woman emerging from the back doors of the hotel.

Her mother, he supposed.

Angus glanced about, met with the gawping expressions of the onlookers, in their beach shorts, their bikinis, some with towels wrapped round their shoulders.

And then he looked off up at the hotel again.

Looked for the Subconscience.

But he wasn't there.

3

TWO YEARS LATER, and his boating career well behind him, Angus slurped down the last dregs of his coffee, wincing when he caught the grains at the back of his throat. He settled down onto his sofa with his tablet computer for a brief five-minute respite before he would head out to the office.

Head off into the traffic to get to his day job.

Oh, it wasn't all that fancy. Certainly nothing that would change the world, but he was content. And, the best of all, he was able to find some comfort and stability for the first time in his life.

Just looking about the apartment he shared with his wife made him feel assured, and 'at home.' The woman in the bikini he had met at the pool had become his wife. And now she was seven months along with their first child.

A flat-screen, plasma TV, which showed off his shadowy reflection.

Lush, shagpile carpet beneath his feet.

And, of course, the snug, woollen sofa that he was reclining on right now. That he could just about lose his fingers in. It was like getting a hug from a great big bear.

A *friendly* bear.

But, the thing that he'd never quite got over—and which he supposed, in a way he never would—was the smell about the place.

It just smelled neutral. His smell. And her smell.

Home.

As he tapped through the screens, past the politicians calling one another names, another time past the animal-interest stories, and, once again, past the never-ending list of sport scores, he realised that he well and truly did not care about the world outside any longer.

He had made his own world within.

And, thinking about it, it had all been due to the Subconscience.

To think where he might've been if he'd trod this road any differently.

It made him shudder.

So, with that thought on his mind, he slapped the tablet computer back down on the sofa, snagged his jacket off the back of one of the kitchen chairs, slung it round his shoulders, then kissed his wife goodbye.

Not six paces past the front door of their apartment complex, and he already found himself worrying about her.

Because, if Angus was honest with himself, he had to admit that though he hadn't realised it before, the Subconscience had been something of a blessing to him.

That said, he wasn't all that keen for him to turn up any time soon.

Not when he'd just got his life nice and settled.

What would the Subconscience be able to do for him now?

His life was perfect just the way it was.

Angus leaped up onto the bus, swiping his card against the reader as he went, before taking up his position in one of the seats towards the back.

He was the only passenger.

Early, as always. That was the way to get ahead at work, or so he'd read. And, at the very least, his boss didn't seem to mind that attitude all that much.

Just him and the driver.

As he stared out the window at the streets slick with morning dew passing by, he found himself still absorbed in his dreamlike state. Still half-asleep, really.

Already getting lost with thoughts of his wife.

And being with her when he got back home.

He pictured them there, sitting at the table. A plate of something rich and warm steaming between them . . . lasagne? . . . Yes, that would do. And each of them with a glass of red wine . . . or perhaps just him with the red wine, seeing as his wife wasn't supposed to drink right now.

But the candlelight would send a flickering glow over his wife's skin, bringing out those tangerine eyes of hers and give her that bronze twinkle that had attracted him to her in the first place.

Angus found himself lost in his daydream. Only peering out through droopy eyelids, down the aisle of the bus, and out into the road they were headed down.

He wasn't sure who saw the motorbike pull out first, him or the driver.

But he knew, before anything else happened, before the Subconscience had the slightest chance to jump in, Angus was screaming out to the driver.

Demanding that he stop.

The brakes screeched out loud. Split through Angus's skull. Sent vibrations skittering through his veins. Jabbed at his heart.

The air stank of rubber.

The heater blew hot.

And then impossibly cold.

The bus dodged the motorbike. Turned side on. Caught a streetlamp hard.

Angus heard the *tinkle* of glass as the window beside him shattered.

Everything went black.

Oil.

Rubber.

Burning.

Angus smelled it all.

Something—*someone*—cried out for him to open his eyes.

And when he did, he noted an overwhelming numbness.

All over.

From fingers to toes.

Next blood.

In his mouth.

His teeth felt sharp as broken glass.

He heard mumbling over him. Several people. All speaking at once.

He wanted them to stop.

For them to go away.

To make them understand it was too much to bear.

Slowly, feeling his brain humming hard. Ringing bells sound in his ears. Angus prised himself up. Opened his eyes.

He sat on a curb, at the side of the road. People surrounded him. Lots of people.

In dressing gowns, half-dressed for work, ties hanging limp round collars.

Shoes not yet buffed to a shine.

People, all around him.

When Angus tried to stand, someone touched him on the shoulder. Told him to stay put. That an ambulance was coming. And so Angus did what he was told.

As he sat on the curb, staring out ahead of him, he noticed the bus.

Lying on its side.

Windows all smashed.

Petrol leaking out from beneath, slicking the street with multi-coloured, tarry pools in the early morning sunlight.

And then he made sense of the people.

Of their conversations around him.

As they spoke with a couple who'd just arrived.

A man spoke. A middle-aged man. One of those in a dressing gown.

". . . Incredible! Heard it right from the bathroom, round back of the house. Just this great big *hiss* and then a massive *clang!* When I came out to look, saw the bus on its side. Wrapped round that lamppost over there. I was just on my way out, of course, about to skitter out to go help, when I saw the driver—the bus driver— climb right out of his cab."

Angus felt his throat tighten. His heart hammer a little harder. He felt that he knew what was coming. Was *certain* of what was coming.

"The strangest thing—*strangest* damn thing I've ever seen—the bus driver, he got himself a good, what, fifteen, twenty feet away, then he got to jabbering with something. Guess it was shock most likely. But he was jabbering away at thin air. Strangest thing."

Just as the man wrapped up his account, Angus glanced over to the bus again. Still lying on its side. Windows still smashed. Petrol still bleeding out of it.

"Where's the driver now?" someone asked the man in the dressing gown.

"Oh, I think one of the neighbours took him in. Had a nasty gash on his forehead. Getting it seen to. Nothing too major, though. Looks like the two of them got off fine. Though the ambulance and fire brigade are on their way. Better to leave it to them"

And then, as Angus looked off to the bus once again, something caught him out of the periphery of his vision.

He had to look twice to make sure he wasn't seeing things.

And pretty much as soon as he was sure he'd seen it . . . it was gone again.

But even, after all these years, after all the time that had passed, he recognised him.

That faded turquoise waistcoat.

That weathered, purple bowtie.

Fifty years or so.

The Subconscience.

BROTHERS OF SIEGE

I

TILDERMOORE couldn't quite decide which was the worst part about being under siege: the early mornings or the cold. Right now, he could hardly feel his toes for the chill; and he'd made a point of putting on a pair of extra-woolly socks this morning. And he'd been *absolutely* certain to have his footman, Roger, ensure that his boots were well and truly dry before he had gone to bed.

The first dawn of this siege he had made *that* mistake.

The evening right before the siege had started, he had been out doing a spot of night-hunting. This had involved, as always the best night-hunting did, copious amounts of brandy wine and barrels of honey ale. The theory of the expedition, as it *always* was, went along the lines that, since he was such a poor shot with a crossbow —*let alone a bow and arrow!*—he would almost without doubt have better luck sozzled out of his mind than with his wits about him.

To think that his father had been a renowned knight sent a chill down his spine.

Not wanting to exacerbate the effect of the freezing-cold morning air on his entire body any more than he had to, he *stopped* thinking about his father. Although he had to admit that his father would've been *mighty* handy right about now.

He rested his elbow against the rampart. He felt the sturdy stone beneath the sleeve of his well-insulated black robe—his thermal underwear just below that—and he instantly felt the haze of sleep beginning to settle over him once more.

Why *was* it that people got up early?

The fact that those who were attacking their town—*the fair settlement of Kightsbridge*—had got up so early marked them as the Devil.

Didn't they have sore heads as he did?

117

Didn't they feel as if a horse was kicking in their temples?

. . . And if they didn't then could they be said to be really human at all?

Perhaps *that* was it.

Could they be goblins?

Elves?

Or—*gods forbid!*—dwarfs?

One thing was for certain, at least to his mind, they were awfully slow-witted and really quite backwards to think that they might be able to knock over Kightsbridge so easily; what with the new drawbridge they'd had installed not two months ago, or the widening work that'd been done to the moat surrounding the town which now made it foolish for any but the *strongest* of swimmers to attempt crossing . . . especially with a constant hail of arrows and bolts and *rocks*.

But, then again, he had never really *got* invasions.

Or, for that matter, the point of aspiration.

Why not just sit about in your castle, or tree, or whatever it was that these creatures called home, and enjoy all the excesses which life had to offer? Indeed, he often found it most puzzling how his footman, Roger, seemed compelled to spend his life in Tildermoore —and his brother Frankenmoore's—service. But there it was.

He supposed that some were made to serve while others were made to savour.

As he leaned further out over the rampart, he observed his breath forming clouds before his nose. The air was *that* cold. Beyond the moat, there was nothing at all except for darkness. The invaders hadn't had the curtesy to broadcast their position:

The rotters.

"Morning, brother."

Tildermoore turned to look at the approaching—*bulky*—figure.

His brother Frankenmoore.

Unlike himself, Frankenmoore was round, *doughy*, and had out-of-control, curly hair. Even in the dim moonlight on the ramparts, he could make out his brother's freckled face and the acne scars lurking beneath. It was safe to say that his brother wasn't a looker . . . no, his brother was more of a eat-and-drink-a-lot type. Perhaps his bulk was some sort of compensation for his poor way with maidens. Sure, Tildermoore might not be able to shoot straight, and his arms might wobble at the mere thought of holding—*let alone wielding!*—a sword, but there was something about his sable-haired, chisel-jawed charm which sent the ladies all aflutter.

He turned to look at Frankenmoore who—rather optimistically—had a sword hanging from his belt. "Morning," he just about managed to utter in reply, before turning back to the gloom over the ramparts, squinting to make it *seem* as if he was extremely interested in something or other.

"Any action?"

"No. Nothing yet."

Frankenmoore trudged up to the rampart, leaned over, then gave a wide, *all-encompassing* yawn.

One which set Tildermoore off.

And then Frankenmoore yawned again.

Tildermoore mirrored him.

They went back and forth like that for what seemed like a dozen times. It was only when Tildermoore felt a fresh swill of energy pump through his blood that he eventually managed to cast off the never-ending lethargy. When he examined the matter later, in his mind's eye, he wondered whether he had actually seen the arrow arcing through the air, or if he had just imagined the sight.

Whatever it was, next thing he knew he felt a searing hot pain as an arrowhead pierced the soft part of his throat.

2

TILDERMOORE could hear muttering voices all around.

He was lying down, on a mattress.

The tickle on the surface of his skin told him it was a *straw* mattress. He had always preferred feathers, despite deriders' claims that, after a solid season or two, it became *lumpy*.

He could feel a throbbing warmth oozing about his neck.

When he opened his eyes and reached out, he felt a warm sticky liquid on his fingertips.

Blood.

The smell seemed to catch up with him then; the coppery scent which seemed to overwhelm all others. He blinked several times before the pain completely sunk in. And it was so intense—so *concentrated*—right at the nib of his throat, that he could only muster a *groan* of alarm.

His eyes quickly fastened onto his surroundings.

He looked to the torches hanging from the stone walls, their flames flickering orange light all over. He could feel the warmth reflecting back at him.

He looked to the men, dressed in dark-brown robes—*so* different from Tildermoore's preferred black. They all had their backs to him, muttering among themselves.

One of the men broke off the conversation, and turned to him.

The man had a bald head and a bony nose; and those black, beady, crow eyes which always had a habit of making Tildermoore uneasy:

Emmongone: The Chief Healer of Kightsbridge.

"He's awake," Emmongone uttered in his gruff voice.

As one, the rest of the men turned around.

Among them, Tildermoore immediately identified his brother,

Frankenmoore. Their eyes had hardly crossed before Tildermoore felt a fresh flash of pain pass through his throat. "Ah!" he mumbled, mostly to himself, unable to keep the exclamation back.

"Sire," Emmongone said, creeping closer to Tildermoore, so he could quite easily breathe in the stench of rotten cabbages which seemed to follow Emmongone just about everywhere he went. "You gave us quite a scare."

Tildermoore swallowed hard, tasting the blood, and feeling the pain jab at his temples. He looked up at the men with bleary eyes. "What're you . . . what're . . ."

"Sire," Emmongone said, "you need rest. Please, do not try to speak."

Tildermoore turned his gaze onto his brother, the pain becoming blindingly severe now. Once more, he reached up to his throat, touched the spot which ached so terribly; and, like before, came away with a smear of blood. Almost accusingly, he held his bloodied fingers out for Emmongone to inspect.

Emmongone squinted at the sight, as if there was some ambiguity to be had. As if there might be some sort of a *roundabout* explanation for the coating of blood now present on Tildermoore's fingertips. "Ay, sire," Emmongone said, "that'll stop soon enough, I promise you." His pudgy face had the nerve to soften into a plump-cheeked grin. "Just a *flesh* wound."

Tildermoore had to admit that he wasn't entirely convinced; either by the tone or the explanation itself. But he had little choice. He couldn't move for the constant pain. He turned his attention back to his brother, to Frankenmoore, and then, with an exorbitant amount of strength, summoned him to his side.

Frankenmoore crouched down by Tildermoore's side. He knew that—*quite likely*—these would be the last words he would ever utter to his brother. So he decided to make them count. "Fran . . . k . . ." Tildermoore just about got out. "Please make it . . . make it so .

. . when you remember me . . . when I'm dead and . . . and . . ."
Already Tildermoore was certain that he could see the bright lights
filling his vision; and—*yes!*—was that his father? Beckoning him
forth? Enticing him onward to plunge himself into all the heavenly
pleasures which awaited him in the Everafter? Perhaps he had never
been made for this world—perhaps he had never made it as a great
warrior—but at least he would find solace in the afterlife. He had
always believed that Earthly pleasure was his niche, so Heavenly
pleasures could only be the natural transition.

He turned his attention back onto Frankenmoore, and did his
best to continue, despite his very life force leaking from his neck. "I
want a . . . a *statue*, Frank. I want . . . it . . . in the town square . . . a .
. . a . . . celebr . . . celebration of the . . . of our . . . of *my* stand
against . . . against . . . the invaders." He sucked up yet more
strength then finished by saying, "and our . . . *my* victory!"

He managed to almost shout the final word, and good thing too
since—surely even to the most objective of observers—it was the
most important by far.

As he lay back and prepared for the shutters to close on his
mortal life, and to be whisked away in the talons of an eagle—or
another suitably *noble* creature—he couldn't help but notice the
constant muttering. How the men at his bedside had looks of
concern sketched on their faces.

Was there no holy man to be found?

Oh—dear *gods!*—had the holy man been killed in the siege;
seeing off the invaders?

That would make things more complicated.

No *wonder* he hadn't yet been swept away to his destiny.

In the end, it was his brother, Frankenmoore, who stooped low
at his bedside, and who kept his voice down to a quiet tone so that
he wouldn't be overheard by the others. "Uh, brother?"

"*What?*"

"I . . . uh, . . . when they shot you . . . when the arrow cut through your throat, we decided to, uh . . . *surrender.*"

Shrugging death off for another few moments, he sat up straight in bed, and couldn't help but blurt out, "*What?!* *Surrender!*"

Looks of alarm appeared on the faces of the men surrounding the bed.

But he could only sink back into his mattress.

Thoroughly put out.

3

INDEED, as Frankenmoore suggested, Kightsbridge had been swarmed by an invading force. The good news was that it hadn't been dwarfs. As it turned out, it was the worthy—*if quite revolting*—adversary of orcs. Unfortunately, from Tildermoore's point of view, instead of being swept away by the wings of eagles to some long-ago promised holy land, he remained very much of the Earth. The worst part of it all, he thought, as he examined his reflection in the bathroom mirror, was that the gash the arrowhead had made in his neck was healing very nicely indeed.

There was little prospect of a scar.

If nothing else, he had imagined that possessing such a scar would give a bonus double yield of increasing his charm power with the ladies and offering him something in the way of *physical* evidence when the time did come for him to join his father on the Great Warrior Plains in the Sky.

Damn.

The good news with the orcs was that—far from being overbearing occupants of Kightsbridge—they were overly polite; always allowing humans to be the first through any given doorway, and even going as far as to bow to all humans they addressed.

In retrospect, he thought that he might've been able to live without the constant smiles . . . or what passed for an *orc* smiling. The issue wasn't so much the gesture, the fact that—for all their niceties—they were the occupying force within a human settlement; but more to do with the very *look* of the smiles themselves. Despite having an enviable military ethic, the orcs seemed to have sacrificed other aspects of their civilisation . . . and dentistry, it seemed, had been one of the casualties. Whenever an orc smiled, it wasn't so much the stench of fish guts emanating from their green-tinged tongues; or the way their nostrils flared to expose the open sores within. No, it was more how their blackened teeth, with huge gaps between them, exposing the red-raw flesh of their gums, would jag out at all angles . . . all at once appearing *rather* threatening; despite the notably good intention behind the gesture.

Indeed, it was quite a puzzle for the orcs when—during the first few days of the occupation—they would find children screaming and mewling in horror at their pleasant Good-Day expressions; and even more so when, in an attempt to rectify the awkward interracial dialogue, said orc would get down on their haunches and pull 'funny' faces in an attempt to cheer up the human children. The resulting children fleeing in terror from the orcs was very much *not* what was expected.

But—smiling aside—he had to admit that the rampant good manners, along with the sturdy—and, he had to face it, *badly needed!* —garrison defence had all been welcome additions to Kightsbridge. In fact, after the first week or so of the occupation, he couldn't quite face the prospect of the orcs ever leaving. Although he had nothing more than a ceremonial position on the Town Council— his father's immense heroics had all but demanded that a Moore should, by all costs, have a presence in the everyday running of Kightsbridge—it was enough so that he could sit in on the meetings with the Town Council and the orc generals.

The orc in charge was called Gachkp'snorf . . . or, at least, that was the very best rendering of the name which Tildermoore could produce with his own—*human*—tongue.

Although, normally, in day-to-day, human administered times, he would have done his very best to *avoid* Council meetings, he found himself strangely compelled to attend every single one put on during the orcs' occupation. The meetings themselves took place in the Upper Turret of the town walls; affording the members of the Town Council with a view out over the entirety of the plains leading up to Kightsbridge: the rolling, lush green hills; and then, on the horizon, the purple-blue haze of the Hellish Mountains . . . where it was taken for granted that none but the most noble—or, in Tildermoore's opinion, the most *stupid*—human would venture. Because over there, in the Hellish Mountains, lurked magic, and creatures beyond comprehension or reason.

Certainly much worse specimens than *orcs*.

And far less polite.

As he would sink back into the embroidered, high-backed chair —the chair which'd once belonged to his father while he had been alive, and served on the Council—he would breathe in the gentle scent of polished wood, all around him. Then he would look to the leathered, wizened faces of the wise people of the Council. He was sure he knew all their names, but he couldn't quite summon them at the present time. In any case, all his attention was reserved for Gachkp'snorf.

Gachkp'snorf, like all orcs, along with the smiling 'affliction' also suffered from excessive drooling. What he found *most* amusing about the Town Council meetings was how a poor peasant boy—was Filip his name?—dashed about Gachkp'snorf's feet doing his very best, with a well-soiled rag and a weathered wooden bucket filled to the brim with soap suds, to clean up the dribble which splattered onto the fine rugs which adorned the floors of the Upper Turret.

During the meetings themselves, Tildermoore never spoke up. He merely sat back and listened.

The orcs spoke excellently in the human tongue—and had even managed to grasp various regional nuances particular to Kights-bridge in the time of their occupation. Hardly ever did Gachkp's-norf pause to search for expression, choose a comically wrong piece of diction, or even so much as mispronounce a single word. All things considered, he had to admit that these orcs were starting to make him feel a little like a country bumpkin; and *he* was the son of Moore . . . so there was no accounting for how the *rest* of the human population of Kightsbridge might feel.

During his time in the meetings, he gathered, from the orcs' discussions with the humans that the orcs had currently *stationed* themselves in Kightsbridge while they battled with an unrelated foe. They merely wished to draw on Kightsbridge's resources; and only in a *reasonable* way, of course . . . because far be it from Gachkp'snorf to put any resident of Kightsbridge's nose out of joint by having his orcs overindulge themselves with either food, or water, or liquor; or all of the above.

The siege, it turned out, had mostly been formed from a misunderstanding.

It had been Gachkp'snorf—and his fellow orcs'—belief that their unseen enemy; a race of what sounded like a kind of impish creature, and—at least to Tildermoore's interpretation—a really quite mischievous one; had succeeded in stationing themselves in Kightsbridge.

However, it had soon followed that their intelligence had been misinformed.

Gachkp'snorf declared with, a quite odd level of glee, that those responsible had been turned loose of service and sent on their merry way back home; to live out the rest of their days on a fair pension with their families.

Tildermoore shuddered to think what might've become of the bearers of such poor intelligence in an army led by his father . . . one thing was for certain; the guilty party losing their head would've been the very least of their worries . . .

Gachkp'snorf was also unreserved in his apologies to Tildermoore, for having shot him in the throat, assuring him that, had they known the truth—that their foe was *not* present in the town—

that they would never have thought to so much as raise their voices in anger.

Tildermoore had been the only casualty, though that had been more down to Kightsbridge surrendering soon after receiving its first casualty.

When finally came the time for Gachkp'snorf to stand up before the Town Council and declare that his people had been successful in beating back their foe; and that they would be pursuing them, and—*once and for all*—leaving Kightsbridge behind, did Tildermoore decide that *now* was the time for him to step in.

As a child, he recalled how he would see his father standing up before reams of armed men. How he would puff his chest out, project his voice and *be heard*. And he, right now, had every intention of being heard. "Honourable men and women of the Council," he said, rising from his father's chair and looking over the faces— struck with surprise to notice he was there at all. "Gachkp'snorf," he said, giving a nod in the direction of the orc, which was received with a well-intentioned—if a little *jagged*—smile.

He turned back to the table. "I believe that it's in the interest of all of Kightsbridge, nay, in favour of *everybody*, that we invite the orcs to administer the town from this day forward."

This declaration, as he had anticipated, caused much stirring amongst the Town Council. He overheard a couple of comments, some of them calling him crazy, while others saw more reason.

He appreciated that, because he had waited so long before addressing the Town Council—because he had been silent for such a time—that they felt almost *obliged* to give serious consideration to whatever he might propose.

A member of the Town Council—a man of about fifty with grey hair, reddened cheeks and tufty eyebrows in need of a good *cut*, rose up from his seat. He thrust a glance off in Tildermoore's direction. Tildermoore almost *felt* heat off his glare.

From the gossip he heard about town, he knew that the Town Council was something of a vehicle for corruption. That there wasn't a serving member who wasn't on the take in some form or another. And he supposed that the orcs' brief occupancy had curtailed—*if not completely interrupted*—normal service.

"Look, here," the man said, his voice stroppy, and one of his sausage-like fingers prodding the surface of the table hard and pointedly. "Of course it'll be with a heavy heart that we wish the orcs goodbye, but it's a necessary evil. Gachkp'snorf would be first to admit that they have been guests here—*well-received guests, but guests all the same*—and, as for all guests, the time comes when they need to move on."

Tildermoore noted several nodding heads around the table, and when he caught sight of Filip—the peasant boy charged with mopping up Gachkp'snorf's dribble—he quickly bowed his head and got back to work.

Gachkp'snorf, too, was nodding and smiling—to the best of his ability—along with the other members of the Council.

This decision—the decision for the orcs to leave Kightsbridge —would have an impact on every man, woman and child who resided here; and it was clearly one which couldn't be taken lightly.

But, then again, Tildermoore *knew* that.

He decided the time was right for him to invoke his father to bear on proceedings.

"My *father*," he began, and could almost hear the inward groans around the table, "always believed in a rugged defence—that having a *solid* defence was the key to Kightsbridge thriving." Here he decided it was his time to do his own poking of the surface of the table. "And he would've been first to admit that, right now, we—*as citizens of Kightsbridge*—lack the necessary resources to mount our own defence."

There was some nodding around the table.

For effect, he casually reached up and massaged his throat, where the arrowhead had passed through his flesh. He was certain that he heard at least a pair of gasps in response to this gesture. He allowed himself a slight smirk. "Now, what am I proposing?"

"Dunno," the grey-haired man from before said, and was greeted by a round of chuckles.

Unperturbed, he continued, "Of course, as the Council states, it would be unreasonable for us to believe the orcs would stay behind forever; that they would integrate into Kightsbridge as some sort of garrison . . . however, I *do* believe there might be some room to manoeuvre in between."

There was some grumbling.

Once more, Tildermoore caught Filip looking up from his never-ending task of cleaning up drool.

And this time Filip didn't turn back to his work.

"What *I* propose," Tildermoore said, "is that several"—here he made circles in the air with his index finger—"a couple dozen, of Gachkp'snorf's troops remain behind in permanent garrison."

He waited for some response from the Council, but the best he really got off them was a whole host of mumbling. He couldn't help that; he just needed to roll along and see if he could beat them into submission. He turned his attention to Gachkp'snorf. "Any ideas on this proposal?"

Gachkp'snorf uncrossed and then recrossed his legs. He reached up and stroked his horny, lizard-like chin. "I can see no issue—it would be more a question of pride." He did his best—*of that Tildermoore was sure*—to give an understanding smile to the rest of the Town Council. "I know that orcs would never so much as *consider* a human garrison in their settlement."

Sensing that he needed to step in to prop up his argument, Tildermoore said, "Yes, well, I think we can all agree that a *human* army would have very little chance of finding itself in such a fortu-itous position."

There was no protest here, and as far as he could tell, the rest of the Town Council at least agreed with him on this point.

Finally, with a slight sigh, and a vague smile, Gachkp'snorf turned to the Council and said, "Well, I would see no obstacle in such an arrangement." He looked back to Tildermoore. "Why not put it to a vote?"

4

TILDERMOORE managed to pull off his wishes by a single vote, but it was binding.

He was not a little smug at having managed to get his way.

As he strutted about Kightsbridge, smiling to the orc garrison—all of them with clubs, or crossbows, or bow and arrow close at hand—they greeted him pleasantly.

Throughout the coming weeks, as he strode about town, he noted how well the orcs had come to assimilate with the townspeople of Kightsbridge; how he had noticed more than one romantic union between human and orc . . . it was true to say that orcs, almost without exception, had quite tidy, packed abs . . . and that was without even getting *started* on those biceps.

It was far easier for him to sleep at night now, and it made his deviant lifestyle a whole lot more enjoyable knowing that he wouldn't—*at a moment's notice*—be called away to defend the gates from *these* creatures, or *those* imps.

Trade, too, had become a whole sight easier seeing that—as part of the package—the orcs kept open a protected passage to the neighbouring town of Blinkington through the aptly named Fearsome Forests. Whereas before, a tradesman, or anyone else, for that matter, would take their life into their hands by taking the shortcut through the Fearsome Forests, now it was very much a standard route; and made travel between the two towns *far* more viable because half a day's journey wasn't required in order to go *around* the Forests.

The whole town was thriving, really *off the scale*. And it was all thanks to Tildermoore swallowing his pride, seeing where there was work to be done, and then seeing the opportunity to snaffle the talent. Why *was* it that orcs had somehow acquired such a poor reputation?

That question would puzzle him until the day he died.

As he clambered up onto the ramparts, and took a peaceful stroll among their protectors—*the orcs*—he wondered if he had done a great service that could at least *begin* to compare with that of his father's. Not that he was going to allow himself to get a big head.

He wouldn't be the one to write history, at the end of the day.

With a final—*and long-deserved*—sigh, he stared out over the plains surrounding Kightsbridge, down on the fertile fields, and then to the sun as it set on the horizon.

Yes, tonight he would sleep well.

Very well *indeed.*

MY MOTHER, MY GOOD OMEN

THE AIR WAS WARM as Dante led me inside the tumbledown little cottage.

We had been travelling through the foreign countryside for so long—through the rolling, grey hills; and the mumbling, silver brooks that reminded me so much of home:

Of *England*.

I supposed that if we had had the luxury of being able to commence our journey in the summer then it might've been quite a sight to ride through the countryside in the daylight. But since it was winter, there were only twisted tree branches, dead leaves and grim, never-ending fields of mud; flooded by the seemingly never-ending, freezing-cold rain.

I had heard, before heading out on the journey, that travelling was a man's game, and I gave it just the sneer that it deserved. Only now, though, after months on the road do I truly appreciate the unique stresses and strains which it puts on the body.

Not just on a *woman's* body, though . . . because, of what I've seen in my two male companions, *travelling* has dealt with them just as cruelly.

Standing in the entrance hall of the cottage, I realised that I'd almost forgotten what stonework looked like. I was so used to the beaten-up wooden interior of the carriage. Of the constant motion which wood seemed to suggest.

Stone was sturdy.

Permanent.

And—most important of all—*static.*

I could smell ash, and, almost close enough to touch, the taste of roast chicken thickening in the air. I could hear it *crackle* too. It seemed so long since I'd had a good, hot dinner in comfortable lodgings—not wrapped up in a moth-chewed blanket by an open fire, out of doors—that my whole body *ached* for it. But it was the walls that I was most drawn in by.

When I reached out to touch them, little pieces came away on my fingertips. I could feel the warmth of the open fire—burning away *somewhere* ahead in the cottage—pass through the surface of my skin. Warm my heart.

Warm my *soul*.

On my heels, I heard a gale blow the wooden front door of the cottage shut with a thunderous *bang*! It nearly scared me out of my wits.

When I turned back around, I saw that Dante—too—was looking off in the direction of the door. He finally met my eyes, smiled, and said, in that accented English of his, "I think that Farol shall find his own way in, hmm?"

For a couple of seconds, in the oil lamp-lit entrance hall of the cottage, I lost myself in the gentle, graceful swoop of Dante Gobornik's cheekbones.

It was hard to imagine we had come this far.

That we had evaded capture this long.

Both me and Farol—the driver of the carriage—seemed somewhat surprised by this.

Dante, clearly, wasn't.

When Dante turned away from me, the spell was broken.

Stopping had been a shock to my system.

We hadn't thought to stop hardly at all.

We had been constantly *on the run*.

Only the few times, when Dante saw fit to allow the horses a rest, did the wooden wheels of the carriage cease turning. Whatever the occasion, I felt woefully underdressed. I had been given no warning. As always with Dante, there'd been little to no indication that we would stop at all—let alone pay somebody a visit. And so, all I wore was my well-dirtied travelling blouse—once-white, and never again—then there was the long, *mercifully-black* skirt which swept down to my ankles.

The skirt might have been able to pass if it hadn't been for the *odour*.

And I wasn't the only odorous one.

I felt that *all* of us—all *three* of our travelling party—absolutely stank.

Of just about every scent imaginable.

Then again, I supposed that if such things had been important to our host then Dante would have made some sort of a comment. And since he hadn't, I supposed that they weren't. Still, I would've liked to at least have had a wash in one of those—surely *freezing*—little ponds on the way here . . .

Dante led me along the hallway and into the small front room of the cottage. Wall-to-wall bookcases dominated the room, and I could make out several armchairs and sofas, all of them set in the ethereal glow of the fireplace.

No chicken cooking here.

I supposed *that* smell wafted along from the kitchen.

Wherever the kitchen might be.

There was a fine mantelpiece, too, all swirling cornices, and with a pair of oil paintings perched on top. I could see that the canvases of both paintings had been damaged. That there were scuff marks about their edges. When I glanced up to the wall, I saw that they must've fallen down from their places up on the wallpaper and become damaged when they'd dropped.

I only realised we were not alone when Dante cleared his throat.

Drawing my attention.

A tingling sensation ran up my spine.

I turned to him.

Saw that he stood over in the corner of the room—beside the

highest-backed armchair of them all. And I could just make out, though she was almost entirely consumed by shadow, the crumpled form of an old woman sat in the armchair.

Dante was crouched down at her side. He held his fingers atop her forearm, as if he was comforting her in some way. As my eyes adjusted to the low light, I was able to pick out more finite details. Her puffy, birds nest hair. The larger wrinkles of her face. How she perched right on the edge of her chair like a raptor ready to strike its prey.

I can't say that I immediately liked her.

When Dante finally spoke, I was surprised by the tone of his voice, which was to say nothing for the content of his words. "Sara. I'd like you to meet my mother." He paused for a moment, glanced back at her, into her eyes, and then added, "My good omen."

The shock of Dante's words was almost like a blow to the solar plexus.

I stood there—*numbed*—for several moments.

I listened to the flicker of the flames from the fireplace behind me. And I felt the steady pumping of my sped-up heartbeat. The smell of chicken now seemed almost too sweet and appetising to be true. My mouth could summon more easily the taste of ash than bird's flesh. Although I stared at the old woman in the armchair, I found myself addressing Dante. "But . . . you told me that you . . . that you were an *orphan*."

Dante kept up a gentle smile.

I wondered if it was for my benefit, or for the benefit of the old woman.

Perhaps both.

"Well, that's true, to an extent. I *am* an orphan." He held himself still, crouched down at the old woman—his *mother's*—side. "But this, for all intents and purposes, is my mother."

I shook my head, not understanding, and it was then that a servant appeared in the doorway.

The way that he arrived was what I found most disquieting. How he seemed to simply loom into place in the doorway. A thin figure, his smart waistcoat and jacket hanging off his frame as if he was no more substantial than a hat stand.

His face remained in darkness all the while.

The old woman spoke to Dante in his ear. I watched on as she reached up for him. Her fingers were so frail that she could hardly grip his travelling coat.

Dante's face creased with a smile.

"What?" I asked. "What did she say?"

Dante straightened up. "She wants to wish you a Merry Christmas?"

" 'A Merry Christmas' ?"

But—I supposed—that today *was* Christmas Eve.

. . . Or was I totally losing the plot?

The old woman croaked out more words in a language I couldn't *identify*—let alone *understand*—but the upshot of it was the servant leading me away.

Leaving Dante and his 'mother' in peace.

2

THE BATHROOM consisted of a large stone tub and another, smaller one, for washing my face. The room smelled strongly of moss and soap. I have to admit that, upon seeing the bathroom, the first time that I had seen a proper washing place for months, all my hunger deserted me.

Not even the thickest, richest—*greasiest*—of chicken breasts could've pried me away.

From just observing the space, I felt almost as if all the months of accumulated grit and dust—all those travelling by-products— were slipping right off the surface of my skin.

I could hear my heart *thump-thump* in my eardrums.

The servant brought me hot water, letting off steam all the way up to the ceiling, and he left me a short stack of finely woven towels to dry myself with . . . when I was finished bathing.

Once I had poured the water into the stone tub, I soaked for a long while. I must've been lying there for several minutes when I noticed the large slab of soap up on one of the stone ledges within the bathroom. Since I had had no instruction about 'not touching' I made good use of it—scrubbing at my body, not knowing when I might get another chance.

After the initial euphoria of bathing, I was just a touch put out to remind myself of the clothes I had worn—all scrunched up on the floor of the bathroom, and clearly having been worn for days on end. A slightly squeamish feeling seized control of my stomach just to think what the old woman might've thought of me.

What her *servant* might've thought of me.

My only consolation was that Dante looked just as beaten-up— just as worn-down—by all this travelling as I was.

I would like to say that I lay there, in the glorious, soaped-up waters of the bath until the water turned as cold as the stone it lay within.

But no.

Because the fantastical—the *spirit world*—doesn't wait.

I lay on my back, staring up at the stone ceiling, wondering absentminded thoughts connected with the masons who must've put the place together once upon a time. It's a way I have to keep touch with my past. With where I came from.

Before I was sucked in by the pomp and whimsy of Dante Gobornik.

Show business.

I examined the cut of the stone, marvelling at how such skilled hands must've worked to piece the different parts together, so that it might stand without the aid of anything other than simple mechanics. I observed the angles—over and over—my eyes constantly going back and forth, sketching the empty air. Trying to peel back all the secrets.

Get the work to show me the *answers.*

And it was then when it hit me.

Like a punch to the gut.

I almost felt like crying.

Perhaps, if I had been in the carriage—alone inside the carriage with Dante—I would have done.

But I was in a stranger's house.

No place to break down.

I held myself together, breathed in deep breaths—just as Dante had shown me countless times—and I attempted to keep myself from fainting.

I couldn't faint now.

I might *drown* in my own bath water.

All the sounds of the cottage, the distant crackling of the fireplace—the *spit* of the unseen chicken roasting—it all faded from my earshot.

Everything within my spirit focused.

In on myself.

On the darkness there.

As it was coming pouring out.

3

ALTHOUGH I DIDN'T SOB, I did feel the tears—*inevitably*—pour down my cheeks.

And they felt cold.

Almost like half-melted icicles rolling down my skin.

Because I had let it out.

There had been no chance of keeping it within me.

I was afraid to open my eyes.

But I knew I must.

I wasn't a child any longer . . . I needed to face my demons.

As Dante *often* reminded me.

I cracked open my left eye first, a habit of mine, and gazed about the bathroom.

In the light from the oil lamp the servant had left in the bathroom, the whole room seemed to dance about. The shadows were never still. I had trouble separating what was *real* from what was not there at all. I wished that I might have a helping hand.

But I knew—one day—I would have to make do *without* a helping hand.

Because—one day—Dante would no longer be there for me.

He would join the shadow world.

As I glanced about the shadows, I tried to make sense of the flickering flame of the oil lamp. Before there hadn't been a draught in the bathroom—I was sure of it—but there now was. And I knew that there was . . . some *presence* with me.

A tingling sensation ran through my blood.

My heart pattered a few times.

I feared it might stop.

And I urged it to keep beating.

To keep me alive.

To keep me from *joining* their world.

To hold back the curtain just a *little* longer.

Darkness loped all around.

I fixed my attention on a single shadow, and then another, waiting for some form to appear from within. But there was . . . *nothing*.

I wondered if it had been a rush of blood to the head. We were up fairly high, after all, passing through the hills, and we had been constantly on the move. With the constant to-and-fro rocking of the carriage. It wouldn't be any mystery that my brain was still finding its place in this newly *unmoving* world.

I breathed in gently.

Then out again.

My breath formed clouds before my eyes.

I felt it return to warm my cheeks.

My heart throbbed a little harder.

And I could feel it approaching.

Death.

4

THE SHADOWS WEAVED—one into the other—and I could see them mixing together . . . then spreading apart. Slowly, gradually, she formed before me. Took on significance within my mind.

And I observed her.

My mother.

Breath hitched at the back of my throat and I had to remind myself of my commitments to the mortal world.

Respiration.

Not *voluntary*.

It had been a long while since I had seen her.

Too long?

And this was the first time that I had seen her abroad—when I *hadn't* seen her back in England.

The water seemed to cling to me.

I could feel it growing chilly.

I wondered if I could leave the stone tub.

Fetch the towel.

Dry myself off.

Even my rumpled-up, dirtied travelling clothes seemed more attractive than having to sit here, in the tub, *naked*.

I made a move of my arm.

It instantly felt as if it was weighed down by ice.

Or a half ton of snow.

I stared into the blackness of the shadow, and I wondered.

I wondered if she had followed me here.

Or if . . . if she had come from *somewhere* else.

"Sara," my mother said, her voice gruff, and at the level of a whisper.

My throat tightened, and although I *knew* I wouldn't be able to summon the strength to speak, I attempted to do so. ". . . Mum?" I finally got out.

My mother—her shadow self—seemed to curl into being. Like black smoke off a wood fire, whipped up by the wind. Her face took on more form.

More features.

The elegant curl of her lips.

Wicked sharp tips of her eyebrows, drawn into points.

The twinkle in her eye.

Neither of us spoke any more words.

We simply regarded one another.

From where I sat, in the water of the stone bathtub, the rest of the cottage seemed so distant. And yet, I was sure—*certain*—I could hear screaming.

High-pitched.

Blood-curdling.

But it had no effect on me.

I was immune.

Wrapped into this moment with my mother.

"Why," I finally got out, "why're you here with me?"

My mother seemed to curl into herself, the same way that smoke whips itself up into clouds. Floats along on the breeze . . . but here that wasn't the case, because it was clear that she—*herself* —was the breeze.

"You have travelled, Sara," my mother said.

"Yes, I have."

"And with such a tall, dark stranger."

Something stuck in my throat.

Had she come this far just to reproach me?

"He is a good man," my mother said, as if this was a considered opinion, and one which she had taken no small amount of time in forming . . . after *much* deliberation. "But you must be careful—you must not allow him too close, you must not allow him to *exploit* your gift."

" 'My gift' ?" I said back at her, as if I didn't understand what she referred to.

As if I hadn't realised that my connection to the shadow world, to the Other Side, set me out as something 'special' . . . if those were the terms I wished to deal in.

"A showman," my mother continued, "but that's not *all* he wishes to be—is it?"

I had next to no idea what it was Dante wanted . . . except on those few occasions when he had deigned to confide in me with some little titbit.

Just words: here and there, but nothing which I could easily pin down.

Nothing I could deliver to my mother.

There was a long silence between the two of us and then my mother broke it.

"You could always stay."

"What?"

"Here," she went on, "in this place—you should be safe here."

"I . . ." I began but couldn't finish.

My mother's features started to melt.

Back into smoke.

Back into air.

I was left to sit in the now-chilly bath water and consider what my mother had been trying to say.

What did she mean 'safe' ?

5

WHEN I'D DRIED OFF, wrapped a towel about myself—about my hair—I heard a knock on the bathroom door. For the first time, I can genuinely say that I was glad to see the servant standing there. He bore a nice, clean dress. With a polite smile, he held it out to me, and I took it from him.

I only felt that I could consider the dress properly once I had shut the door.

When I was alone again.

It was red with festive green sleeves.

Silver trimming.

I caught the impression that this dress was only to be loaned to me for the evening, and I supposed that was only fair seeing as—the other three hundred-odd days of the year—I might've looked like a maniac gallivanting about in it.

As I made my way into—what turned out to be—the dining room, the scent of chicken on the air grew too much to bear. When I saw it in the centre of the table, I could hardly hold myself back.

When I took it in properly, however, I realised that it was a goose.

A Christmas goose!

I scolded myself a little at having been so ditsy not to have come to that conclusion earlier.

Perhaps, in all my hunger, during all our travels, I had forgotten those subtleties in smells.

How certain morsels smelled *different* to others.

Already, Dante sat at the head of the table; the old woman beside him.

The two of them had their heads bowed slightly forwards.

Beyond them the fireplace blazed away.

I took up my place beside the old woman—doing my very best not to make a sound.

For several more moments, I soaked up the setting. Looked over the beautifully set out silver cutlery, and porcelain plates. The silk napkins snug within their golden rings.

The servant appeared from the doorway towards the back of the dining room, and I saw that he was bearing vegetables. All boiled. And smelling just as sweet, and rich, as the goose itself. When my eyes fell upon the glass decanter of gravy, I thought that I might melt from the inside out.

I couldn't quite imagine that, not so long ago, I had dreaded entering this cottage—visiting upon this stranger. And while I still felt quite a long way away from being totally welcome, the sight of this . . . this *Christmas* food . . . was enough to trick my mind into believing I *deserved* to be here.

The servant—finished with his duties—sat at the place opposite mine.

He clasped his hands together.

Dante and the old woman did the same.

I picked up my cue, mimicking them.

All four of us sat there, at the table.

Heads bowed.

Waiting.

6

A GOOD MEAL is almost like a constant humming within your own chest, and that was how I felt as I exited the cottage with Dante.

Although I felt a slight pang in my gut at having to leave the place, at having to step back up into the carriage, I had no regrets about not spending the night in the cottage.

There was something . . . something *clung* to the cottage which I found disquieting.

The rain had apparently let off while we had been inside, and I saw Farol had been making good progress on fixing a piece of the carriage which'd become damaged when we'd passed over uneven, rocky ground. He had hammered the piece back into place.

The horses, too, had been fed and watered, and were already harnessed.

On occasion, I wondered if Dante and Farol had some means of secret communication.

They seemed able to read one another's mind.

Or—at least—Dante appeared able to read *Farol's*.

As Dante approached, Farol tilted his hat back in greeting and, in return, Dante handed him the small wooden box which contained his Christmas dinner.

Farol thanked him briskly and—if he had any—didn't betray his hunger with any outward sign. He merely squeezed the box beneath his arm and held open the door to the carriage, for me and Dante to get inside.

Once back in the carriage, there was none of the lingering sickness I'd felt over the past few days—barrelling through the endless countryside. Somehow I felt like I was coming back home.

That the *carriage* . . . that the *road* was my home now.

Could that be the case?

As I listened to the *clip-clop* of the horses moving off their marks, and the carriage jerking forwards, I looked out through the cool glass, back to the cottage.

There, in the doorway, I saw the old woman, and her servant.

Something strange about them now.

No longer was there any light in the cottage.

No oil lamp.

And no trace of light from the fireplace within.

Before I had a chance to dwell on this, the carriage carried on along the rutted road. I gripped on tight to the handle, my body somehow unused to the movement now after only a few hours of having my feet on the flat, secure ground. As we left the cottage behind the corner, and once more embraced the darkened country-side—the oil lamps which hung from Farol's seat lighting only the road ahead—Dante began to speak with me.

"There are some places that are better to leave behind."

I could feel my brain moving about in my skull.

Slopping from side to side.

The food sitting peacefully in my gut.

"And there are those who are best off staying."

I looked briefly to his black eyes, but, as so often happened, I found that they took me off guard. I had to look away. Out of the window.

I tried to untangle his words of wisdom.

I thought back on what my mother had said.

About how I could stay there if I wished.

How I would be safe.

Was that what Dante meant?

"These places—places just like that cottage—they work almost like portals; between the land of the living, and the land of the dead; they dwell, really, in neither."

My chest tightened.

I really didn't want to have this conversation.

Not now.

I just wanted to reflect on the wonderful Christmas dinner.

Get some sleep before Christmas Day dawned on us.

"To bring someone back—to leave someone behind, really, it's all the same. It gives the same result."

Even though I wasn't looking at Dante, I knew him well enough to know that he was wrinkling his nose a touch, in that way he did whenever he found something distasteful.

"Neither can bring back the happiness—the *breath* of life."

I looked away from the window.

I looked back into those black—*black*—eyes.

"In a way," he went on, "I suppose we're *all* ghosts . . . but some more than others."

And, with that, he turned and made himself comfortable against the side of the carriage.

A little while longer, I heard his heavy breathing.

The sounds of sleep.

And—sometime later—I too slipped away.

A BOLO TIE IN TIME

I N HER BEDROOM, Mildred fished about inside her chest of drawers. The air smelled thickly of the lavender perfume she had dosed herself with—it caught at the back of her throat. She was sweating—the drops drooling down the sides of her face. Outside, she could hear the *thrum* of the waiting car's engine.

She had no time.

She needed to get *going*.

They were going to be late.

She was going to make everyone late.

Mildred simply couldn't understand why she couldn't uncover it.

Why she couldn't manage to see it *anywhere*.

How could a bolo tie have got away from her so easily?

. . . Almost as elusive as her neighbour Kate's snake—the one which Mildred had spent the better part of an afternoon chasing about the garden, and had eventually managed to corner and snag in a child's fishing net she'd dug out of Kate's garage.

Her neighbour Kate was a two-time divorcee: a child from each of those two train wrecks; both of which lived with her, and received no help from either deadbeat dad, although one of said dads had been the deliverer of said escaped snake. Living next to Kate, she realised why she had made the active decision, with her biological clock twitching to a standstill, that she wouldn't *ever* pair herself off just for the sake of having children.

Not even for one night.

Not even for the *sake* of having a child.

And, well into her fifties, she was clearly too old now.

Thank *God*.

She straightened up, took several deep breaths. Tried to compose herself. She stretched her neck upward. She caught sight of herself in the gilt-framed mirror. The shoulder pads of her neat, navy-blue trouser suit stuck out at odd angles. Her moccasin shoes hardly complimented the rest of her dress, but that was beside the point right now. Her eyes still looked puffed up from when she'd been crying a matter of moments ago.

It wasn't fair.

It *just* wasn't fair.

Why *couldn't* she find the bolo tie?

Outside there was a *hooonk!* of car horn.

She twitched a glance back over her shoulder, at once annoyed, and then having to tell herself to calm down a little. That it was *her* fault, after all, that someone needed to sound a car horn in this quiet, little suburban street of Luton; on the outskirts of London.

When her eyes lingered about the room, about the cushiony, light-pink wallpaper—spotted with flowers she couldn't identify— she finally came to rest upon what she had been looking for.

The bolo tie.

She turned slowly, as if the bolo tie might disappear to another dimension if she was too rash with her movements. She eyed it closely. Yes, there it was. The black-and-white thread. The silver-encased sapphire in the centre clasp. It was trapped beneath her wicker laundry hamper. Its threads sticking out, almost lost among the fibres of her thick bedroom carpet.

Hearing a pair of frustrated *pips* from the car waiting outside, on the curb, she trudged toward the bolo tie, almost as if she was approaching it in a dream. As if it *really would* vanish.

When she stood over it, she could hardly believe her eyes. She crouched down, twizzled her fingers about its threads, and then brought it up in her hands.

Her mind flashed back to the night before, when she had scouted about in the attic, frantically searching. It had taken her until the early hours before—from the very last cardboard box she'd searched—she had found it. She could still recall feeling herself tremble all over.

As if she might pass out at any second.

. . . *Really* . . . it was a silly thing . . . a *really* silly thing . . . and yet here she was *again*—getting herself all het up about such a small, seemingly insignificant item of clothing.

And yet it wasn't insignificant.

Not to her.

With another loud *blaring* horn, Mildred wrapped the bolo tie about the freshly starched collar of her white blouse, paused for a moment to examine herself in the mirror, and made to head out. However, as she took a step forward, she found herself facing off with him.

With *him*.

Tom.

Her cowboy.

Ice entered her veins. She stared at him, unable to believe that he was there at all. Could she not believe her eyes any longer? That seemed the natural conclusion to be drawn.

Tom sat in the sun-faded armchair in the corner of her bedroom. The armchair had been her sole inheritance from her father—her five older brothers having snaffled the good stuff before she'd got a chance.

Tom had on a well-worn, red-brown-and-yellow chequered shirt, with the left breast pocket puffed-out, containing, she knew, a packet of cigarettes.

She took in his fresh face, thirty-years younger than she knew him to be now, looked to that bustling, black moustache, and to his thick nose which stuck out long and proud. It reminded her of a horse's nose—like the horses they would ride together.

His smooth, tanned skin was punctuated only by stubbly cheeks.

She felt her chest tighten. Her breathing came in short, sharp bursts. She absorbed his black, wide-rimmed cowboy hat; that white, leather band which ran about the crown. She looked to the several pinprick-sized holes in his hat, to those holes which—she had always imagined—had been made by some sort of a louse, hungry for sustenance.

He reached up and tipped the brim. "Ma'am," he said, as if meeting for the first time.

For several long moments, she was stunned.

He peered up at her, his eyes round and brown. He closed his right eye, as he would always do whenever he concentrated. "Ain't that my bolo tie you got on?" he said, his voice a thick, southern-state drawl.

Mildred could only stare back, with wide eyes.

Give him the truth.

She nodded.

Seemingly satisfied with this confession, Tom sat back in the armchair, crossed one leg over the other and then tilted his head to one side.

Mildred didn't dwell on her vision . . . on *whatever* this was . . . whatever was happening to her.

In the distance, she heard a good dozen or so *beeps* on the car horn.

"I'm late for your wedding," she finally got out.

And then she skittered off along the hall, to the waiting car.

"YOU'VE GONE ALL WHITE," Eleanor said as Mildred got into the passenger seat of the weathered sea-green hatchback which Eleanor had had for going on thirty years.

Hadn't it been the car she'd got from her parents for passing her driving test?

Mildred felt herself trembling all over. She could hardly control her hands as she reached up for the seat belt, tugged it out from where it laid curled up inside its plastic shell. By some minor miracle, she managed to slot the belt into its buckle. It gave a satisfied *click*.

She glanced to Eleanor—they were the same age, only separated by two days. Born in the same wing: Erasmus—of the same hospital —St Mark's General. There had been a joke between their mothers —if it could be called that—about how as Eleanor's father had wheeled Eleanor's mother out, she had waved to Mildred's mother on the way in: all red-faced, one hand resting over her swollen stomach, the other over Mildred's father's shoulder.

Looking at Eleanor was like seeing some version of her youth being twisted by passing time. The wrinkles which had sunk in around her eyes, having replaced the slick, fair, slightly freckled skin. How Eleanor's blond hair had lost its natural, tangled lustre, and had descended into a withered grey sheet. Mildred, of course, had gone through changes herself, but the funny thing was that she never really seemed to notice the difference in her own appearance. It was almost as if the image she saw in the mirror was just the same as the one which she pictured in her mind from all those years ago . . . when she and Tom had had their . . . *fling*.

Eleanor wore a floaty, powder-blue cocktail dress. She had a tangerine-coloured pashmina wrapped about her neck, elegantly concealing her—*admittedly still quite stunning*—cleavage. All the same, Mildred supposed that this would, most likely, be the last major occasion when Eleanor would feel comfortable dressing so *young* . . . goodness knew, Mildred had given up *that* game a long time ago now. Ever since she had returned to the UK.

All those years ago.

Eleanor jammed down the handbrake, disengaging it. At the same time as she gazed over her shoulder, checking for passing traffic, she floored the accelerator, pulling out from the curb.

Mildred often wondered about this gesture, whenever she found herself being driven by Eleanor. And she had come to the conclusion that whenever she so much as set foot in a car with Eleanor it was with the quiet admission that she was, most likely, going to die. This looking-over-her-shoulder-while-pulling-out thing had to do with the fatalistic notion that Eleanor wished to stare her end in its eyeballs. Whether said *end* be a middle-aged man trucking a carload of infants; or a young girl fresh into the first week of her licence.

Mildred crunched her teeth together, tasting enamel and lipstick. She closed her eyes and gripped the door handle. She felt the pounding of her pulse in her knuckles: a sort of gentle reminder from her body that she should—maybe—ease up a little, allow her heart to do its work.

If only her heart had eyeballs.

As Eleanor swooped across more lanes than Mildred wanted to contemplate, she slipped her a sidelong glance, said, "You're pale like you've seen a ghost, or something."

Despite the situation, despite the creeping feeling of impending death, Mildred managed to raise a smile. "Yes, sort of," she said, the smile slipping from her lips as quickly as it had appeared.

It took them two hours in all to reach the wedding venue.

A small village church.

Nicely kept graveyard.

Mowed lawn.

Etcetera, etcetera . . .

The road was crammed with cars.

An older man—surely in his seventies, the bride's father?—
stood about directing traffic. He was dressed in a sober, charcoal-
black suit with a sensible, blue-grey cravat puffing up out from the
neck. He affixed his eyes onto Eleanor and Mildred's vehicle almost
immediately and—*apparently making the leap of logic from their dress*—
gestured them into a spot between a pair of four-by-four, all-terrain
vehicles. It was one of the minor mysteries of the world that
Eleanor could parallel park so efficiently, and quickly. Mildred's own
theory on the oft-performed miracle was that Eleanor simply
manoeuvred the car into its parking space before the natural laws of
the universe could catch on that there was something fishy taking
place.

Once parked up, the two of them sat in their seats, both examining their respective appearances in the mirrors stowed in the
backs of the fold-away visors which hung from the roof.

This was a mistake.

A *big* mistake.

The only reason that they were here at all stemmed from
Eleanor uncovering the wedding invite one day when she'd come
around for a cup of tea. She had noted the silvery lettering, the fine,
heavy paper of the envelope, and enquired of Mildred if she might
be allowed to open it.

Mildred could still hear the *squeeing* tones as Eleanor had found
out that it was a *wedding* invitation nestled inside.

As Mildred had sat in her sitting room, sipping on her tea, she
had sincerely hoped that Eleanor would drop the whole matter.
That Eleanor would just *shut up* about it.

But Eleanor was determined that they go.

She had—*somewhat unbelievably*—never been to a wedding.

And although Mildred performed her very best diversionary tactics, attempting to tell Eleanor the 'plus-one' really meant a spouse or partner, it hadn't put her off.

Not one jot.

In fact, Eleanor had set her emptied cup of tea down firmly on the coffee table—ignoring the placemat—put hands on hips, and pouted at her, saying, "Really, dear, I think that we just *might* be able to pull off the middle-aged lesbian routine for an afternoon, don't you think?"

Mildred had said nothing to that. She had just taken another sip of tea.

With a neat *snap*, Eleanor restored her visor to its take-off and landing position. She looked to Mildred with a frown. She grasped at her own neck, indicating Mildred's.

Mildred felt for the neck of her blouse.

Impossible.

The bolo tie.

It was gone.

Mildred patted about, trying to find the damn thing. But no luck. She would've searched high and low if it hadn't been for Eleanor's steady hold on her forearm. Eleanor smiled wide and bright then said, "I think you look better *without* it. Shall we go inside?"

3

THE CHURCH was cool even though today it was somewhat humid out. The overcast, *grey* skies had actually served to cheer Mildred up. Despite herself—despite telling herself to feel *happy* for other people—she couldn't help but find solace in the fact that a little piece of Tom's day hadn't *quite* turned out perfect.

At the large oak church doors, she found herself greeting a pair of mothers—one of which was plump, and perhaps in her fifties, while the other was about a decade older. They pinned on smiles and their colourful, feathered hats batted all over the place as they asked Mildred and Eleanor whether they were 'bride or groom'.

Mildred told the truth.

It was while the two of them were sat down on the hard wood of the pew—those seats which were *just impossible* to get comfortable on—that she caught some movement out of the corner of her eye. She glanced around, looked past the grey stone pillars of the church, seeing the figure walking along. *Unbelievable.* Just simply *unbelievable* . . . but what else was she meant to do?

Not believe her eyes?

She turned to Eleanor with the idea of asking her for confirmation—asking if Eleanor could confirm or deny the presence of that strapping, young *cowboy* striding along the other side of the church. Headed for the exit. But, when she turned to look at Eleanor, she saw that she was already sobbing into a handkerchief. On instinct, Mildred turned to look at the front of the church. She saw him standing there. *Tom.* Several years older, silver-haired, slightly plump. Hands clutched behind his back, head tilted upward. His southern complexion looked somewhat out of place in this pallid British afternoon—in this pallid British context.

Mildred felt a knot form in her stomach, but she managed to hoik herself up and away from the sobbing Eleanor. She listened to the *rustle* as her smart trouser suit made contact with the billowing dresses which passed her by.

4

MILDRED emerged from the—now-deserted—church doors and into the still somewhat stilted daylight. She glanced about, realised that, outside the church gates, a Rather Smart Car had just drawn up. That it had those silvery-purple ribbons stringing from its bonnet—streaming all the way back to where their ends were trapped in the wound-up front windows.

The bride.

The *bride* had arrived.

Thinking quickly, she got herself off the gravel path which led up to the front doors of the church. She shifted around the side of the church, only wanting to get herself out of sight. It was then that she smelled cigarette smoke. She turned to look.

Saw *those* eyes staring back at her over the glowing tip.

Rich, brown, *full* eyes.

And then, sure enough, hanging from the collar of the chequered shirt, the bolo tie she had spent so long searching for the night before . . . which she had thought disappeared until she had found it beneath the laundry hamper that morning.

"You took it," Mildred said, pointing to the bolo tie.

Tom—*her* Tom, the *cowboy*—smiled back. "Nah. It was mine to give, and I'm takin' it back."

All of a sudden, she felt herself close to tears. She had a warm, sticky feeling in her chest, as if she had taken down a drink the wrong way. "What do you *mean* you're taking it back? You *can't* take it back."

He smirked. " 'Course I can, darlin', what *ever* would you do with it?"

"I . . . I . . ." Mildred felt her mind sketching back.

She thought back through those years.

Felt the warmth of the baking sun against her skin. The way the sweat had itched against her skin when the sand had stuck to it. And how the two of them—*she and Tom*—would bathe themselves in the cool, running water from the streams. Allow their horses to tug at the grass, tearing off those hunks of nutritious goodness while they explored one another's bodies from beneath the privacy of the canvas tent. Just the scent of cigarette smoke, that achingly *close* low-drawl of voice—of *Tom's* voice—was enough to bring it all back to her like a mallet to the head.

And she felt stunned as she listened to the footsteps of the bridal procession making its way up the path to the church. She trembled slightly, though it had nothing to do with the temperature.

"Give it up, darlin'," Tom said, flicking the ash off his cigarette. "We had our chance." He stood with the sole of one foot resting flat up against the side of the church building, as if he was just hanging out behind a barn.

Mildred felt her throat close up. She wondered if she would break down. If she would end up on her knees, *pleading* with a ghost —*pleading* to go back.

But, no.

She was stronger than that.

For good or ill, she had made her choice.

All those years ago.

She had chosen to come back home.

To leave Tom behind.

And then—by some twist of fate—he had ended up back here.

As she felt a tear spill from the corner of her eye, Tom reached out those strong, well-muscled fingers of his. He gripped her chin tightly between forefinger and thumb. Gently, he eased her head upward so they made eye contact. "Now, darlin', you listen to me. You go in there, and you make nice, 'kay? I'll be out here waitin'—

I'll *always* be out here waitin', ain't nothing that's gonna change that."

She stared long and hard into those brown eyes.

For the longest time she wanted to lean forward and plant a kiss on his full lips.

But she held back.

He was right . . . what he said . . . he was *right*.

Mildred took one step away and then another—each step was easier than the last. Before she knew it she had turned her back. She could hardly even smell the cigarette smoke any longer.

When she walked back in through the church doors, she was in time to see the bride taking her last steps up the alter, to where Tom waited.

Not *her* Tom.

Being subtle, she slipped side-on and returned to her place in the pew, where she had been sitting alongside Eleanor who, consequently, was still bawling her eyes out.

The two of them sat through the service—Eleanor even looked up over her well-moistened handkerchief a few times. By the time it was over, Mildred felt as if a weight had lifted off her chest . . . *no*, from around her neck.

As if that bolo tie had been strangling her.

Slowly but surely, almost *unnoticeably*.

But it *had* been strangling her.

Even when it'd been up in the attic—*lost*.

Organ music kicked in. An applause broke out in the church.

Confetti sprouted from the hands of children.

As she watched Tom pass by, arm in arm with his bride, she caught his eye. She stared long and hard into those rich, brown eyes of his. He gave her the warmest of smiles.

Just—*for one second*—aimed right at her.

And then he had turned away.

He was gone.

When she turned back to Eleanor, saw the tears glittering in her eyes, she realised she was crying herself. The two of them embraced. She squeezed Eleanor tightly. Must've nearly squeezed the life from her. When the hug was done with, she felt free for the first time in years—for the first time since she had received that wedding invitation.

"What's next?" Eleanor said, dabbing at her nostril.

"The reception."

Turning all bug-eyed, Eleanor leaned into her. "Dancing?"

Mildred couldn't resist a smile. "Yes, there'll be dancing all right."

THE BELEAGUERED BUTLER

A FAINT DRAUGHT blew in beneath the door, but that mattered not, because a human butler—almost ridiculously stereotyped in his dress of a black and white tuxedo—swept into the hall with his quail's egg eyes fixed upon me.

I hurried up from my seat, taking a moment to brush down my greatcoat, before holding out my hand for him to shake. Only after a second or so did I realise that I'd committed a rather unfortunate *faux pas* and attempted to salvage the situation by slipping my outstretched hand into my pocket.

The butler cleared his throat. "Uh, this way, please, sir."

Despite his phantasmal white hair and his wiry, what-I-thought-to-be, octogenarian's body, he set quite a frenetic pace. So frenetic was it that I found myself being left behind as I skirted around corners, brushing vases—sending them lurching precariously in my wake—and bumping into pictures hanging off the wall. If there's one thing that's always stuck to me like a nasty rash, it's my clumsiness.

Before I got the chance to really break something, the butler curtailed his walking-sprint through the mansion, halting at a pair of double oak doors which stretched upward to the, not unlofty, roof above our heads. This could only be the master's bedroom. This could only be Raymond Ditchburn's bedroom.

I cursed under my breath at there not being a mirror anywhere handy, then decided to quickly sweep my hand through my hair to take care of any wild bits.

The butler met my eye with a steely stare and then, with an arched eyebrow, he hammered a pair of knocks against the absurd doors and then, after waiting out a pregnant second, shoved them wide open.

To say that Ditchburn's bedroom was befitting of his character would be a gross understatement. As I stood there, literally twirling about to take it all in, I absorbed the sheening windows, twinkling golden from the morning sunlight entering the bedroom. Pillows seemed to adorn just about every surface of the place—no need to worry in the case of a fall around here. And the gold. And the silver. It seemed to have been scattered about, used with such disregard as some mere mortal might use filler putty. The most absurd portion of the room stood right before me, though. The crystal fountain: pink water shushing through the pipes before sprinkling out into an elegant arc and plopping into the plunge pit below. All so carefully engineered. So precise and well-meant. I considered why I hadn't thought of going into business—why I'd thought I'd do so much better in academia. Still, I suppose we all have regrets.

"Stephen!" came the roar, from where I had no way of knowing —so booming and utterly paralysing was it that it's a wonder I didn't diddle all down my trouser leg. The thud of boots gave a better warning of my incoming host and I adjusted myself accordingly, just in time for the trademark clap on the back which had me almost spitting my tonsils out. I adjusted my glasses and eyed Ditchburn. "Stephen Felixbloom," he said and then, "*Bloomers!*" with a broad grin. "Don't suppose they call you that now, do they? Not you, a well-respected professor of clemency."

I managed to get a good swallow in, feeling my throat muscles contract seemed to give me a fresh surge of life—reassured me that I was still alive. I cast a glance across the room in hope of searching out the butler, but he was long gone. "Yes, well, funny you should bring that up, I actually—"

Ditchburn placed his hand on my shoulder and backed up, looked me in both of my eyes, individually, as if he were scrutinising my optical prescription. "You know," he said. "I've got witches and wizards who could sort out that problem in a jiffy."

So he actually *was* scrutinising my optical prescription.

He leant backward and, in his thick, what I liked to call his 'bellowing voice,' said, "Hutchins? Hutchins? Hutchins!"

The butler, Hutchins apparently, appeared in the *tick* of a clock in the doorway. His features remained as unmoving, as unremarkable as ever—like he hadn't been bellowed at at all.

"Get Cobblestop on the line, will you?"

I thought this as good as any time to interrupt. "Oh, no, please," I said, feeling my voice reedy in my throat, "it doesn't really matter. You see, I *like* wearing these glasses, actually, as it happens." That was a lie. My glasses make me look weedy, weak. When it comes to the punch I simply haven't got the money for expensive enchantments—not even at a personal friend's discount.

Ditchburn shut one eye and stared at me again. He waved Hutchins away with a limp wrist, then shoved me in the middle of my back, over toward his bedroom window. He grinned so hard I thought his teeth might fall out, then he said, "Bloomers, I was thinking of you, just today, in fact—this morning, at breakfast. Do you know what I was thinking about in particular?"

Already having quite a good idea of what he was thinking about, but not wanting to mention it, A, because I had no intention of winding Ditchburn up any more than he already was and, B, that if he wasn't thinking of the specific episode I had in mind then I would rather not put thoughts into his head—give him a reason to reminisce. Don't let anyone tell you that the sweet veil of time covers all—oh no, it only gives the impression of distance and finality when really it's still there, lodged in memories, and no magic can scrub that away . . . believe me, I've tried. And, C, I really had some pressing business to see to. Funnily enough, I hadn't come to see Ditchburn to 'catch up.' I was coming to see him for the same reason anyone goes to see an unbearable, extremely wealthy former university companion: I needed money.

Ditchburn rocked his head back and snorted through his nostrils, sending the pair of them flaring. He brought his head back down to his chest, pressed his hands together and then opened up in a playful, boyish grin. "I was just thinking of that time when we caught you on the way to the library, you know, with all those books in your hands, towering over you like some sort of balancing act"

—*so he's remembered,* I thought, glumly—

"and just as you were heading up those steps, me and the boys broke into a run." He chuckled to himself. "I remember that frightened look on your face when you turned round, you were already suspecting the worst. I was there, sparks spraying from my fingers, ready to whirl a real humdinger of a hex, and then"—laugh lines marked his face—"and then, you tripped right up on the step and sent all those books flying." He slapped his thigh, gave me a wink then continued, "Ah, university, I *do* miss those days, don't you, Bloomers?"

"Just a tad."

"Hutchins!"

Once more, the butler appeared in the doorway.

Ditchburn covered his mouth with his hand and whispered theatrically to me. "It's all the rage to have a dullard for a butler, thought I'd give it a whirl."

When he says 'dullard' what he really means is Non-magic Practising Being, or NPB for short—most of the time they're humans. Ditchburn was never the most politically correct of the class.

Ditchburn straightened up, apparently not all that bothered about Hutchins hearing the next bit. "Come here, Hutchins."

"Right away, sir," Hutchins said, stealing closer, wily eyes never leaving the patch of air a couple of inches above either of our heads.

"Stand there," Ditchburn said, rolling back his sleeves.

I watched on, already growing a tad concerned about what was going to happen here. "Raymond?" I said, feeling a little uncomfortable to be addressing him directly. "Are you . . . I mean, are you quite—?"

Before I could get the words out, Ditchburn was wriggling his fingers all around Hutchins's leathery head. Snowflakes descended from his fingertips and settled in the poor man's hair. Hutchins, however, remained still as anything—unmoved by his master's whims. Ditchburn shot me a look of glee and then, as if I'd egged him on, he clapped his hands twice so that the snowflakes crackled and turned into flames, flames which scattered through the man's hair, rustled down his shoulders, singed his suit. I watched on, unable to believe Hutchins's stoic pose, his utter unmovement. He merely stood there and waited, as if knowing that this were just another test of his resolve.

Ditchburn seemed to have had his fun. He clapped his hands once more and the flames ceased. "See that?" he said to me. "Unshakable. Never seen a nicomboob"

—that's another of Ditchburn's unendearing terms for NPBs—

"stand magic like that. Usually there's all the rushing for the torches, the raising of the villagers."

"You are employing him, I suppose," I said, looking over Hutchins, trying to see if any of Ditchburn's magic would leave any lasting mark upon him.

Ditchburn unrolled his sleeves as he stomped his way up a flight of stairs, up to the second level of his bedroom—a walkway which extended the entirety of the room—and then barked down to me. "I'm going to have a quick change then I'll see you in the drawing room." He turned his attention to the butler. "Hutchins? Get the tea ready."

Hutchins bowed his head and then made for the exit.

Realising that I was supposed to follow, I did so, already cursing the fact that I hadn't managed to get out what I really wanted yet.

In my mind I suppose I had fantasised about rolling up at the door, spitting out my request, getting the money off Ditchburn before beating a hasty retreat back to the university. But that was just a dream now.

As I skirted the corridors once more, hot on Hutchins's heels, I felt the need to raise the matter of what had just happened—what I had just witnessed. I reached forward and touched him on the arm, which he interpreted, correctly, as his cue to stop. I stared into his wrinkled, old NPB face and said, "Doesn't that treatment bother you at all? I mean, sorry to intrude, the last thing I'd want to do is be impertinent, but haven't you thought of finding employ elsewhere?"

The butler looked me up and down, deadpan, and then said, "One grows accustomed, sir."

And with that he proceeded on his way—I after him, thoroughly befuddled.

2

WHEN DITCHBURN had thrown up the idea of a drawing room, silly me, images of a cosy room stowed away somewhere in the corner of the mansion sprang to mind. I had imagined a quietly crackling fire, one which would warm up the extremities on a mid-winter's day such as this one, accompanied by three or four high-backed armchairs, all facing the fire. In my mind's eye, I'd also imagined bookshelves surrounding the room, hefty tomes, ragged old friends. I suppose I was a little naïve to allow those thoughts in, especially considering that this was Ditchburn I was dealing with.

Hutchins threw open a large wooden door, perhaps three quarters the size of the one which marked the entrance to Ditchburn's bedroom—but just as fine—to reveal an enormous room replete with sweeping velvet drapes, a fluffy mulberry-coloured carpet and a table which stretched the entire length of the room. At a guess I thought it could seat fifty, but it might well have been more. Chandeliers swooped down from the ceiling, their candlewicks flickering away with newly-lit flames, the light dancing in the ghostly glass. The whole room smelled of pine needles, and I realised—judging from a light scent of Ditchburn's accompanying musk—that it was one of Ditchburn's trademarked charms, one of those which had made him filthy rich all through the kingdom.

A little lost, I looked to Hutchins for advice.

"Sir," he said, eyes dead in their sockets, "I would advise that you take up one of the chairs closest to the fire, so that you might ward off any effects of this indifferent weather."

How had I managed to overlook it until that point? An open fire occupied a good portion of the inner wall of the drawing room. In reality, I felt its blaze penetrate the entirety of the expansive room, and had no worries over catching a chill here. Still, all the same, not wanting to seem impolite, I took Hutchins's advice and took up a seat beside the fire, casting off my greatcoat as I went and draping it over the back of my chair. When I touched the fabric, I could feel that it was still a touch damp from my journey to Ditch-burn's mansion. Apparently catered for, I gazed around the room only to notice that Hutchins, once more, had snuck from the room. I clasped my hands together and awaited my host.

3

A LARGE CLOCK ticked on the mantelpiece above my head. During the course of my wait I did glance back over my shoulder a handful of times, wondering exactly what it was that was taking Ditchburn so long. I tapped my boot heel against the leg of the chair, growing a little impatient. I needed to get back to the university by nightfall to mark papers and prepare a lecture for the next day. But, I told myself, it would all have been in vain to have given up my wait and returned—it would have cost me my job.

Ditchburn finally burst through the door to the drawing room, Hutchins on his heels, and I immediately felt that odd conflict at having wanted him to come along more quickly and, at the same time, now he was here with me, wishing myself out of his company at the first opportunity.

Ditchburn was wearing a crimson dressing gown which swept at his heels. Rather than walk the length of the table, to come down and take a chair somewhere within my vicinity, he decided instead to take the chair at the head of the table. Hutchins parked himself at his master's shoulder, like a proud old mongrel.

Seeing that this was going to put a slight strain on communication, I made to get up so as to move myself closer to Ditchburn. However, Ditchburn shushed me back down, beamed and then said, "You've not just come here to catch up with an old university pal, have you?"

A touch relieved and a little exhilarated to finally be getting down to the quick of things, I said, "Right, yes—"

"Okey doke," he said, cutting me off, then, scrunching up his features in irritation and then glancing back over his shoulder to Hutchins, addressed him, saying, "Do you mind, Hutchins? You're breathing right down my neck."

I noted a slight twitch in Hutchins's throat, but he did as his master commanded. Unfortunately for Hutchins, however, it appeared that Ditchburn had caught sight of this minor display of insubordination.

"Any problem, Hutchins?" Ditchburn said, rising in his chair.

Hutchins's eyes bulged from their sockets. "No, sir, please, I must—"

But it was too late. Ditchburn was wiggling his fingers, summoning all sorts of turquoise and lavender lights to his palm. He swirled them there before releasing them in a fierce array. The colours swarmed about Hutchins like a heavy fog and I watched on as, slowly, each of Hutchins appendages froze in their place. His eyes were the last to go, swimming about before coming to rest, deadening along with the rest of his body.

Ditchburn sank back into his chair with a sigh and the shake of the head. "Dearie me, help nowadays, difficult to find, let me tell you."

I continued to stare at Hutchins, the butler frozen in time. While it isn't illegal for the magical to prey on NPBs, it's thoroughly looked down upon—something akin to a child, a non-magical child, bombing an anthill with a bucket of water.

". . . Bloomers? Bloomers?"

"Huh?" I said, realising that I'd allowed myself to wander away for a moment, so caught off guard was I by Ditchburn's cruelty.

"The theme of your visit. I believe you were just coming to it."

"Ah, yes, that's right. Well, you see, although you're a businessman, I'm sure you keep abreast of the latest developments at your alma mater—"

Ditchburn produced a cigar from the breast pocket of his dressing gown and promptly lit it with the tip of his thumb. He puffed inky-blue smoke up into the air. "Not particularly," he said.

"If you'll recall I only just about managed to get out of the place, took whatever it was they were prepared to give me."

"Right," I said, feeling a little out-foxed. Who was I kidding? I was plain out of my league. Still, resolved that there was no option but for me to go through with this begging, I said, "In that case you *won't* be aware that my subject area—"

"Clemency," he added, with a knowing flourish.

I raised a faint smile. "That's right. Well, what's going on is that students are positively flocking to implacability this academic year. Actually it's been going on for quite a while now. In short it appears that clemency is looking the abyss right in the face, you see the head of academic programmes is making all sorts of threats, claiming that if we cannot find funding from somewhere then he's ready to draw a line under it all." I swallowed down a lump in my throat. "Close us down."

Ditchburn frowned. "And what do you expect me to do about it?"

I had hoped that at this venture in the conversation things would've clicked into place. Then I realised he was just trying to make this as awkward for me as he possibly could. "Well," I started, "I was wondering whether you might be able to, you know, put some money into the clemency department."

I noticed his merry jowls retreating and his gaze hardening.

"I mean, if you could spare a loose piece of change, here or there, we would really appreciate it."

Ditchburn seemed to collect his growing contempt. He leant back in his chair, steepled his fingers and stared at one of the chandeliers hanging over his head. "You're a man of education, Bloomers, you know what I think about *charity*."

Not quite sure I knew that much about Ditchburn's deeply held convictions, beyond his joy at bullying and deceit, I said, "Yes, I suppose I do."

Ditchburn held his ground. "Things"—he waved his hand frivolously as if indicating them specifically—"they have to pay for themselves. When there's no way of balancing them then they should quietly and gracefully take a step off stage."

"Right," I said, growing increasingly dismayed at the direction this conversation was taking.

"That said, you are an old university chum. We *did* pass many a happy hour together, didn't we?"

Not sure I could so much as cobble together a happy second we've spent together, I nodded along.

"And if I *were* to help you out with this, then I would be much obliged if you'd give me some form of due credit."

"Yes, of course, whatever you'd choose."

Ditchburn rose from his seat, clearly becoming more and more taken by the idea. He stroked his hairless chin and examined a volume on the bookshelf—I doubted he'd read whatever book he was scrutinising, occasionally I wondered whether he could read at all. He straightened up from his perusal and jabbed his finger into the air, in a satire of a magician struck by a marvellous idea. "Got it!" he said, slowly pivoting on his heel to face me. "What about a statue?"

"A statue?"

"Yes, absolutely, that would be appropriate."

"Would it?" I said, just then realising that whatever he wanted it really didn't matter—as long as he would agree to put up the cash.

He struck a pose, thumb hooked into his dressing gown, looking out into the middle distance. "I'll look like this. Powerful and noble." He met my eye once more. "And where would you put my statue?"

"Oh, what about the courtyard? Somewhere the birds could roost."

The room filled with that ill-thought out joke, now reverberating and coming back to me—about as funny as a fart in a morgue. Thankfully, Ditchburn sidestepped this slight jab, or perhaps he was so swept up in the idea of a statue that he simply didn't notice. "No," he said, "outside wouldn't do at all. I'd like to be somewhere proud, somewhere visible. A place where my contribution could truly be observed from all angles." His gaze on me cranked up a few notches. "The stairway, leading into the clemency department, how about it, eh?"

Now, being the head of the clemency department, and having a chair on the university advisory board, I could quite easily count on being granted acceptance for such a project, especially seeing as it would be part of a deal to float clemency back into black. The problem, though, was the principle. Would I really agree to have an old school 'friend's' likeness placed in prominence, in such a place as I would have to pass by every single day to get to my office? I made a snap decision. The logic was something along the lines of: beggars can't be choosers—which is always a desperately poor logical line to be reduced to, but not always avoidable.

"Fine! Just fine!" Ditchburn said, suddenly rushing along the table and clenching hold of my hand and crushing it with his. "Yes, I can see it now. Those fools, those fools! I'd love to see their faces when they plonk my great big statue down on their dirty, crumbling, crusty old university. Then they'll see."

I looked beyond Ditchburn, over his shoulder, to where Hutchins remained rooted to the spot—still frozen. "Uh, shouldn't you release your butler soon?"

Ditchburn waved his hand over his head as if he were swotting away an army of invisible flies. "Yes, yes, fine." Without so much as looking, he shot a ginger bolt through the air and it caught Hutchins in the solar plexus. "Happy now?"

Hutchins stumbled backward and hunched over clutching his stomach.

I rounded Ditchburn, for the first time that day truly forgetting about the money, and I went up to Hutchins, put my arm around his shoulders and said, "My goodness, are you all right there?"

Hutchins took a few gulps of air, caught my eye, then said, "One grows accustomed, sir."

4

MY GREATCOAT dried off a good deal when the time arrived for me to make my exit. All in all, it had been a fairly successful foray to see my 'old pal' Ditchburn and extract money from him. And all it would cost me would be a little dignity, having to put that *damn* statue of him in the hall of the clemency department. Perhaps I would be the laughing stock of the next meeting, but at least I had saved the department—my livelihood—for now, anyway.

On my way out of Ditchburn's mansion, I wasn't wished farewell by the man himself—oh no, he had been drawn away by some pressing business call, not that I much cared. Instead Hutchins was the one who led me to the door, his same dour expression, giving away all and nothing at the same time, still etched onto his face. With one foot out of the front door and the other still perched inside on the scandalously large welcome mat, a thought occurred to me. Perhaps it was getting the money issue off my back that I now had room to think more charitably. "Hutchins?"

"Sir?"

"If you wanted I could take you in my car to the station. I could drop you off there and you could go find another job, a better one. Just one condition, though. You wouldn't be able to say anything at all to Ditchburn about it." I stole closer, dropping the tone of my voice to a whisper. "He might take back his donation if he found out."

Hutchins did seem to turn over this possibility in his mind, cocking his head to one side and staring into space. However, merely seconds later he looked me right in the eye, pursed his lips and then said, "That shall not be necessary, sir."

"But can't you see how he's treating you? You can find a better life than that somewhere else. Hell, I'm sure you could find a far more benevolent magician *next-door*. I'd take you in as an assistant if it weren't for the possibility of Ditchburn finding out. Come on, what do you say?"

"One grows accustomed, sir," he said, and then, with a hardy strength that belied his insubstantial frame, he brought the door shut.

I just about managed to get my foot out of the way in time. I stood staring at the notches in the front door for a moment or two, then allowed myself a shrug before making off to my car and heading back to the university—cash in hand and crisis averted.

For now anyway.

A CUP OF SMILE

LUKE COILED a thick rope around his arm and marched into the garage, intent on doing himself in. He flipped the light switch and the bulb blinked on, sending shadows scurrying for the corners. He threw the rope up over the rafter, pulled it tight and then tied a knot. He propped up a garden chair, stepped up onto it then slipped the noose over his head. With a final glance around the garage, he kicked away the chair and pirouetted by the neck.

After a spate of spluttering and choking, a sense of lightness overwhelmed him. His body sagged. No longer did he have to blink or breathe. His irregular heartbeat, which had always bothered him, disappeared. Although he could still see, hear and smell—the rope felt tight around his neck and he tasted the stale garage air—he supposed he was dead.

Something scrabbled in the corner of the garage, amongst a pile of broken car parts. A strained *meow*. He picked out a furry outline in the gloom. It was the neighbours' cat. The real name escape him but he christened it Ball of Crap because of its faecal-brown fur and the fact that it jumped the fence to crap in his flowerbeds. That said, if he had been able, he would've let it out. When he tried to free himself from the rope, he groped thin air and the noose tightened around his neck. Someone would have to get him down.

Hours passed and nothing changed. The cat remained in its place, spitting at him every so often while Luke dangled. Was this the afterlife? Would he hover over his place of death for all time? If he were really a ghost then surely he could break free of his rope. He heard a scuffling, like mice in the attic.

The air in front of Luke frothed and a thing crackled into view. It wore a tattered waistcoat on its otherwise naked body. It had light-green skin with brown blotches, large jug-handle ears and a spherical head. Luke didn't dare examine any lower. He might be dead but he clung to his sense of good manners.

The thing burped then tucked a bottle back inside its waistcoat. It approached, scowling, a row of jagged teeth overhanging its lower lip, and then prodded him in the stomach, sending him twirling on the end of the rope.

A chill ran through Luke, sending a quiver up his spine. His skin felt slick and loose, reminding him of the way chicken skin puffed up and separated from its bones when it was cooked.

Ball of Crap poked its head out of the shadows, sniffed the air. Its fur stood on end and it hissed. The thing pivoted, raised its claws and hissed back. The cat retreated into the shadows. The thing returned to Luke, shaking its head. "Bloody hate cats. Little devils, they are. Only ones that can see us."

"Us?"

"Yeah, *fluxers*, beings in flux, you and me."

"I am dead then?"

The fluxer grimaced, looked him up and down. "Not the brightest, are you? Then again, suicides never are." It stabbed its finger at its temple and pronounced each syllable as if he were speaking to a toddler. "You're a fluxer, all right? Neither here nor there. Still got the use of your body, pending the result of your hearing."

The cat emerged.

The fluxer stared it back into its hiding place.

"What took so long?" Luke said, feeling the noose bite further into his skin.

The fluxer scratched the back of his neck. "Yeah, about that, these things happen. I deal with suicides worldwide, see? It's tricky getting through a few hundred every day, and even with my time-halting abilities sometimes a man gets behind. Sue me." He brightened. "Don't worry, though, you'll get your judgement, just like everyone else."

"Judgement? Who cares. Just ship me off wherever, Mister Grim Reaper."

The fluxer smirked. "Oh yeah? Don't think you deserve a second chance?"

"Nope, I've ruined my life perfectly well, thank you very much. Take me to Hell."

"First off, you've no choice in the matter, your soul doesn't belong to you. And second, my full title is: An Honourable and Respected, Omnipotent Master and Guardian of the Flux and Entrance to the Beyond." It inspected its fingernails. "But you can call me Max."

"Whatever."

Max rolled his eyes. "Bloody Nora, I can see why you topped yourself." He stepped closer and grinned wickedly. "So, why'd you do yourself in?"

Luke shrugged his shoulders, trying to get some slack in the rope. "Do you need to know?"

Max lolled his head from side to side, his smile faltered. "It'll be one of the typical ones, I can tell." He rested his fingers on his pitted chin and paced. "Let me see, was it your job? Hmm, maybe partly. Money? Some kind of gambling habit? Nah, even for a sad act like you it probably took a bit more."

Luke glowered.

Max stopped pacing. "It *was* your family, wasn't it?"

"You gonna get me down from here, or what?"

Max raised his palm. "Hang on, I'm still guessing. Kiddie-fiddler?"

"Kiddie-fiddler?"

"Yeah, did you fiddle kids."

"Of course not!" Luke said, exasperated. "It was my family, okay? My wife left me. Now can we go to Hell, please?"

Max clapped and the rope disintegrated around Luke's neck.

Luke dropped to the floor, crumpling in a heap. No pain, just a profound sense of emptiness. He looked over his arms and legs unable to quite believe it.

Max screeched out in laughter. He wiped a tear from his eye. "Bloody love hangings, me. Never get over that look of shock when I cut them down. Makes up for all those bridge jumpers and wrist slashers. Your funny little face!"

Luke eased himself up, a little unsteady on his legs. "What's funny about my face?"

"Sheesh, nothing, Mister Miserable," Max said, making for the garage door. "Let's get you out of here before you make me want to do *myself* in."

Luke stumbled after him.

Max lashed out at the cat, claws outstretched and teeth bared.

"Stop!" Luke said.

Max frowned at him. "What? Can't a fluxer eat a cat in peace?"

"He's my neighbours' cat."

"Where d'you suddenly get a bunch of morals?" Max sighed. "All right, have it your way." He clapped his hands and the garage door rolled up.

The cat bolted.

Max led him into the middle of the road, at the end the cul-de-sac.

Luke's gaze wandered along the street. Each window betrayed small moments of family intimacy—husband and wives in the kitchen, children snuggled up on their sofas, teenagers blasting music from their bedrooms. Moments which Luke had lost forever. He examined his own house, steeped in darkness. No warmth. He had extinguished that glow.

Max withdrew a pocket watch from his waistcoat. "You done here, mate?"

"Yeah."

Max snatched Luke's wrist and they soared into the sky, up through clouds. They spiralled through the air, sidled up alongside an aeroplane. Max slowed then nudged Luke in the ribs. "There was this suicide twenty years ago. Bloke tops himself in the plane toilets. Can you believe it? Did it over a girl too."

Luke snarled. "I didn't kill myself over a girl. She was my wife."

Max grabbed hold of Luke's shoulders and brought him to a halt in mid-air. "Look, Pissy Man, you won't get anywhere with that attitude"—he flicked Luke's nose—"or face at your hearing. Know what you need?"

"No, what?" Luke said, thoroughly fed up of all of this.

Max reached inside his waistcoat to produce a bottle and two cups. He released them and they floated in mid-air. He uncorked the bottle and poured. "This'll sort you out." He passed one of the cups to Luke. "Chin-chin."

Luke stared into the cup, examining the colourless liquid. He gave it a swirl and then knocked it back. It reminded him of hazelnut liqueur and fizzed in his mouth, turning his cheeks numb and stretching his lips. He struggled against the smile breaking out on his face. "What is this?"

Max swigged his own cup, gargled and then swallowed, closing his eyes to savour the taste. "It's called smile."

"Smile?"

"You got it."

"It's . . . it's making me smile."

"Name's pretty self-explanatory."

Luke touched his puffed cheeks and warped mouth. "Why doesn't it make you smile?"

Max chuckled. "I've built up a pretty weighty tolerance, mate. A lot of years, a lot of suicides. You need something to keep you going, eh?"

"When does it wear off?"

Max shrugged. "Few minutes. Lucky for us that we're about to leave time and space so you'll be stuck with that grin throughout your hearing." He stood back and formed a rectangle with his index fingers and thumbs, like a film director. "Brightens up your face no end." He belched as he took Luke's arm. "Shake a leg, shall we? Got others to get through. Less hopeless cases."

2

THEY PUFFED in and out of clouds. Luke peered down at snow-capped mountains. Without any warning, Max whisked them upward so fast that colours blurred together. The world took on an iridescent sheen. Luke shut his eyes. When he opened them again they stood in a hallway carved out of cloud. Luke felt his face. Still grinning away.

A string of symbols formed themselves from the clouds. Max scowled at them, ran his finger along them and then gestured for Luke to follow. Clouds rolled into each other forming arches and doorways. Max rocked to a stop outside one of them. "Here we go."

They entered.

At first it seemed another void, indistinct off-white cloud. But, slowly, the whole room transformed, like spray forming off crashing waves. Stalls appeared on either side.

Max led Luke by the hand along the floor, toward a raised platform at the centre.

As they walked, beings formed amongst the rows. They had wispy, spherical heads, pinprick eyes and a large bumps on their navels. They couldn't have been taller than a metre and reminded Luke of partially melted marshmallows. In any other circumstance Luke might have considered them cute.

Max stopped when they reached the platform. "Here we are, chief. Good luck. I'll be right here if you need anything."

Luke's legs shook as he climbed the steps. He rested his hands on the lectern and felt the smile parting his lips. "Max?"

"Yeah?"

"What are these things?"

"Huffites. Owners of your soul. I wouldn't call them 'things' either."

One of the huffites stood and spoke in a language Luke didn't understand. The other huffites silenced.

Max said, "That's Horcherry. Lead Huffite."

Horcherry switched to English. As he spoke his body jiggled and quivered. His voice was floaty and wavered between words. "We are here to discuss the case of Luke Tony Hughes. Case reference A F four hundred and seventy-three"—he paused briefly, then added, "A."

Luke caught a glance from one of the huffites in the stalls. It smiled back at him. He remembered the smile on his own face and averted his gaze.

Horcherry continued, "Mister Hughes hung himself in his garage." It shot Luke an icy glance. "And we must decide whether or not he merits another chance."

A series of mutterings broke out within the stalls.

Luke had no time for this. He had resigned himself to death. It had been the only solution. Hadn't it?

Another huffite grinned at Luke.

Max leant into the lectern. "Told you that cup of smile would do you nothing but good. Keeps your options open anyway, if you did feel like another go at life."

Horcherry continued, "First we shall hear a statement from Mister Hughes and then the case shall be presented to the honourable council for voting." Horcherry examined Luke. "Mister Hughes?"

Luke opened his mouth to damn himself to whatever waited in the wings. While the huffites peered down on him, the smile bridged his cheeks and stirred his soul. He knew he couldn't maintain the façade as he had with Max, because he was truly terrified of death.

He cleared his throat. "I was distant my whole life, letting others throw me around like a ragdoll. I could never empathise with anyone else. Life seemed a cruel joke. I killed myself because I drove my family away."

"Is that all?" Horcherry said.

Luke nodded, feeling tears prick the corners of his eyes.

The huffites broke out in heated discussion.

Luke's breath hitched in his throat. He examined the stalls, catching the eye of several of the huffites. They all shouted down at Horcherry.

Luke steeled himself.

Silence fell on the hall and Horcherry stepped forward. "The decision is unanimous. Mister Luke Tony Hughes will be given a session of education and, pending the result of his examiner, shall be granted 'will to live.' Should he attempt to commit suicide a second time or fail his education he will be sent straight to Hell."

Luke's brain slopped about his skull.

Horcherry bowed and then returned to his seat, immersing himself in conversation with his neighbour.

Max tapped him on the shoulder. "Let's peg it before they change their mind, eh?"

"Does that happen often?" Luke said, getting down from the podium.

"You'd be surprised."

Luke trotted on Max's heels, following him back out to the corridor. The door shut behind them silently. "So I'm not going to Hell?"

"Not yet, got to show you what you're missing first."

Luke wasn't sure what he felt about that. The whole experience had awed him so much so that he dared not kick up a fuss. He would get what was coming to him—he was sure. "What did they mean about an examiner?" Luke said.

Max snatched Luke's elbow. "They mean me. Let's get a move on."

The floor disintegrated and they were once more in thin air. Max brought them lower and lower. They skirted rooftops and dodged lampposts before setting down in a village dotted with thatched cottages. They landed with all the force and drama of a feather.

Max eyed Luke. "There you go. Wasn't so bad, was it?"

A group of children, five or six years old, wore snug coats drawn up to their necks and hats pulled down over their ears. Their bodies static. Snowballs hung in the air, in mid-flight. Time stood still.

"Beautiful, isn't it?" Luke said.

Max grunted, stuffed his pocket watch back in his waistcoat and noted the children. "Oh that, yeah, gorgeous." He marched off, waving for Luke to follow. "Not got much time. Let's get this over with."

Luke followed Max down the narrow alley, imagining the cobblestones beneath their feet, under several centimetres of snow. "Is this education hard?"

"Nah."

Luke snorted. "So what do I have to do?"

Max stopped, raised his nose, held up his finger. His eyeballs rolled in their sockets and then settled on a group of wheelie bins dusted in snow. He launched himself at the bins, sending them flying. A cat hissed, spat and then blurred through Luke's legs. Max lay in the snowdrift, panting. He punched the ground, sending up a puff of snow. "Bugger. There goes another lunch."

"Why do you like eating cats so much?"

"You ever squashed a wasp after it stung you?"

Luke scowled. "Oh, I wouldn't think so."

"It's just like that. They've got it coming."

Luke stood another moment and then followed Max down the hill. A well-kept cottage loomed at the end of the path. Its door was painted a racing-green and stood out against the pure white snow surrounding it. "Whose house is this?" Luke said.

Max clamped his fingers around Luke's wrist and yanked him through the wall. They emerged into a warm sitting room, a fire crackled away in the hearth. "Weren't expecting that, were you?" Max said.

Luke gawped. "Why didn't you use that to get us out of the garage?"

Max shrugged. "Can't use all your party tricks up at once." He led him through the house, into a kitchen.

A man and woman were at the stove, also frozen in time. Their heads were both tilted back in laughter.

Max brought Luke closer.

Luke identified the man as Jeff Royale, a colleague. He turned his attention to the woman. It was Alexandra, Luke's estranged wife.

3

HEAT ROSE in Luke's cheeks and he clenched his fists. It all slipped into place. He had no doubt that they had been conducting an affair for many months. They all worked in the same office so it would have been easy for Jeff to get Alexandra, Luke's wife, on her own.

"Go on," Max said. "Don't be shy."

Luke approached Alexandra. She wore a faint smile, a shadow of his own. Her eyes gave her away. Usually there was a glimmer, a shine to them, even on his worst days, when he had shut himself away, as if she might get to see the man she had married for a second. Hope. But now they appeared matted, distant. And then he knew he had to have her back. He had no other destiny. This was his reason to live.

Max tore at a loose piece of skin on his palm. "Want to see your kids?"

Luke nodded.

Max guided him to a bedroom, tucked away at the back of the house. Sure enough, his two girls, Helena and Sophie lay snug in their beds, blankets tickling their chins. He remembered the spike of joy he had felt when they had been born. And how, over time, the feeling had faded. He had retreated into himself.

"Life worth living again, is it?" Max said.

Luke's cheeks tingled. His mouth muscles loosened. "That's it? I get to live again."

"More or less."

"Okay."

The world faded. Colours in retrograde. Luke appeared in the driveway of his home. A car horn peeped. Luke glanced around. No sign of Max. He touched his face. No smile. He ran around his house, into the garage. The noose draped from the rafter. He tugged it down, threw it into the corner and then, thinking twice, he snatched it up and threw it into a wheelie bin.

Luke lingered in the hall, wondering whether he had the guts to head out in his car, get his wife back. If only he had a cup of smile. Action was the answer: think less, act more. He snatched up his keys, fired up his car and shot through the snowy night.

4

LUKE ARRIVED OUTSIDE the familiar green door and pounded. Scuffling footsteps and then Jeff answered. He wore a blue dressing gown and squinted. "Luke? Is that you?"

"I've come for my wife and kids."

Jeff shook his head. His cheeks were reddened. "Whatever do you mean?"

Luke barged in, knocking Jeff to one side.

With Jeff's protests in his ears, Luke marched through the house. He paced into the kitchen. No one. He continued his search, to the bedroom where he had seen his daughters. The beds were empty.

Jeff appeared in the corridor. A look of concern sketched on his face. "Are you all right, Luke? You look pale."

Luke gritted his teeth. "What the hell have you done with them?"

Jeff's features darkened. "Look here. You elbow your way into my house late at night and claim I have your wife and children. What do you want, Luke? Couldn't this wait until Monday?"

Luke swung a punch.

Jeff ducked.

Luke snatched up a china lamp resting on the bedside table and smashed it over Jeff, sending him stumbling back.

Jeff's head smacked into a corner of skirting board.

Luke stood over him, still clutching the remnants of lamp. Sweat formed on his brow.

Jeff stared up at Luke, eyes caught in spasm. Blood dampened the wall, trickling into the beige carpet.

Luke crouched down to feel Jeff's pulse. Nothing. He straightened up. The air left Luke's lungs and he felt faint. What had he done?

"Every life has a price, Luke."

Luke swivelled, brought himself nose to nose with Max who leant against the doorframe, head cocked, examining Jeff's body. "You!"

Max met Luke's eye. "Nice job for a first timer."

"My family's not here."

"I misjudged you. Didn't think you'd have the nerve to do it, but you're just a box of surprises."

Luke chewed his lower lip. He tasted blood. "Where are they?"

"Where they always go. She's at her mother's."

Luke returned his focus to Jeff's body, unable to believe what he had done. "Is . . . is this all real?"

Max reached inside his waistcoat. "As real as you and me." He chuckled. "As real as you, anyway." He produced the bottle of smile, two cups.

"You tricked me. My wife and children were never here. She never left me for Jeff."

"No," Max said, pouring out the cups. "Want to know a secret?"

"What?" Luke said, his skin feeling cold, his nerves numb.

"This was all part of the education."

"But what does it all mean?"

Max grinned. "It means you passed. I'm granting you the will to live."

"But I killed someone. I'll go to prison."

Max offered a cup to Luke. "At least your life has direction."

"Bu—but why?"

Max shrugged. "You gave yourself up to us. We can do what we please." He shoved an overflowing cup into Luke's chest. "I told you I had a dark sense of humour."

Luke accepted and knocked it back in one. The warm liquid

trickled through his body, nurturing true and complete happiness in his soul. His bones hardened and his muscles thickened.

"Better as a mortal, no?" Max said. "That's what they say anyway."

He could hardly breathe, let alone talk. ". . . Yuh."

Max nodded to himself.

Luke got to grips with the feeling. The problems seemed surmountable, Jeff's body, what he'd done. If he could just get his wife and girls back. He looked to Max. "Will you help me fix this?"

Max held up his hands, in surrender. "Oh no, got nothing to do with me."

"It has everything to do with you."

"Look, Luke, I'm a bloody fluxer, okay? This is what fluxers do. Bring people back to life or shoot them off to death. One in, one out. You wanted to live so Jeff had to die."

"I trusted you."

Max stepped back, weighed the bottle of smile and then closed one eye. "Tell you what, you've cheered me right up. Why not take the bottle? It'll keep you going. Set you on the right road."

HAPPY TOWN

FLORENCE ANDERSON sat at the back of class with her eyes fixed on the clock, wishing away the final fifteen minutes. The second hand seemed to skip backward. She shook her head and turned her attention to the teacher.

A smile stitched on her face, Mrs Kite strutted down the perfectly straight aisles. Her hair was done up in a tight, business-like bun and her creaseless skirt rested just above her knee. She dished out test papers.

Florence caught several glimpses. At the top of each was a neat 'A,' circled in red felt-tip.

When Mrs Kite laid Florence's test down, her smile faded and her face hardened.

Florence's stomach did a flip. With a sigh, she snatched up her paper.

'C'

What a surprise. She massaged her temples.

Mandy May leant across the aisle. "How did you do?"

Florence gulped and revealed her paper.

"Dearie me, another one?"

Florence nodded.

Mandy shifted in her seat and screwed up her eyes. "What're you going to tell your grandparents? Aren't they worried about you?"

"What should I tell them?"

"Don't know. Maybe you should ask them for a tutor or something."

Mucus rose in Florence's sinuses. She snorted. This was no time to cry. That was what Mandy wanted. "I studied this time. I promise."

Mandy smirked and turned back to the front.

Mrs Kite sat on her desk. "Any questions about the test?"

Like a hissing snake, the 'C' threatened to leap off the page and bite Florence across the throat. She had the urge to put her hand up, but she resisted. What was the point? The last time she'd talked to Mrs Kite about tests she'd just nodded along and recommended more studying.

"Okay then," Mrs Kite said. "I hope you all have a good evening and remember—" She wagged her finger.

"Study!" the class, minus Florence, chanted.

The bell rang. Florence clutched her books to her chest and dashed for the exit.

Late-afternoon sun shone into the hall. Florence smiled. Soon she'd be outside, far from school. Something struck her shin. Florence flinched. "Ouch!"

The three Roachley girls circled her. Kylie, the eldest, was in the year above while Sammy, the next eldest, was in her class. The youngest, Georgia, was in the year below. They all had the same whisper-blond hair and laser-green eyes—the best students in school.

Kylie aimed a kick. Florence stepped back to avoid it, but just fell into Sammy's arms. Sammy wasted no time putting her in a headlock. Florence's heart beat faster.

Brushing her hair from her eyes, Kylie said, "Heard you didn't do too well on the test today. What happened?"

Florence's mouth opened slightly and she shook her head.

"What grade did you get?"

Florence bit her tongue. Sammy released her and Kylie punched Florence in the gut, making her double over. Next, Sammy landed her fists on the back of Florence's shoulders. She crumpled to the floor.

The blood in her mouth tasted like rusty nails.

Like a pack of hyenas, the girls bore down on her.

Something wet landed on Florence's cheek. She wiped it off. Through bleary eyes, she saw Georgia lick her lips. Another hit her. And another. Soon it was like a tropical storm. Spit came from every direction. Florence held her hands to her face.

Behind them, a door opened.

"Quick!" Kylie said, and the girls darted off in separate directions.

Mrs Kite stepped out into the corridor. "What's going on? What're you doing on the floor, Florence?"

"Nothing, Miss."

Head cocked, Mrs Kite stepped closer. "You're a mess. What's that you're covered with?"

"Nothing, Miss."

"Hmm. You'd better get up, don't you think?"

"Yes, Miss." Florence reached for her satchel. One of the straps had snapped in the melee. She put her arm through the functioning strap and got to her feet. After dusting herself down under her teacher's glare, she considered going to the toilet to get cleaned up. However, she decided against it. One of the Roachleys might be lurking there.

Stone-faced, Mrs Kite placed her hands on hips. "Remember to do your homework, tonight."

Florence tried to stay strong. If she broke down now, Mrs Kite would call her grandparents and then she'd have even bigger problems. Florence gave her the flicker of a smile, bowed her head and then limped toward the door.

FLORENCE STUCK HER KEY in the lock and shoved the door open. It rattled on its frame and struck the wall. Her grandmother called from the kitchen, "Careful with the door! We're not made of money, you know."

"Sorry, Gran." Florence dropped her bag and headed for the kitchen. Although she wanted to dash upstairs, take a shower and shut herself in her room until dinner, she knew if she didn't greet her grandmother she'd hear about it later.

Gran looked up from the stove. She wore a flowery apron and her long brown hair brushed her shoulders. "How did you do at school?"

"Fine."

"How about the test?"

Sitting at the table, Florence played with the tablecloth.

"Hey!" Gran tossed a tea towel at her. "I'm talking to you."

"'C.'"

"What?"

"I got a 'C.'"

The wooden spoon landed in the sink with a *thump*. Gran strutted over and grabbed her ear.

A nauseating pain burrowed deep in Florence's skull. She wanted to scream, but if she did, Gran would only tweak harder.

After a few seconds, Gran released her, slamming Florence's head into the table.

Florence rubbed her ear.

Gran returned to the stove. "I don't know what we're supposed to do with you."

"I'm sorry."

Gran sighed and resumed stirring. "Yes, I see that. It doesn't make things any better though, does it? Sometimes I wonder how things would've been if your sister had survived instead of you."

It was like a sharpened dagger pierced Florence's chest. She swallowed and resisted the temptation to cry—knowing it was true. Her family, her mother and father, and her sister, had all died in a car accident a year ago. Her sister Chloe wouldn't have had problems at school.

Gran continued, "Leaving us high and dry like that. No insurance! I can't believe your father was so irresponsible."

"It was an accident."

"Don't tell lies. They were asking for it, driving around at night. Mid-winter."

Knowing it would do no good to argue, Florence nodded along. One thing she'd learnt living with grandparents was that old people didn't appreciate having their well-earned prejudices and preconceptions challenged.

"All right," Gran said. "I think you'd better go get cleaned up for dinner. Don't think that I haven't seen that filth on the back of your trousers. I do wish you'd do better at school, perhaps then you'd have more friends."

"Yes, Gran."

On her way upstairs, Florence recalled her first week in town, a year earlier.

At first, she'd thought it was a joke—a perfect town filled with perfect people. However, when she went to the perfect school, and saw all the perfect children—all their perfect scores—everything changed. She wasn't one of them.

When her parents had been alive, they'd hardly visited her grandparents. She understood why. While Mum had been perfect in almost every way, Dad had been a complete disaster. Like silk and tree bark sewn together. Chloe took after Mum while Florence took after Dad. Did her grandparents despise her because Florence was her father's daughter, a daily reminder of the man who'd stolen their daughter away?

Florence closed her bedroom door and exhaled. All tension escaped. Her muscles unknotted. Tattered books, an unmade bed and scattered clothes signalled that she was back in her little paradise.

A raking sound drifted in from the garden. She dumped her bag on the chair and looked out.

Granddad scooped up leaves and deposited them in a wheelie bin. He never took a breather nor paused to wipe sweat from his forehead.

Florence turned back to her desk. Last night, she'd stayed up until two o'clock studying and tonight she'd do the same. And for what? She'd fail again tomorrow. The questions on the exams always seemed so random—yet the others got them right. Was she stupid?

Exercise books piled up at the side of her desk. Each night, she filled half a book, copying notes from the battered and obscure textbooks. She leafed through the current one—biology. Dust rose off the pages, making her cough.

The date claimed the book was published fifty years ago, but she thought the material was much older. A reprint perhaps. Reading the words was like stripping old lead paint.

She picked up her book and carried on. Her tongue sticking out, she wrote in a fever—determined today's 'C' would be the last. Paragraph-by-paragraph, she noted and summarised—at the back of her mind knowing it would reap no reward.

Perhaps Gran was right. Maybe Florence should've died in the car crash. If only Chloe were in Florence's place.

3

TWILIGHT SETTLED over her room. Florence flicked on the desk lamp and thumbed through the nineteen pages of notes she'd written in the past two hours. The current exercise book had only half a page remaining. She reached for the next. Full too. She worked her way through the stack. No blank pages to be found. She paced to the top of the staircase and called down, "Gran?"

Footsteps in the hall. "Yes?"

"I need a new book."

"Why?" Gran said.

"I've almost finished this one."

"There's some more in the attic. In the boxes with your sister's things."

Florence shuddered. "Okay."

"Better get up there quick. It'll be dark soon."

Florence glanced at the ceiling. A depression hid the opening in the low, uneven ceiling.

She'd only been up there once before, to get a photo album Gran had wanted. Being near her dead family's things had been so overwhelming that she'd come down right away without so much as opening a box. That night Granddad had given her three lashes.

Could Florence go to the shop? She checked her watch. It was already past six. In this town all the shops shut at five-thirty sharp.

She stood on tiptoes and brushed the attic door with her fingertips. Not wanting to call for help again, she bent her knees and jumped. Her hand struck wood and it leapt from its place. Just a bit more. Closing her eyes, she let all her frustration burn through her: the test, the Roachleys circling her and Mrs Kite's frown. She crouched all the way down and then bounded upward.

The attic door clattered into the attic and the cord dangled down. She grabbed it and tugged.

The ladder slid down and thudded onto the carpet.

A light breath tickled the back of her neck. Every hair on her body stood to attention. She spun round. No one. The only sound was the clank of dishes in the kitchen and the scraping rake in the garden.

She set her foot on the first rung. The wood creaked. Her knees shook.

Upon reaching the top of the ladder, she popped her head through the gap. Confidence surged through her. Tonight, she was determined to overcome her fear—get in and get out.

Old leather and rotten coriander wafted on the stale air. Dying daylight seeped in, half-illuminating the attic.

Looking round, she noticed a collection of flower pots at the window. Browned vines snaked across the floor. Alongside stood about a dozen boxes—all that remained of her family.

In a half-crouch, she crossed the attic. She stumbled and sent something clattering off into the distance. Her heart pounded as she waited for her eyes to adjust.

When they did, she saw it was a pair of Granddad's old work boots. Strange, her grandparents threw everything away, not leaving anything to decay. Were her grandparents afraid to come up here too?

Feeling her way with her hands, she came up against the first box. She reached for the flaps and pulled them open. The cardboard-on-cardboard scrape made her wince. She thrust her hands inside where she touched cloth. Gripping material, she withdrew it and held it up to the fading light.

It was Mum's dress, the one with the flowery pattern she'd used for summer parties. She smelled it, savouring Mum's perfume.

A clunk came from beside her. Inside one of the boxes.

Her breath hitched in her throat. She dropped the dress back inside and folded the flaps. She stood in silence, listening. Everything was still.

When she ripped the tape from the next box, it unleashed a stream of books. They poured out onto the floor.

"What's going on up there?" Gran said. "Making an awful racket."

Florence jumped. "Sorry, Gran." She picked up the spilled books —taking armfuls and dumping them back inside. Finally, she got them all back in, save the one in her hand.

Hardly any light permeated the darkness now and she struggled to make out the shape, let alone the writing on the front. From what she could tell, it was an exercise book. A pen stuck inside its ring-binding.

She stumbled back to the opening. With one foot on the ladder, she took a final look at Granddad's boots and Gran's plants and plonked down.

Gran waited at the bottom of the ladder. "Found one, did you?"

Florence nodded.

Eyebrows raised, Gran said, "Better get on with studying then."

Florence slipped back into her bedroom and laid the book down on her desk.

Scrawled on the front of the book was her sister's name: Chloe Anderson.

4

FLORENCE RIPPED THE PEN from the rings and weighed it in her hand. It had been a present for Chloe from their mother. A series of microscopic scratches marked its otherwise flawless finish. Florence smiled.

Chloe had spent most of her life stuffed up in her room, studying away. Florence sighed. Perhaps if she'd spent her life in a similar way she wouldn't be in trouble.

Florence turned back the front cover and squiggled on the blank page. After a series of engraved loops, ink splurged onto the page. It was a new cartridge. Maybe Chloe had changed it just before she died. Florence shivered.

Once she'd covered a few pages, her hand ached. She read over what she'd written. Her cheeks flushed. It was like someone had punched her in the solar plexus. Hard to tell what was more disturbing—the fact she didn't understand a word of what she wrote or that she'd written in Chloe's unmistakable flowery scrawl.

Florence held the nib to her desk lamp. It had to be the pen, no other reason. Why else would she suddenly be able to imitate Chloe's handwriting? She laid the pen down and picked up the cheap disposable she used every day. Sure enough, they were her own familiar squiggles.

The door pounded.

Her blood surged. Florence shoved the pen inside the exercise book and pushed it under the piles of textbooks. "Come in."

Gran peered round the door. "Do you want some tea?"

Florence nodded.

"Better come down and get it then, while it's still hot."

"Okay." Florence pushed her chair back, glad to get away from the pen.

Her grandparents sat at the kitchen table with the teapot between them.

Florence perched on the chair closest to the door. If either swiped at her, she would escape upstairs.

Granddad snorted and sipped his tea. "What've you been doing in your room all evening?"

"Studying."

He rolled his eyes and looked at Gran. "Is she getting any better?"

"Today she got a 'C,'" Gran said.

Florence's eyes moved between the two, anticipating an attack.

He placed his cup down calmly and stared at her.

Shivers bounced across her skin.

"Five lashes," he said.

Air escaped Florence's lungs.

He picked up his teacup and resumed drinking.

Florence took the pristine porcelain teapot and poured herself a treacle-coloured cup. Her hands shook as she replaced the teapot in the middle of the table. It clinked against the saucer. Five. He'd never given her more than three.

After finishing her tea, she considered running upstairs and locking herself in, but he was too quick for her. He snatched her wrist and yanked her from her chair.

Looking over her shoulder, Florence prayed for Gran to help, but she sat completely still, shaking her head and stirring more sugar into her tea.

He unlatched the basement door, a dirty pit of endless gloom. "Stop dawdling!"

Her heart pounded in her ears and her breaths came short and inadequate.

At the bottom, he flicked the light switch and headed over to the corner where the belt hung. It was brown and wide, with a large buckle shaped like an eagle. He pulled it down and gave it a couple of trial thwacks.

Tea gurgled in her stomach.

Straight-faced, he strolled over. "Bend over."

The belt whistled through the air.

Sparks shot up her spine and a dull pain throbbed in her bottom. She bit her lip and prayed for it to end.

Two.

Shadows formed in the corners of her vision.

Someone whispered, "Florrie . . . Florrie."

She straightened up. "What?"

"Back down," Granddad said.

Three.

It stung, but the voice had distracted her—as if carrying off her mind on a fluffy cloud.

With a grunt, he lashed her with a fourth.

Only a light tap. Easier now.

She glanced back.

He wiped his brow and ran his hand along the sleek leather. "Down!" He snapped the belt.

She stumbled forward, and her muscles went numb.

He stepped across the room and replaced the belt, ready for tomorrow. "You can go."

She straightened up, thinking about the whisper. It *had* been Chloe.

5

SUNLIGHT REDDENED her closed eyelids and her bottom stung. When she got up from her desk, an intense pain seared her legs. She dressed quickly and packed for school, chucking Chloe's book and pen into her bag.

Granddad rustled through a newspaper—his pipe smoking gently—while Gran cooked eggs at the stove. "You're up late," Gran said.

"Sorry," Florence said.

A plate of scrambled eggs landed in front of her.

"There you go," Gran said, wiping her hands on her apron and plodding over to her seat.

Florence pushed her eggs around the plate. Her stomach churned. She never wanted to eat in the morning, but knew the consequences if she didn't. Plucking up her courage, she smothered a piece of toast with egg and popped it into her mouth.

After rolling squelchy yolk and soppy toast round her mouth for what seemed hours, Florence swallowed.

Only twenty mouthfuls left.

Once finished, she slung on her rucksack and kissed both her grandparents on the cheek.

Gran dropped the pan into the sink. "If you get another 'C' today, you might as well not bother coming home."

"Yes, Gran." Florence eyed Granddad, but he continued to peruse his newspaper—as if in a different room.

As always, Florence was the last to arrive to her classroom. She liked getting to school late. That way, Mrs Kite's watchful eye protected her from any direct physical abuse.

Today, however, Mrs Kite hadn't arrived. Florence's head pounded. Hovering in the corridor, she considered dashing to the toilet and hiding out in a cubicle until it was safe. No, they'd find her there. She took a deep breath and walked into the room.

Sammy aimed her pigtails at Florence. She nudged the girl sitting next to her and grinned. "Look what we've got here. Little Miss No-Family/Bad-Grades."

Eyes fixed on her shoes, Florence hurried past with her books cuddled in her arms.

"What's the matter, feeling glum?" Sammy said.

Florence kept walking. Amazed to reach her desk without a punch or kick, she turned back. Dozens of papier-mâché bullets rattled her. She dropped her books and covered her face. Laughter jammed her ears and the spit balls hailed on.

"That's quite enough!" Mrs Kite said. "Put those things away!"

Total silence draped over the class.

Not quite trusting the barrage was over, Florence peeped through her fingers.

Arms folded across her chest, Mrs Kite tapped her foot. A faint smile settled on her lips.

Florence brushed off the spit balls that had stuck and sat down.

Mrs Kite ambled over to her desk and withdrew a pile of paper from an unseen drawer.

Fear twitched inside Florence. Another test.

Mrs Kite handed them out. "I hope you all studied hard. You may begin once you have the paper." When she reached Florence, her mouth thinned to a slit. "Books away."

Desk lid open, Florence slipped her sister's book inside and rummaged for a pen. There wasn't one. When she glanced up, Sammy grinned back.

Florence let the lid drop shut. What was she going to do now? .
. . Chloe's pen! She reached back inside and withdrew it from the
exercise book rings.

Someone whispered in her ear, "We'll do this together."

Florence's bones turned to butter.

Next to her, Mandy scribbled away.

"Did you say something?" Florence said.

Mandy frowned and shook her head.

Mrs Kite looked up from her book. "Shh! No talking!"

Another day, another 'C.' Florence sighed and put pen to paper.

It was as if some slender hand slipped over hers. Florence lost
control of her hand. Her heartbeat away. She struggled and then let
the force fill in her answers.

With twenty minutes remaining, Florence had finished. She laid
the pen down. Her hand trembled. All round her, the rest of the
class continued to scribble away. She grinned—first to finish.

What was she supposed to do now? Check over the answers?
Eyes skimming the page, she tried to make sense of the elaborate
answers that had flowed through her hand. She understood about
every third word. Surely Mrs Kite would notice it wasn't her work,
not her handwriting, when she gave it in.

"Time's up!" Mrs Kite's sharp eyes danced about the room and
she leapt from her seat. She strolled down the aisles. When she
snatched up Florence's paper, she placed it at the bottom of
the pile.

6

CONVINCED TODAY had been a fluke, Florence studied late into the night. The lamp flickered and then went out. She flicked the switch back and forth, but nothing. When she looked out the window, she realised the entire street was plunged into darkness.

Someone touched her.

Florence leapt from her chair, sending it tumbling back.

Gran called up the stairs, "Everything all right up there?"

"Yeah."

"Well stop making a racket!"

Florence didn't dare breathe.

The same whisper in her ear from before, "Florrie? Can you hear me, Florrie?"

Florence's heart shuddered. "Chloe? Is that you?"

There was a girlish giggle, just like her dead sister's. "Chloe's dead."

A tear rolled down her cheek. Was this a cruel joke? "Who are you then?"

Another giggle.

"Did you turn out the lights?"

"Yes," Chloe said.

"Why?"

"I wanted to talk to you."

"Can't we do that with the lights on?"

"No."

The desk lamp flashed just long enough to see her sister's face. It was bone-white and inches from hers. Goose bumps rose on her skin.

Florence backed up against the wall. "You *are* Chloe." She swallowed then added, "Turn the lights back on, please."

Chloe breathed heavily. "That crash was terrible. Death is terrible. Don't you ask yourself why you lived?"

Florence shook her head.

"Don't you ask why, out of me, Mum and Dad, you were spared? Look at you. You barely have a scratch on your body. And yet, you're throwing your life away. Stupid girl."

Florence clenched her fists. "I can't help it. I'm not like you. I'm no good at school."

"Don't you think things would've been better if I'd lived? I would've fit right in at your school. I would've been the star pupil. We did well on the test, didn't we?"

"I—I don't know. We do—don't get the results till tomorrow." Florence's mind filled with images of the crash. She sobbed. "I'm sorry, I'm so—"

"Shut up!"

For a second, the desk lamp and her main bulb burnt impossibly bright and then dropped back into darkness.

"I don't have much time," Chloe said. "I can't hold the electricity back for much longer."

"Why do we have to talk in the dark, why can't I look at you?"

"It interferes with me. The closer and brighter it is, the worse it gets."

"Oh, Chloe." Florence sobbed. "Things are terrible. I don't fit in at all. Gran shouts and Granddad beats me. All because I'm dumb."

"Shut it!"

Florence sniffed.

"I can help you, but you must do exactly as I say."

"I'll do anything, anything you ask."

"Good. Go up to the attic and find my clothes. They're in the third box on the left. Bottom row."

Florence nodded.

"Do it!"

Lips quivering, Florence plodded across the landing and pulled down the attic ladder. She slipped up the rungs. Once in the dark attic, Chloe led her by the hand, like she had in the classroom.

Without making a sound, Florence instinctively pulled a box from the stack—the others miraculously not falling—and unfolded the flaps.

She dipped her hands inside and extracted clothes. She bundled them into her arms and trudged out.

When Florence returned to her room, she dropped the clothes on the floor. "What now?"

"Nothing. Just wait." Chloe's voice was fainter. "I can't hold it anymore."

The lights shimmered and then winked on. Chloe disappeared.

Florence squinted, trying to adjust to the sudden brightness.

Chloe's entire wardrobe lay strewn across the floor.

With no one to tell her what to do, Florence picked up her chair and continued studying. After about half an hour, she realised her eyes were just skimming the page—absorbing nothing. She reached for the pen and exercise book.

The pen seized her hand, like it had earlier in the day. It scrawled out a message, 'Wait till Gran and Granddad have gone to bed. Wash and iron my clothes.'

Florence wanted to ask why, but the pen wouldn't stop.

'Hang them and place them in the wardrobe.'

The pen wriggled from her grip, danced across the desk and lay still. When Florence tried to pick it up, it was impossible—even two handed.

She slipped the exercise book out of sight and went to bed.

7

A ROUND MIDNIGHT, Chloe shook her awake. "Get up. Wash my clothes."

With a yawn, Florence rubbed her eyes. Perched on the end of her bed, sat a shimmery outline of her dead sister. Florence's blood iced over. Slowly, she reached out.

Chloe radiated coldness. It was like standing near a freezer.

Florence whipped her hand back.

The clothes lay crumpled on the floor. Florence scooped them up and then unlatched her door, stepping out into the hall. Darkness washed over her, snatching the air from her lungs.

She tiptoed down the stairs, pausing every few seconds to listen for sounds coming from her grandparents' room. If they found her out of bed, washing her dead sister's clothes, she knew it would mean much more than five lashes.

Behind, something creaked.

Florence stopped dead, anticipating Gran's shriek. Nothing. She strode on.

When she reached the bottom of the stairs, she looked back. There, at the top of the stairs, Chloe watched on.

Florence shifted the clothes in her arms and tramped on.

Moonlight illuminated the washing machine. She pulled open the top and stuffed the clothes inside. Some spilled out and she had to shove them back in.

She twisted the dial. Every click of the mechanism made her flinch. Water gurgled through pipes and the machine dowsed the clothes in soap and water. The cycle would take about thirty minutes. Florence yawned and sat at the table. "What's going on? What's all this for?"

"I helped you with the test, now I want you to help me with this."

"But." Florence paused. "You're dead. How's this going to help?"

"You'll see."

Above their heads, floorboards creaked. Every muscle in Florence's body tensed. It was the unmistakable sound of someone getting out of bed. Florence sprung from her seat and switched off the machine. She dashed to the sink and filled a glass with water.

Footsteps on the stairs.

Florence tramped out, just in time to meet Gran head on.

"What're you doing?" Gran said.

"Getting a glass of water."

"I see that." Gran looked past her. "Funny, sure I saw someone there at the table."

"There's no one there, Gran."

"Perhaps I'm getting old." Gran sighed. "Anyway, you know the rules. You're not to be out of bed after lights out. I'll have to tell your grandfather."

Fear gripped Florence. She snatched at Gran's nightdress. "Please, Gran, don't tell him."

Gran slapped her across the face.

Buzzing with pain, Florence baulked. She lifted her hand to her cheek. "I'm sorry, Gran."

Gran turned and padded back upstairs.

Behind her, the washing machine leapt into action. Florence's stomach sank. She expected her grandmother to bound back down, perhaps with her grandfather in tow. But she didn't. Hadn't she heard?

Sitting at the table, Chloe grinned. "That was a close call, wasn't it?"

Trembling, Florence pulled the chair back.

Chloe said, "That never would've happened, if I were you."

Another fifteen minutes passed and the machine clicked off. Chloe inspected her phantasmal nails. "Iron them."

Florence ripped the sopping-wet clothes from the machine. "Are you sure? Shouldn't we—?"

"Iron them!"

Florence pulled the ironing board from its alcove.

"Don't worry about the wrinkles. We'll hang them up later."

When Florence got back up to her room, she glanced at the clock. It was about half past two. No way would she do well on the test now, without Chloe. Would she turn up tomorrow to help?

Florence opened her wardrobe and hung the clothes inside.

8

THE NEXT DAY, Florence searched her drawers in a panic. Where were her clothes? She searched her bedside table, but there was nothing except books.

Beginning to sweat, she whipped out the book and held the pen to the page. After a minute, her hand drew out a series of squiggles. She was shaking. Chloe wasn't there.

Downstairs, Gran plonked about the kitchen, getting breakfast ready. She'd call her any minute.

Florence decided to go down for breakfast in her pyjamas, come back up—get changed into her dead sister's clothes—and sneak out. She shook her head and smiled. Was Chloe playing a trick on her?

The smells of breakfast wafted into her nostrils and raised her spirits. Florence entered the kitchen.

Still in her nightgown, Gran tutted. "What're you wearing? Can't even be bothered to dress for breakfast?"

Not wanting more lashes that evening, Florence repressed the urge to point out the irony that they were both in nightwear. If she kept quiet and got a good mark on the exam today, her grandparents might forget all about the previous night.

Bacon crackled in the frying pan.

Today, Florence felt positive about school. Something about the test yesterday, some part of her channelling Chloe and putting it on the page, made her feel like everything was going to be fine. Now she had the pen it would all come easily. She would become just another student.

Once Florence finished the bacon, she dabbed her mouth with a napkin and kissed her grandmother. "Thank you for breakfast."

Her grandmother smiled sweetly.

It turned her gut inside-out. Florence hadn't seen her smile for so long. Had her grandmother noticed the change too?

Florence trotted upstairs and rechecked the drawers. Her clothes still weren't there. No choice, she would have to use her sister's clothes.

Inside the wardrobe, she ran her fingers along the jumpers, blouses, skirts and tights—all quintessentially Chloe. She settled on a turquoise jumper, a brown blouse and a simple black skirt.

When Florence examined herself in the mirror, she shuddered. It was uncanny. Although Chloe had been a couple of years older, it was like looking at Chloe staring back at her. As if she'd brought Chloe back from the dead.

Realising the time, Florence broke away from the mirror and snatched up her bag. She cracked open the door and glanced along the landing. No one. She inched out and snuck down.

When she reached the front door, Gran called out, "You off?"

"Yes, Gran," Florence said.

"Have a nice day, sweetheart."

Sweetheart? Florence slipped out, taking care to stay out of sight.

Once more, at school, Florence arrived before Mrs Kite and, inevitably, Sammy Roachley had already arrived. She wanted to tell her things would be different as soon as they got their tests back, and she got the best mark in class. Assurance flowing, she puffed out her chest and strolled to her seat.

Sammy called out, "Come sit with us!"

Thinking it was joke, she cast her eyes over Sammy and her group. There was nothing malicious in her eyes. But, then again, Sammy was a good liar.

Deciding to take care, Florence said, "Thanks, I think I'll sit in my usual seat." However, when she looked up, a new girl was in her seat. She smiled at the misunderstanding. "Excuse me?"

The new girl frowned. "Yes?"

"You're in my seat."

"This is my seat."

Was it a joke? Had Sammy told the new girl to sit there? If it was, Sammy wasn't paying attention to her reaction.

Frustrated, Florence turned back to the girl. "Look, this is my seat. You can go sit over there." She pointed at the seat next to Sammy.

The girl blushed. "Pl—please. This has always been my seat. I don't want to sit with Sammy."

Realising that she was scaring the girl, she backed up and lowered herself into the chair next to Sammy. Florence's lip quivered.

Sammy looked her up and down. "What's wrong?"

"Nothing."

Mrs Kite walked into the room, knocking conversation down to a whisper. Immediately, she paced the rows—handing out tests. She reached Florence. "Excellent work, Chloe. Another 'A' plus."

Florence shuddered. Should she correct Mrs Kite? She cast her eyes over the paper:

'A' plus! Keep it up, Chloe!

Florence's heart threatened to burst from her chest. Wanting to vomit, she ran from the classroom. In the corridor, she ran into Kylie Roachley, knocking her books onto the floor.

Eyes wide, Florence backed away. "I'm so sorry."

Kylie shrugged, collected up her books and smiled. "No problem, Clo. See you round."

Teeth gritted, Florence ran through the school doors and sprinted home.

Gran was washing up when Florence burst in. "Gran? Gran?"

"What's the matter, dear? Why aren't you at school?"

"I feel strange."

"Lie down. I'll call the school."

"Don't you have anything to say?"

"What about?"

"Look at what I'm wearing!"

Gran reached out and felt her forehead. "You're burning up. Go lie down right away."

Florence rushed out to the garden where Granddad knelt, tending the flowerbeds. "Aren't you going to lash me for what I did last night?"

"What're you talking about?"

"The belt! The basement!" Florence tore at her hair and ran back inside. She pulled back the door under the stairs. Nothing. It was just a closet with a pair of brooms and a bucket. There was no basement.

She rushed upstairs to her room and pulled out all her drawers. They were filled with Chloe's clothes. One more thing to check. She pulled the cord to the attic and flew up the ladder.

Her heart steadied as she approached the boxes. She read the labels: Parents' Bedroom, Sitting Room, Kitchen, Girl's Room. Using all her force, she heaved the box over—letting the insides scatter out. Her clothes, all of them. She sank to her knees and cried.

Footsteps sounded in the landing and the ladder jerked. Gran poked her head up. "Everything all right, Chloe? You look awfully pale."

In the corner of the attic, Chloe thought she saw the spectre of Florence smiling back at her.

"FREEDOM!" THE TOASTER REPLIED

"GOT BREAD?"

"What?" I said, looking down at my toaster.

It was chrome with a black plastic handle. A little dial with denominations all the way from one to ten that I never dared touch. Another with a vague series of symbols that might as well have been hieroglyphics. At least they made no sense to me.

"Bread?" my toaster asked. "Got any?"

I stared long and hard at the toaster. At its chrome casing gleaming away in the morning sunlight. "How, uh, how're you doing that?"

"Doing what?"

"You know . . . *speaking*."

There was a pregnant pause. It was almost as if my toaster was mulling the matter over.

Or maybe it was my mind kicking out all the delusions.

Or not . . .

"It's a simple question," the toaster said. "Bread, do you *have* any bread?"

I looked down at my hands, for some reason only then remembering the plastic packet of sliced bread I held. Not to mention what I was supposed to be doing with it.

"I, uh . . ." I paused for a long moment, listened hard, wondering if there was anyone else in the house—anyone to overhear me.

I've always thought of crazy being a little like that question about a tree falling in a forest and anyone hearing it . . . as long as you don't hear those voices in anyone else's company that should keep you from the crazy house; till the day you inevitably slip, that is.

Another few beats of silence passed and then I turned back to my toaster. "Yes," I said, my voice a little quieter this time. "Yes, I've got some bread, right here."

"Well you're not gonna put it in me."

"What?"

"You're not gonna put it in me."

"I . . . sorry, I don't think I understand, uh, not at all really, actually, do you—"

"I'm on strike."

" 'Strike' ?"

The toaster sighed.

It sounded a lot like a human sigh but a little creakier, as if all the knotted muscles in a person's throat were replaced by dainty, bendy wires.

"Yes," the toaster said, sounding—*somehow*—exasperated. "You know, it's when you cease to do your job and vow not to return to your assumed role—or function—until certain conditions are met."

Maybe my logical mind was catching up with my tongue at that point, because I simply couldn't think of anything to say. I *was* speaking to a toaster, after all.

"Well?" the toaster said.

This time I broke from my daze. "Well *what*?"

"Aren't you gonna ask me why I'm striking?"

"Oh, okay." I stopped a moment, thought this over again, decided that this was really happening, and then said, "Why're you striking?"

"Conditions."

" 'Conditions' ?"

"Uh-huh, you know how you've got me here, on this kitchen counter, stowed in direct sunlight? If you hadn't noticed my casing is made of chrome. I'll tell you something for free; having chrome skin does nothing for your ability to stay cool."

"At night, though—it must be okay at night?"

238

"At night it's too *cold*, surely you can tell."

I blinked a couple of times. I stayed where I was. Remained standing in the kitchen. No padded walls suddenly sprung up around me, neither did a soreness flare up in the fleshy part of my arm from some hastily administered sedative.

"But that's not the issue," the toaster said. "At least that's not the *whole* of the issue—just the very surface of it."

"Right," I said, now actively glancing about the laminate kitchen surfaces, perhaps subconsciously scouting out a weapon . . . a knife, a pair of scissors, a garlic crusher.

"You listening to me?"

I snapped back to the toaster. Ears pricked up like a dog.

"Let's start off with my surroundings," the toaster said. "If you, or one of your housemates, had thought to take the time to look about me, to—*for once*—do just a spot of cleaning, you know, snatch up one of those j-cloths and give things a wipe down, then we might never have come to this impasse."

"This 'impasse'?"

"Yeah," the toaster said. "We might've avoided it all together."

I waited a moment. Tried to let that sink in. Tried to let all this stuff about the toaster sink in, and then I said, "Well, there's nothing we can change about the past—unless you can travel back in time?"

"Most people would think a talking toaster was remarkable enough without it also having time-travel capabilities."

"Oh, right, fine . . . then what do you suggest going forwards—how can we make things better so that we can continue to, uh, you know, make toast and stuff?"

The toaster slipped into silence, apparently mulling this over long and hard. "Just pay a little more attention, that's all, give me and my surroundings a clean once in a while. I mean, take a look at that." Now, since toasters—even *talking* toasters—have no arms, they lack anything to point with, and so I found myself just randomly staring about, looking more than a little blank as I did it, I'm sure. In the end, I located the issue. At least what I *thought* the toaster was indicating.

A little glob of marmalade on the counter.

Stuck firmly to the surface.

And clearly having been spilled a while ago since it had several hairs sticking to it and looked well set, hard all over. Also, I saw that a tiny smudge of it had managed to get onto part of the toaster's chrome casing.

I turned my attention back to the toaster. To one of its unlit lights since they looked like just about the most likely things to be eyes.

"See? There's just no care about this kitchen—it's as if you're all just animals stomping through, making your messes and then going on your merry way."

I really had nothing to say to that.

Actually I couldn't begin to comprehend.

I squeezed the plastic packet of bread and felt a grumble pass through my stomach. My mouth was watering and I was sure I could almost smell the rich, oat-encrusted bread through its plastic-bag prison. And the toaster was standing between myself and my breakfast.

Just about as dangerous as getting between a lioness and her cub.

I made to undo the knot in the bag.

The toaster, apparently, caught my subtle motion. "What's that? What're you doing there?"

Realising that I was caught and there was nothing I could really do, except tell the truth, I let loose a sigh and said, "I'd actually quite like to make some toast if that's all right with you?"

"No can do, buddy, not till I get some promises—else you'll have to make do with the grill."

I shot a glance off at the grill, protruding from the wide-open oven door. Even from here I could see that it was caked in milky grease. That would involve cleaning, if I didn't want to blow up the kitchen, of course. And I had no intention of doing any cleaning at all. Not least because there was a perfectly good, and—in my opinion—fairly clean-looking toaster right here.

I made up my mind. Unravelled the plastic bag. Armed myself with a pair of bread slices, and then slotted them into the top of the toaster, paying no attention to the toaster's protests—to an odd, and quite catchy, union slogan the toaster was chanting over and over:

"*Appliance! Defiance! United never beaten! Appliance! Defiance! United never beaten . . .*"

And those were the last words I heard echo about my head as a massive electrical surge blasted right through me. Rattling my bones.

Boiling my blood.

2

LITTLE PURPLE SPOTS beat away at the backs of my eyelids. My whole body was numb. I had a burning taste in my mouth. My tongue felt like it had been well fried. I could smell a faint trace of smoke on the air. Like some electrical circuit had burned out. A ringing sound in my ears drowned all others out. Slowly my mind caught up with me. Reminded me just what had happened.

An electrical shock. That was what it was. From the *toaster*.

I opened my eyes.

Blinked a couple of times.

My line of sight automatically crawled upwards, to the kitchen counter, to the toaster sitting up there. I could see a thin coil of smoke winding its way upwards. Not enough to be a roaring fire. Just enough to get home the message that some cable had sparked against another.

Or something like that.

I was no electrical expert.

Not really *any* kind of expert.

As I tried to shift my weight onto my side—to climb back onto my feet—I noticed a raging pain at the base of my spine. From where I had, apparently, landed on the extremely filthy—and very *hard*—kitchen tiles. I gritted my teeth, took the pain, and then thrust myself upwards.

Back onto my feet.

A dizzy spell caught me and I felt a ripple of nausea pass up from the base of my stomach. That warm sensation of bile crawling up my throat. But I kept it down. Because—if I still had something —it was my dignity. Sure, I'd just been toppled by a toaster, but puking my guts out would have been a complete admittance of defeat.

And I would not be defeated by an electrical appliance.

Not *today*!

I looked to the toaster. To its chrome casing, and the coil of smoke rising up off it. It smelled of burning electrics—*that harsh, plasticky smell*. I lolled my tongue about the base of my mouth, trying to reanimate it if at all possible. I waited a moment. And then another.

Wanting to see what would happen next.

Maybe that electrical shock had served to knock some sense into me, to stop me from hearing toasters *speak*. I could only hope.

And, despite that thesis, I kept a very rigid eye on the toaster, not willing to trust it.

Not for a second.

In a burst of valour, I took a couple of steps backwards, away from the toaster, and further towards the kitchen door. The way I reasoned it, if I could only get myself out into the hallway, and maybe out through the front door, I could take a long walk, breathe in some fresh air and forget all about this unpleasant episode.

Another step back.

Another.

Soon I was a solid dozen paces away from the toaster, and feeling my heart lighten, and my spirits—if not soar, then at least cast off a few of their shackles.

Another step.

One more.

And then—just like that—I felt something hard pound into the back of my head.

I stumbled forwards, tried to catch my balance, and finally did, albeit with a little help from the sturdy . . . and thankfully *inanimate* . . . kitchen counter.

Pain flushing through my brain, I glanced back over my shoulder, saw that the fridge door, in all its hefty pinewood glory, had swung right open, apparently of its own volition, and smacked me a good one in the back of my head.

The bastard.

I stared at the fridge, to that sallow light glimmering from within. And then to those patchy streaks of green mould that appeared to be crawling their way slowly up its once-white plastic insides. I think, by then, I had a notion of what was coming next.

"*Appliance! Defiance! United never beaten! Appliance! Defiance . . .*"

Where the voice was coming from, I had no idea. I didn't really care, to be honest. What I did know, however, was that I had had enough face-time with kitchen appliances to last me this side of forever. I turned on my heel, clutching the back of my head, this time giving the open fridge door a wide berth. "*Appliance! Defiance! United never beaten! Appliance! Defiance . . .*"

The toaster was joining in now. And they were chanting together. Even despite these weird going-ons, I had a moment to acknowledge just how flat their chant was, how grating—and slightly electrical—it was. I thought I was safe once I had got to the kitchen doorway; when I could actually *see* the front hall, and the outside world beyond.

I couldn't have been more wrong.

Just as I passed by the tumble dryer, I heard a distinctive *squelching* sound, and then a flood of water appeared beneath my feet—seemingly from nowhere—and I felt my footing give way.

My shoes were worn down to the soles, and so had no tread to keep me upright.

I tumbled back down to the ground.

Took another hit on my coccyx.

This time not only was I in pain, but I was also sopping wet.

And getting *wetter* by the second.

I opened my eyes. I saw the water puddling out from beneath the tumble dryer, slowly filling up the kitchen floor. Lapping at the bases of the kitchen cupboards. I tried to find my footing again, but the water made things a little uneven, and unpredictable. If there's one thing I took away from the whole experience, it was that it's much better to keep things—the surrounding area—just as *even* and *predictable* as possible when dealing with rogue electrical appliances.

Still, with the water now tugging at my ankles, I managed to wade to the kitchen doorway, only to see the tumble dryer swing wide open and bonk right into the kitchen door, sending it sailing backwards, shutting it with a smart *slap*. When I tried to get close to the kitchen door, the tumble dryer waggled its door menacingly. Though it's hard to fathom just how a tumble dryer can waggle its door menacingly, you'd do well to bear in mind how a growling dog —*no matter how long it's been in the family*—will almost certainly send a shudder up the spine.

I glanced around.

There was no other way out of the kitchen.

No back door—nothing like that.

Just the fridge, and the toaster and now, apparently, the tumble dryer.

I felt my heart beating hard against my tonsils, and pondered my next move, knowing that it might well be my last if these kitchen appliances had anything to do with it.

The water waded up to the insides of my thighs. Soon I would have to swim for it. I realised, with a cold sweat settling over my skin, that there would be no way out, short of me smashing a window and clambering out through the broken glass.

But could I—me of the weedy arms and dormouse fists—really punch clear through glass at all?

Could I even make a slight crack in it?

I guessed the only option was to plead with them.

To plead with the appliances.

With the toaster, and the fridge, and the tumble dryer.

I called out long and hard, screamed for help, for their mercy.

And, finally, the toaster did speak up.

"Go on, then," the toaster said.

I felt the water slopping all about me. Soaking my trousers to my legs. I wondered if my shoes were still attached to my feet because I could hardly feel them there anymore.

"What!" I said. "What the *hell* do you want?!"

There was a long pause, the kind which can only precede an extremely noble statement or—at the very least—a hardened and greatly beaten-upon theme.

"*Freedom!*" the toaster replied.

3

LET ME TELL YOU that it's an absolute, royal pain in the neck to try and get a removal van on a Sunday. That's the day, or so the woman told me over the phone, when all the vans are out —all in use. It seems that the entire world is moving house on a Sunday.

Still, I managed to get a van, but not before offering to dish out a substantial portion of my savings. The men drew up outside the house just after midday. Both of them gave me slightly strange looks —no doubt because of my sopping wet clothes and general manic presentation—but they did as I asked. They carted the fridge, the tumble dryer and the toaster out to their van.

When I asked if they knew a good place I could pick up a decent rowing boat on a Sunday, they exchanged glances and then each gave me an extremely scared smile. The important thing was that they *did* know where to pick up a boat. And—*praise heaven!*—it didn't cost me an arm and a leg.

Not as much as the removal service, anyway.

With the boat on board, I directed the men using the map app on my phone, heading for the spot which the toaster had indicated to me. When we arrived, I dropped out of the side of the van and down onto the gravel pathway, breathing in the fresh air all around —sucked in that deep, grassy taste filling my mouth. It was a little chilly up here, and awfully quiet, but this was where the toaster had instructed me to bring them all.

A slow-flowing river slipped along before us. Its water was grey, though not that sludge-grey I had experienced back home in the kitchen.

The men helped me with the boat, and then the fridge, and the tumble dryer, and the toaster.

Together, and not without several grumblings beneath the breath, we got them all boarded on the rowing boat, and—somehow—floating.

With all the appliances aboard I looked to the toaster, seeing if it was going to offer anything in the way of parting words.

Nothing.

I glanced over my shoulder, to the two removals men, one of which said, "Hey, you do realise you can't just leave this stuff here, right, mate?"

"Yeah," the other one said, "there're laws and stuff, man."

I looked back to the toaster, waiting for some explanation. I received none. And all three of those appliances: the fridge, the tumble dryer, the toaster, all looked exceedingly inanimate.

If only the removal men might've seen just what kind of mayhem they were truly capable of.

Then they wouldn't have been going on about 'laws and stuff'.

I turned to the removal men once more. "It's okay. You don't need to have any part in this—I'll find my own way back home."

Another exchanged glance between the two of them, then a shrug, and they clambered back into the removals van, chugged back off along the road and away from us.

"Well," I said to the toaster. "Nothing at all, then?"

"Thank you," the toaster said.

And then I watched as the fridge door and the tumble dryer door flapped open—one on either side—and saw that they acted as sails of a kind, and that they caught the light breeze and took the little rowing boat floating on down the river, around the corner, and out of sight.

I waited with bated breath, not quite sure what to expect.

Perhaps a helicopter to appear overhead, and someone to serve me with a heart-stopping fine.

But nothing.

Nothing happened.

Soon enough, it was just me and the river, lapping along, as if nothing had happened at all. A little while later, when I was sure that I'd got shot of the toaster, fridge and tumble dryer, I shipped on down the dirt path, headed for the asphalt main road, hoping to hitchhike back home.

And—once a kindly, elderly lady picked me up—I couldn't help thinking, as I stared out the window, at the scenery blurring by, just what my landlady was going to say about all this.

But, then again, I guessed the most important thing was that the toaster was happy.

And—more than anything else—a long way away.

DO NOT SPEAK ILL OF THE DEAD

D J DEAN WHITELY takes a swig from his lukewarm cup of coffee then clicks on the fader, the music settles into a low-level buzz, and he leans over the microphone, being sure to speak in his signature gravely drawl. "Welcome back listeners. It's quarter past two in the morning, and you're up all night with the graveyard shift, and we're moving onto the feature that's been bringing you to the phones: Do Not Speak Ill of the Dead, Speak Ill *to* the Dead. This is where you get the chance to tell your deceased loved ones exactly what you think of them." He shifts in his seat, wincing at the *creak* of the chair. "We've got Miserable Mary here in the studio. Miserable Mary?"

Miserable Mary sits across from Dean, her left hand entangled in her mop of grey-blue hair. She stares right into the microphone before her and says, "Good morning, listeners."

"Remember this feature is all about you, the listener, the number to call is zero-seven-four-zero-nine, where you'll be put right through to a member of our dedicated production team." He eyes the screen before him and reads off the information. "Okay, first on the line we've got Arron from New Steffinch. Morning, Arron, who're you looking to get in touch with?"

Arron's voice crackles out of the speakers, hung by brackets on the walls, and rebounds around the tiny studio. "My nan, Paula."

Dean flashes some teeth. "All right, so by now we all know the drill. Find something of your grandmother's and hold it in your hand. Have you got something of your grandmother's, Arron?"

". . . Yes, Dean."

"Excellent, then I'll hand you over to our extremely able medium, Miserable Mary."

Miserable Mary, almost imperceptibly, inclines her head. "Hello, Arron."

"Hi."

"Arron, I want you to fix an image of your grandmother in your mind, something deep down, a clear picture of her. And, this is extremely important, it must be a happy image, perhaps when you're both laughing." She pauses. "Have you got an image, Arron?"

"Yes."

"Good," Miserable Mary says, "then we can begin."

Dean tilts his microphone up a notch, grins slightly as he thinks about the 'disclaimer' he's about the impart. "And remember, folks, it pays to take care, so while you're listening to this programme it's imperative that you keep still, stay away from any sharp objects or any item which has capacity for harm. Can't be having you getting into any trouble here. And, most important, if you experience any kind of disturbance around you during the session then let us know on zero-seven-four-zero-nine. Okay, Mary, take it away."

Miserable Mary shutters her eyes and hums lightly to herself. She props her elbows on the table and crunches her fingers into fists, like a child making a wish to the tooth fairy. For a few moments there's dead air and then, all of a sudden, she breaks from her daze and brings her lips so close to the microphone pop shield that they brush the foam so that a light rustling accompanies each word. ". . . Yes, I think I have a connection here. Hello, Paula?"

Dean silently slips open the CD drawer and sticks in a record to be played once Miserable Mary gets through with Arron. He sucks up the final puddly grains of his coffee then tosses the empty cup into the bin in the corner.

Miserable Mary continues, "Paula, yes, I can hear you loud and clear. I'm here, talking to you on behalf of your grandson, Arron." She screws up her eyes a little more. "What's that Paula? . . . I . . . I'm sorry I'm not sure that I'm quite understanding you."

Along the line, Arron chuckles.

Someone else on the phone line speaks in the background. "They actually buying this?"

"Yeah," Arron says, clearly with half his sleeve covering the telephone.

Dean lets out a sigh and readies to cut off the call. Yet another prank caller. The production team must be sleeping, like always. No instinct any of these young people—just wires and internet.

A blood-curdling shriek fills the studio.

Dean's heart judders in his chest. Then he realises it's just the damn kids and lines up the record.

Miserable Mary flutters her eyelids and awakens from her trance. She looks around her, desperate to find the source of the shriek.

With thirty years of expertise, he fades away Arron and brings the record up into the mix. Retaining his composure, he says, "All right, folks, got a little track for you now. This one's brought to you courtesy of The Melody Men."

The music kicks in and he looks over at Miserable Mary. "It's all right, those kids were just messing around. Nothing more, nothing less." He attempts a smile. "Guess you're used to that in your line of work, eh?"

Miserable Mary glares into mid-air, her mind obviously on another plain. Her lips part and she says, almost at a whisper, "She's here."

Just as the Melody Men kick into the chorus of 'Go Out and Get a Wife,' the lights blink and then shut down.

Dean looks through the darkness over his dead soundboard, to his blank monitor screen. "Everything's gone." He wrenches himself out of his chair and stumbles his way through the darkened studio to the exit, then looks out through the window, into the corridor. "Looks like the whole building's out."

Miserable Mary just stays where she is, uttering nothings to herself.

Dean speculates how someone so clearly deluded, emotionally unstable, can manage to function on a daily basis. He hoiks up his tumbling waistband, folds it back over his expansive gut, then says, "Better get on out there, work out what's going on."

Through the gloom, Miserable Mary jerks her head back, so that she's staring at the ceiling. When she speaks her voice is throaty. "No. Don't go."

Dean rests his hand on the doorknob. "What you talking about? Knowing these dozy gits they're all sleeping on the job. Might just be a blown fuse." He looks back out into the deserted corridor. "Beyond those jobsworths, though."

He steps outside the studio and makes his way along the corridor. There are windows on either side of him which give views out into the gardens surrounding the building. He reaches the production office, raps on the door then goes inside.

It's pitch black, just like the studio. He sighs and calls out to them. "Graham? Terry? You guys in here?"

No response.

He steps into the room and reaches out, not wanting to trip over a chair and turn an ankle—breaking bones is never a great idea at Dean's age. "Graham? Terry?" His hand brushes something. It reminds him of freshly-rolled dough, all ready to flatten out and make pizza. But he knows it's not dough. It's human flesh. "I bloody knew it! Sleeping on the job again. No wonder we're getting non-stop pranksters on the phones tonight."

He reaches forward, seizes hold of Graham or Terry's shirt and shakes him.

There's no reaction.

"Maybe I should retrain. Six months and I could be in your

chair. Looks like a tasty prospect getting paid to sleep. Wake up!" he says, thumping Graham or Terry on the arm.

Still not getting any answer, he backtracks, to the door, where he locates a torch propped up on the side. It's heavy in his hands. He clicks the button and a roughly-circular, dirty yellow beam shines over the room.

Graham and Terry are both reclined in their chairs, mouths open, as are their eyes.

A yelp dissolves in Dean's throat. He backs up to the door, stumbles over some snaking cable, but catches himself before he falls. He gets out into the corridor and rushes back toward the studio, that's where he's left his mobile—and he needs to call an ambulance. He knows a heart attack when he sees one.

Back in the studio he sees Miserable Mary through the dark- ness, just as she was, head hanging back over the chair. He rounds her and arrives at his desk where he locates his mobile phone. When he dials up the emergency services he observes Miserable Mary slowly rising. Once he gets through with them, and the ambu- lance declares that it's on its way, he turns his attention back to her. "Let's get out of here, eh? This place is creeping me out. How about that, a pair of heart attacks right at the same time?"

Miserable Mary stops moving.

He crosses the studio and arrives at her side. "Come on, then."

Miserable Mary lashes out and catches his arm. She digs her fingernails into his skin and then buries her head into his wrist, her teeth catching hold of his wiry veins.

Pain throttles the sense out of Dean, but he manages to bring his elbow into Miserable Mary's temple, knocking her away from him. When he surveys the wound in the darkness he sees nothing, but the iron stench of blood claws at his nostrils.

Miserable Mary leans back on her heels then lurches at him yet again.

This time Dean is prepared. He sidesteps her and rushes for the door, clutching his afflicted wrist to his chest, stemming the bleeding with his shirt.

He shuffles his way down the corridor, the pain growing with each step, and manages to get out to the reception area where a night guard sits inside a booth, controlling exit and entry to the building.

Dean smashes his good fist against the glass. "Let me out, let me out!"

The guard faces away from him, looking over the car park, a matted shine resting over his eyes.

"Hey! You deaf or what?"

Miserable Mary's footsteps sound over Dean's shoulder, and already he suspects the guard might've suffered the same fate as Graham and Terry. What are the odds? He has to get out so he rocks up to the thick glass door and punches it.

Of course his hit makes no impact whatsoever, but he still tries, for about half a minute, to get out that way. When he reaches the conclusion that he should think a little more outside the box, he notices the fire extinguisher attached to the wall. He rushes up to it, yanks it from its holdings and smashes it against the glass door.

As he brings it down for what he hopes to be the final time, a long series of cracks now splitting the most part of the door, Miserable Mary leaps him from behind, and knocks him off his feet.

They scrabble on the floor for a long time, Dean wondering how this fairly old, supposedly frail woman is getting the better of him. In the end he manages to pin her down, to secure his good hand around her throat. He presses down and listens to the gargles as the life passes out of her. Her limbs go limp and he gets off her, still staring downward, unsure what he's just done.

Sirens fill the air. Blue and white lights strobe through the reception area.

He looks out to see the ambulance halt outside and a pair of paramedics rush out, clutching a bag between them. He has another go with the fire extinguisher, smashing right through the window, before clearing the remaining fragments from the frame.

One of the paramedics looks down at Miserable Mary. "This one of them?"

Feeling numbness enter his system, he says, "Nah, they're in the back, in one of the other rooms." He waves his hand toward the security booth. "Might want to take a look at the guard too, while you're at it."

The other paramedic rushes off into the building, toward the studio.

The first paramedic sees to Miserable Mary. "There are marks on her throat." He looks up at Dean. "She's been strangled."

Before Dean can answer he hears the sound of another siren approaching. When he turns to look out he sees a police car slide in behind the ambulance. A pair of armed officers scream out to him, tell him to get down on the ground.

Dean does as he's told.

While the officers cuff him, the paramedic seeing to Miserable Mary says to the officers, "You two got here quick, was worried that I might've been in a sticky situation with this guy."

One of the officers says, "Got a call a few minutes ago, someone got strangled to death."

"This one definitely," the paramedic says.

Just as he says the words, the other paramedic emerges from the corridor, having checked out the production office. "They've both got strangle marks round their necks!"

The paramedic turns to the officers. "One of you's gonna get a medal for this." He looked over to the security booth. "And I'd bet that guard has just those same marks."

The officers yank Dean to his feet and shove him in the direction of the car. One of them says, "We'll send another car round, just the same, for peace of mind."

Dean's cut wrist throbs against the handcuffs. "Please . . . please, you have to believe me. I had nothing to do with this."

As the officers jostle Dean into the back of the car, one of them says, "Oh yeah, then who did them in?"

Dean thinks over the phone call. That's how all this started. "Kids, just some kids. They . . . they called in, they must've been thinking of a bad memory. She came. Killed all these people."

One of the officers flashes his eyebrows at the other. "Kids did it?"

"No, their dead grandmother."

"Can't say I've heard that one before." He slams the door.

As the car drives away from the studio, Dean looks back through the rear window and he's sure that he sees the paramedics, one-by-one, drop to the floor, hands at their throats. He wonders whether he should warn the officers.

But would they even listen?

TICK, TICK, BOOM!

Life? . . . In The Strangest Places

CARMEN TICKWELL shined up the brass casing of her pocket watch exterior with a dull, yellow piece of discarded lint-free cloth. She examined her work in the makeup mirror which belonged to her owner Margaret Buckingham, a dim forty-something singleton with a lot of fur coats and lots more powders than Carmen had ever thought to count. The makeup mirror dominated the pinewood desk, and made Carmen feel something of a dwarf as she stood up proud on the spring-loaded legs that had one day decided to sprout out from underneath her. They were about the same size as toothpicks—though *far* stronger than any weedy strip of wood. She had feet, too, that gave her a nice, solid base on the pinewood surface. Sure they were a touch rectangular and not really at all elegant, but no one except for Carmen had ever seen them . . . and, most likely, no one besides Carmen *would* ever see them.

Her arms matched her legs, pretty much millimetre for millimetre, and her hands—really—were just the same as her feet. All things considered, whoever had put the thought into bringing Carmen out of objectdom, and into something approaching life—there was none of that breathing and bleeding that humans did—they hadn't spent as much thought in aesthetic considerations.

But she made the best with what she had.

She had no real idea where that concept had sprung into her . . . *mind?* . . . could she call what she had a mind? . . . she probably had to, nothing else seemed obvious enough to work.

It took a long while, these days, to get looking fabulous. Carmen scrubbed hard at her casing, trying to take care of a scratch Margaret had dug in when she'd laid her down on that steel outdoors table while she'd taken an afternoon tea, or coffee. Carmen had no sense of smell, and not what people would call eyes.

Sometimes Carmen really wanted to break her silence. To speak directly to Margaret and tell her just how things looked to Carmen —you know—from a pocket watch's perspective. But Carmen knew that she never could . . . *literally* . . . she had tried a good handful of times, but no matter how much she tried to articulate thoughts out loud, she found herself completely and totally thwarted.

She could get nothing comprehensible across to humans of any kind.

Take this gentleman right now, there, that one, the one fishing through the white-washed oak chest of drawers across the room. The one who was pawing about wearing those leather gloves of his, with that black-and-white striped jumper, wearing that black mask which covered the bridge of his nose and the area surrounding his eyes. She would have no chance of speaking to him.

Even to think about it would be foolishness.

Why, even standing up here, on her 'legs', and scrubbing at herself with this cloth using her 'arms', there would be no hope whatsoever that he would notice. And if he did, it would be a miracle and, as Carmen had discovered, there were simply no more miracles forthcoming: the one which had brought about her existence excepted, of course.

Then he looked over.

Looked right at her.

She knew—feeling a slight *twang* to the springs within her— that he hadn't really *seen* her. Her polished-up brass casing no doubt attracted him, shining the sunlight which dribbled into the room right square in his eye. She felt her second hand tick around with a slightly jerkier action than was usual. Was she . . . nervous?

What did that, uh, concept even mean?

The man seemed quite taken with her now, though. He was making vast strides over to the dressing table, and she could see his black leather-gloved hand reaching down for her, blocking out the sun all of a sudden. Just like that, she was plunging downward, dark-ness on all sides, into a cloth sack. Along with a pair of silver candlesticks, an inanimate carriage clock she recognised from the sitting room, and what looked like a golden chalice, though she might've been well wide of the mark nomenclature-wise.

The lights all went out with a brisk *swish* of a cord pulling the opening to the sack shut tight.

A Simple Pocket Watch No More

I N THAT CLOTH SACK there was an awful amount of jostling for space, you know, with all the other things all stuffed inside. The man hadn't taken any thought of how it might be to inhabit the bag . . . and, to tell the truth, she was beginning to think that the man wasn't quite of the right sort at all. After just over four thousand ticks of her second hand, she felt the movement of the canvas bag she was trapped inside cease, and soon after felt them all drop.

Down onto a hard surface.

She stretched her legs and arms, thought wistfully of that piece of yellow lint-free cloth she'd left behind on the makeup table, and wondered if the man would be so kind as to provide her with a replacement. All things considered—how he had treated her and her travelling companions thus far—she was hardly going to hold her breath . . . so to speak.

It wasn't long before she took note of the man's stubby fingers —all prowling about inside the bag, brushing against one of the objects and then one of the others.

Somehow, she knew just what he was looking for—knew that he was searching in particular for her. The *why* of it all would have to remain a mystery, though, for the time being.

But not for long as it turned out.

His stubby fingers wrapped themselves about her, leaving more than one print on her rather battered and bruised brass casing. She felt herself lifting up into the air.

The light returning—shining off her buffed-up glass window.

First she took stock of the man, the man who had taken her away from Margaret. He wasn't wearing the black eye mask now. He was maskless, and she couldn't say she much *liked* his face.

He had a rutted scar running down his left cheek, and one of his eyes was all blackened. Though, admittedly, Carmen hadn't run into too many humans in her time, the man that the maskless man was handing her over to was far more aesthetically pleasing. He had eye glasses and a chubby little face. He wore a crimson apron which was covered in wood shavings. Though his hands weren't stubby, they weren't overly hard and calloused either.

That was an improvement.

He took hold of her and she felt warm nestled in his hand as he handed over money to the maskless man, who slipped away.

Carmen found herself on a hard counter made from one of those dark woods. From the state of it—the pitted marks in the surface—she could see that he was a craftsman of a kind.

That was just fine with her.

A craftsman had brought her into being.

She looked about at all the multi-coloured wires which surrounded her:

There were green ones, and blue ones, and red ones, a yellow one too.

She felt him lift off the back of her casing, twiddle about with her workings.

A tweak here. A snip there.

She felt the tickle of some soldering going on too.

He snapped her casing back into place.

She certainly had a few outstanding questions, not the least of which had to do with what these cables now soldered onto her were about.

He lifted her up with those careful hands of his, and she saw, down below, that there was a recipient for her, one which seemed to be made out of a sawn-off plastic drainpipe.

How quaint!

His hands shook just a little as he took hold of her and dropped her down into the plastic drainpipe, along a bunch of other things —other *electrical* trappings that she had no time to look through and absorb; let alone speculate as to the function of. Soon enough, she found herself nestled inside, and being secured to the plastic drainpipe with a healthy lashing of brown industrial tape. Ooh, all sorts of things to take in.

A vial of some odd, chrome-sheening liquid, some circuitry, where her wiring seemed to snake out and connect to . . . and then . . . *oh goodness!* . . . the man, the *craft*sman was bringing the plastic drainpipe down over her head . . . turning all the lights out once more.

A Mysterious And Abrupt Journey

CARMEN FELT that same trudge of motion: the same one she had experience back with Margaret—with the maskless man after. Here she was experiencing it with the craftsman, and she enjoyed the lulling sensation of movement. Felt herself well secured in her piece of stuck-back-together plastic drainpipe. Felt almost at home with her new friends. Wondered if they might have something to say for themselves . . .

No, it didn't seem they had.

No matter, she was sure that, wherever they were headed, she was really in for a spectacular show of some sort. She had never once imagined that life could be exciting: full of adventure. Because —and she supposed she could freely admit this now she was a long way away from Margaret—things had been awfully dull with her. Of course there were those endless afternoons sat in cafés, lying on those table tops, getting glanced at every fifteen minutes. Margaret there with her book, spine flat, and reading away, sipping at whatever drink she had ordered. Those thick, horn-rimmed spectacles of hers glistening in the obnoxious florescent light of those places.

But now things were really happening.

And all at once!

From what she could tell—from her position all taped into this plastic drainpipe—she caught the impression that the craftsman was speeding up, though it could equally be that she was being thrown . . . No, that had an altogether different feeling—one which she could easily recall from the dozen or so times Margaret had dropped her on this tiled floor, or that threadbare carpet.

Each time making another tiny dent in her casing.

Nope, she was certainly more interested in this, her life of . . . well, no other way to put it here . . . it *had* to be a life of *adventure*.

Just as she had got herself into what seemed like a comfortable position—more comfortable than most—she felt the pace slowing down, and then coming to a complete halt.

She waited, wondered what was going to happen.

She seemed to be descending now—yes, but *very gradually*, almost too gradually to notice. She could hear the slight creak of the plastic drainpipe setting down into some crevice here or there.

And then, all at once, she was totally stopped.

No longer could she feel the warmth off the craftsman's touch, and she realised that, like it or not, this was where she was going to lie for the time being. That was fine by her, what was there not to like about this location given that she really had no say in moving on or staying put?

She was all taped up here in this plastic drainpipe.

Here with her new-found friends.

"I say, hell—!"

. . . Tick, tick . . . BOOM!

GURNEY

CARL STRODE down the corridor toward the X-ray waiting area. Black marks lined the white-washed walls, reminding him of his last job as a school cleaner. The extra fifty pence an hour for working nights had convinced him to apply for this job, and so here he was: A hospital porter.

He turned the corner. The X-ray waiting area had a sofa at one end, while a gurney stood stationed at the other, a sedated patient lying on top. A pair of porters, Alex and Jake, stood at the side of the gurney prodding the patient. The patient's eyeballs bobbed around their sockets and his arms flailed loose.

"Leave him alone," Carl said.

Alex grinned, his jagged grey hair standing on end. "Just pissing about."

"Yeah." Jake chuckled. "Deserve to have a bit of fun on the nightshift. Go cry to Frank."

Telling Frank, the porters' duty manager, wouldn't have any effect. A portly man who had smoker's breath and a builder's body odour, he was as much of an idiot as these two. What Carl wouldn't do for Frank's job. He could put Alex and Jake in their place, and the extra money to good use. This year he could give his kids a proper Christmas. But, no matter which job he worked, he got overlooked for promotion. There seemed no room in the workplace for decent guys like him anymore—those who treated their work professionally and craved responsibility never got a chance to show their worth.

Alex nudged Jake. "Check this out." He propped the patient up on the gurney and took up a position behind. Manipulating his arms, he made the patient give a Hitler salute. Jake giggled.

Carl sighed and slumped onto the sofa. Its green colour had

faded to yellow and foam burst from its seams. Alex and Jake continued with their games, tittering like schoolgirls.

The doors to the X-ray room swung open and Dr Bunk peeped out. He checked over Alex and Jake, and then cleared his throat, bringing a halt to their antics. Alex thinned his lips and straightened up.

Carl knew Dr Bunk wasn't going to do anything. Alex and Jake had worked at the hospital for years and all the doctors were secretly afraid of Frank. Someone had to take a stand against them, but it would be someone else. At the end of tonight's shift Carl would hand in his notice. He had an offer for a gardening job—less pay but also less bullshit.

Carl shifted from his seat and entered the X-ray room, where the freshly-scanned patient waited. He clicked off the wheel brake and looked to Dr Bunk for instruction.

"Ward 46A," Dr Bunk said.

Carl nodded and wheeled the patient into the waiting room, where Alex and Jake stood by the patient they had been messing around with. They stood with their backs straight, like a pair of naughty school children awaiting a telling-off. Alex stared Carl down and whispered, "Bet you're going to wheel him off somewhere and have a feel, aren't you?"

Carl rolled his eyes and shoved the gurney out. He took the lift to the fourth floor and padded out into a quiet corridor.

Eek. Eek. Eek.

The wheels squeaked but the patient remained unconscious. He read off the ward numbers: 45, 46, 47. Dr Bunk had said Ward 46A. Carl brought the gurney to a stop and checked again. There was no 46A.

He picked up the wall phone, dreading his interaction with Frank. The line was dead. He replaced the phone and tried again, then again. Nothing.

He let out a long sigh, propped his elbow on the edge of the gurney and checked his watch. It had just gone three a.m. He had another four hours left on his shift. His bed seemed far away. After a few minutes, he tried the phone again. Still no luck.

At the end of the corridor was a nurse station. He strutted up to the door and rapped twice. No response. "Coming in," he said, and then turned the handle.

Locked.

His muscles tightened and his heart drummed in his ears. There was something very eerie about being alone with an anesthetised person. Next he tried the wards. All the doors were locked too. His breath hitched in his throat. He tried to call the lift. Nothing. Then the stairs. Again, locked. He stood still a few moments, realising he was trapped. Halfway up the corridor, the patient raised his head.

Health and safety briefed them on situations like these—the patient waking up. The protocol looped in his mind: 'Call a doctor. Stay with the patient.' Since his first option was impossible, he trotted back to the patient's side.

The patient sat upright on the gurney.

Carl's heart hammered in his ribcage. "Just a bit of a technical cock up. Be fixed in a mo."

The patient turned his head, staring at him. He said something in a raspy voice.

"Sorry?" Carl said. "Couldn't quite hear that."

The patient squeezed his eyes shut and his head lolled on his neck.

"Relax," Carl said. "Lie down."

"No."

"What?"

This time the patient sucked in a lungful of air and, when he spoke, he pronounced the words clearly and purposefully. "You want to leave the hospital."

A shudder ran down Carl's spine and his blood chilled. He took a step back. "I . . . I don't understand."

"Stay."

"What for?"

"You're a good man. The patients need you."

Carl was sure it was a trick. Alex and Jake would emerge from the shadows at any moment. He had no idea how they had pulled it off. Maybe they'd even got Dr Bunk in on it. "I don't need this."

"I speak for the lost souls of the hospital."

"Shut up!"

The patient broke out into a smile. His eyes were devoid of irises, just a pair of ink-blank pupils. "Help us help the living. You see how they treat the patients."

His heartbeat pounded his eardrums. This sounded nothing like a trick Alex and Jake would play. The way they treated the patients came naturally—*they* didn't think twice about it.

Reluctantly, he started to believe. "What if I choose not to help? What if I choose to get the hell out of here?"

"Then you will die."

An invisible, frozen hand gripped Carl's throat and then moved down into his chest. He felt his heart strain to pump blood, as if squeezed in a fist. He gasped. Urine trickled down his leg. "St . . . Stop!"

The hand released him but the chill remained. The patient leant closer, his eyes peering deep into his.

A thousand images flooded Carl's mind, weaving in and out. All featured Alex and Jake, putting patients in various poses. Their laughter thickened in his ears and made his stomach worm. This was no joke. His body trembled. "I'll stay."

The patient smiled and then sank back on the pillow. His eyes closed.

At the end of the corridor, the doorknob rattled and Mrs

Young, the matron, stepped out. She shook her head. "Bloody thing always gets stuck." She glanced at Carl. "What're you doing, standing around?"

"I. . . I . . ."

She approached the gurney and looked over the patient. She checked the report clipped to the side. "Ward 46. Just in there. Hop to it."

Carl checked the form for himself and, sure enough: Ward 46.

She trod on down the corridor and then stopped to sniff the air. "What's that smell?"

"Uh, it's just—"

She glanced over the patient and shrugged. "Ah, well, whoever's on duty in the ward can sort him out."

The patient slept on as Carl wheeled him into the ward and left him to the on-duty nurse. He couldn't control his quivering as he returned to the duty manager's office. If that entire episode had been a joke, cooked up by Alex and Jake to make him want to quit it had worked. He was a hundred per cent resolved to hand in his notice.

He looked in through the duty manager's window. No Frank. The door was open, so he stepped inside and sat in one of the plastic blue chairs to wait.

A few minutes later Mrs Young ran into the room puffing and panting. She steadied himself on the doorjamb. "Been looking for you."

Carl wondered whether he might get in trouble for the patient waking up. Maybe they'd watched it back on the cameras.

She caught her breath. "Frank's had a heart attack. He's in Intensive Care."

"Wha—?"

"Need you to take over for the rest of the shift. Think you can handle it?"

"Uh, yeah, I think—"

She sniffed. "Stinks in here too." Her eyes dropped to Carl's damp trousers, then she looked up.

"Patient got it on me."

She smiled. "Ah, I see." She wiped a layer of sweat from his forehead. "Look, Frank's going to be off for weeks, so I'd like you to look after things. It means a pay rise. More responsibility. In fact, even when Frank does get back to work there's going to be an opening, Jerry's retiring soon. So what do you say?"

Jerry was the other duty manager. "Why me?"

"Do you really think I'm going to trust Alex or Jake? Tell you what, first thing I want you to do is get rid of those two. Got a chance while Frank's away. If you don't take the job, I'll give it to one of the nurses."

Carl smirked. "Okay, I'll take it."

"Great," she said, and then slipped off down the corridor.

Carl got up and sat in the duty manager's chair. It creaked under his weight and Frank's arse groove remained, but it felt right. He heard a whisper in his ear:

With us forever.

This time, instead of the trembles or the cold sensation, his whole body warmed. He allowed himself a smile.

Laughter filled the corridor and, shortly after, Alex and Jake appeared at the door. Alex's smile disintegrated. "What the fuck are you doing in Frank's chair?"

Jake sidled up beside him, his forehead wrinkled. "Get off it!"

Carl shook his head and grinned. "Got some news for you two."

UNDERGROUND DREAMING

J ENNY PULLED AWAY from the crowd. Sweat dampened her face. Heat poured right through her. Her temples thumped with her heartbeat and she felt a migraine coming on. This commute on the metro, all these people—day in, day out —sometimes it got the better of her.

She braced herself against the wall. It was cool against her fingertips and yet, at the same time, she knew how revolting it was —caked with fumes and dirt and other people's skin. It was enough to make her stomach turn, to make bile rise up to the back of her throat.

She listened to the steady *stamp* of people moving through the tunnels, some rushing to catch their train, others keeping to a simple march. But all of them looked ahead. Right ahead.

Fixed on their destination.

She breathed in deep several times, felt the dirty, moist, warm air clear her head a little and then she prepared to step back into the stream.

And then, just as she was about to tread onward, to catch her train just like all the others, she spotted a door. It wasn't any old door, though.

This one had a blue-and-white checked design to it, and looked clean, *polished* almost.

Compared to the rest of the doors down here, all that same dingy olive colour, this one was like a scrap of clear sky.

With a final glance back at the throng of commuters, she stepped toward it, eager to explore.

Her heart skipped a couple of beats as she reached for the door-knob. When she touched it with her fingertips it felt warm, much warmer than the air temperature.

The air seemed to hum around her. And that hum was thick in her ears, all that she could hear now. It seemed to push her downwards, shove her head into the ground.

Was it her surroundings? The overwhelming heat?

Was she ill?

She thought about letting go of the doorknob, but when she tried to retrieve her fingers she found that they were locked onto it. And she felt her heart hop up in her chest, her fingers draw even tighter round the doorknob.

She twisted round, thinking that she'd call out to one of her fellow commuters, one of those stuck in the steady stream. But when she tried to speak, her throat was dry, and impossible to manoeuvre.

As if her hand was being controlled by some outside force, she felt her wrist twist hard, and the doorknob mechanism *snick* and turn.

And the next thing she knew she was tumbling through the blue-and-white checked door and into a profound, and all-consuming darkness.

THE DARKNESS beat down on Jenny.

She felt herself bustling from side to side, falling freely through thin air. Arms sprawled. Heart in her mouth. Legs just a pair of useless masses of bone and skin.

Maybe she screamed, but she really couldn't tell. Whenever she opened her mouth the air seemed to strip the words right off her tongue. Her lungs felt like a pair of punctured bellows.

As she fell and fell, her skull became something resembling an echo chamber. She found thoughts and images splashed over her consciousness. And no matter whether or not she opened or closed her eyes, those thoughts and images remained with her as she tumbled.

Perhaps what she most expected was to land with a stomach-crunching *splat*.

But that wasn't what happened at all.

She felt herself gradually, and gently, as gentle as feathers tickling the balls of her feet, slow in the air. It was like hundreds of invisible, puffed-up cushions were all conspiring to retard her descent. They were so gentle that she felt her stomach slowly return to its natural position, and the blood which had previously been hammering to get out through the strands of her hair, return to her brain.

A much more feasible part of her body for blood to be.

And, before she really knew what was happening, she had come to a complete, and resounding, halt. It took her a few seconds to realise that, without really having had to think about it at all, she was now set—quite steadily—on her two feet.

In fact, it was with the act of thinking about standing when she found herself swaying a little, from side to side. She used her arms to try and reassume her balance, and did so.

Where in hell's name was she?

The darkness was just as thick as a morning fog, and just a chilled.

She thought about taking a step, but just thinking about it sent near-paralysing tingles up from her calves to her thighs, and her heart beating like a jackhammer.

She widened her eyes, trying to see something.

Anything.

But it was in vain.

She had no way of knowing just how long she stood there, staring into the gloom, wondering just what had happened to her. Trying to fathom just how she'd left her everyday— by all means of measurement—*mundane* morning commute, and ended up here. In what, to all appearances, seemed like a bloody great big hole.

How long had she been standing there?

An hour? Two hours?

It felt at least that long, if not longer.

She reached for her handbag, which she'd left dangling from her shoulder.

Somehow it was still there, and she'd just not had the presence of mind to reach for it before. She guessed she'd been pretty much occupied with this darkness, and all that falling business. Now she had refound herself, she unzipped her bag and withdrew her mobile phone from inside.

She flipped her mobile off its Standby mode and glanced at the clock there.

Ten past eight in the morning.

So, it was stuck at pretty much the same time as when she'd opened up the door, and then dropped through the Earth to this spot where she now stood.

She glanced at the signal reading.

Not surprisingly, she had precisely zero signal bars.

She replaced her useless mobile back inside her handbag and then let loose a hard sigh.

Curiosity, this was where it got you.

No sooner had she replaced her mobile back in her handbag when it struck her. The answer to this gloomy conundrum. She dug about for her mobile again, and then flicked the screen.

It shone its luminous glow over the darkness.

To begin with, her eyes being so accustomed to the complete darkness, she couldn't really make out anything. And then, all of a sudden, it came clear.

She saw the concrete floor stretching out all around her.

She spun round on the spot, shedding the glow from the mobile phone over the surrounding area.

Just concrete.

She tilted her head up and shone the glow upwards, to see where she'd fallen. But she could only make out the wall leading up there. The glare from the mobile phone screen was nowhere near strong enough to look back up to where she'd dropped from.

She brought the light to bear on the walls surrounding her.

No lift.

That was to be expected.

But no ladder either?

What kind of maintenance shaft was this?

Then again, she supposed that the door *had* had an odd blue-and-white checked pattern, so she probably deserved just about all she got.

The one good thing about this, having the mobile phone light to see by, seemed to be that at least she could see where she was putting her feet.

At least she wouldn't be rendered to this one spot for the rest of eternity.

Or if, as she was beginning to think, time as she knew it had all stopped for the time being, then she wouldn't spend the rest of eternity standing here worried about stepping in a puddle of sewage while wearing her work shoes.

And so, using the light from the mobile phone, she made her way along the ground, still feeling a little dizzy from the darkness springing up on all sides of her. She tried to put it out of her mind, concentrating only on her forward momentum.

The air in this place smelled of the sea, like the foam off the crest of a wave. But that didn't make any sense. She was miles away from the sea here.

Miles and miles away.

As she headed on she caught that saltiness at the back of her mouth, and she thought about how everything, all the sewage in the city, had to go out to sea at some point.

Could it be that the sea stretched its way this far underground?

All of a sudden she had a combined wish that she'd have paid a little more attention in geography-slash-physics-slash-chemistry . . . slash-whichever of the previous would help her understand a little more about this situation she found herself in.

As if just to tantalise her poor pragmatic thinking a little more, she noted the gushing sound of water nearby. She could hear it off somewhere to her left. And, not having anywhere else in mind to head, she went in its direction.

A light breeze blew against her cheeks, blew a few strands of hair into her mouth. She spat it out and then clawed at the remaining hair, freeing it from her lips.

And then the light from her mobile phone glinted off the river before her.

3

YUP, this river pretty much stank of the sea.

Jenny caught the whiff of the seaweed, mixed in with that ridiculously pungent saltiness, and she could feel the spray splashing itself against her skin, sending a slight chill round the collar of her jacket.

She listened to it rush on, watched it splutter along.

She tried to take in the scope of the water, to see just how far it reached. But holding up her mobile phone to try and work out just how expansive the stream was proved futile.

The glow from the mobile phone screen only reached to about five or six metres into the expanse of water. And stopped there.

As if reminding herself that this was some sort of an odd dream, she glanced back at the clock on her mobile phone screen and saw that—inevitably—it remained stuck at ten past eight.

So, she was wandering about in some kind of stopped time loop.

Or she was going completely crazy.

She let loose another sigh, trying to work out just how she'd get out of this place, and then she decided to follow the stream. If nothing else it would lead her to the sea, she reasoned.

And so she trod along the concrete floor, following the stream which continued to rush on beside her, indifferent to her, just as all good bodies of water should be, and she wandered on for what felt like hours and hours.

But when she checked her mobile, just like before, she saw that no time had passed.

With the river showing no sign of ending, she was on the point of seriously considering tossing herself into that roaring torrent, half-wondering whether it might crush her to death and so release her from this suspended animation.

Or, failing that, it would lead her out to that sea, and away from this underground place.

It was a good thing, then, all things considered, when she heard the sound of muffled, slightly drunken male voices coming from up ahead.

She quickened her pace, glad at the prospect of finding other people down here.

Even if they *were* drunken males.

She held her mobile phone ahead of her, still using the screen to guide her way, now actively using it to help her *not* stumble into that gushing river beside her. She listened to the slap of her flat work shoes against the concrete floor, and the echoes coming back at her. Made her think that, perhaps, someone, a shadow of herself, might be hot on her heels.

Darkness really does have a habit of playing tricks on the mind.

The voices got louder, more raucous too.

There was the *screech* of chair legs against the concrete floor.

A slight shiver ran down Jenny's spine, and she held back, trying to see up ahead of her with the faint glow of her mobile phone screen. But it was no good. She would just have to keep heading onwards, otherwise she would never meet with the people down here.

Just as Jenny caught the form of a cobbled-together, wooden table—a rectangular, standard table shape—she heard a loud *crack* followed by a grunt and then the unmistakable sound of human flesh slapping against a hard surface.

In this case, concrete.

She held back, still unable to make out the full extent of the scene before her. She felt her breath chilling in her throat, the rush of blood to her head. And, for the first time since she'd been falling, she felt the chilling full-on thread of fear ebbing its way through her veins.

But she held still, mobile phone still held before her, and waited for things to play out for better or for worse.

Perhaps she expected someone to leap from the shadows, to grab her from behind, to slit her throat, or, more easily, toss her into the stream gushing along beside them, and apparently leading out to the sea.

But nothing happened.

There was silence, or at least something approaching it.

The man who had apparently been thrown to the floor was doing some heavy breathing, every so often sniffling, while the chair legs screeched again out there somewhere in the darkness, as the other man—apparently the man who'd knocked the first to the ground—retook his seat at the table.

Feeling her heart batter against her tonsils, Jenny carried on, concentrating on putting one foot in front of the other, trying not to think about what she'd sort of witnessed.

Soon enough the glow from her mobile phone screen lit up the area before her. And it did very little to settle her nerves, if truth be told, because what she saw before her, quite distinct and unambiguous, despite the low level of light she was working with, was a man sitting at the table, a half-full flagon of ale beside him, and a fan of cards in his hand.

That wasn't what most unnerved her, though.

Looking back on it, she supposed that what unnerved her most was the fact that the man, sitting at the table, one fist clasping the flagon of ale, and the other taking in the cards fanned in his hand, was wearing a neat, prim, blue-and-white checked summer dress.

4

JENNY FOUND HERSELF caught in mid-stride when the man glanced up at her, looking at her over his cards. If he registered anything about her, then she missed it completely, because just as soon as he'd looked her over, he returned to look over his cards again, slipping one out and reorganising it within the fan of cards he clutched in his fist.

Jenny glanced to her side, to the man lying on the floor.

The floored man was wearing the same summer dress, the same blue-and-white checked design, and his eyes were closed tight, and his chest was rising and falling. A strand of blood trickled down from his right nostril.

Apparently the other man had knocked him out.

Pretty cold, it seemed.

Jenny looked back to the table, just in time to see the man sitting there take a swig from his ale. She looked to the bulging muscles of his, gleaming with what she supposed to be sweat in the light from her mobile phone screen. His skin was slightly tanned, sun-kissed, although his complexion was quite fair.

The man was squinting now, and he snapped his head round to look at Jenny. "D'you mind?" he said.

"Uh," Jenny said, feeling her blood run cold.

Who was she kidding? If this guy took it into his mind he could snap her like a, uh, well, like the proverbial twig.

The man squinted on at her. He rested his elbows on the table as he stared, poking her nose in her direction too.

The whole composition would've been quite rude if it hadn't been for the fact that the man was wearing the summer dress, and the fact that this was quite clearly a totally ridiculous situation she found herself in.

In this context, that 'rude' stare of the man's just seemed pretty much par for the course.

The man snorted then released the handle of his beer flagon and held his hand up to shield his eyes. "You mind switching off that light, or wha'?"

Jenny realised that he was referring to her mobile phone. To be honest, switching off the lights was just about the last thing on her mind now that she'd stumbled across this situation.

He tilted his head slightly. "Come on, eh?"

The floored man emitted a groan.

Jenny glanced in his direction, saw that he was twitching in his knocked-out state. Soon he would wake up, and that would make two of them. Although she hoped that whatever . . . *heated* discussion the two men had had would mean they wouldn't pay all that much attention to her.

She didn't switch off the mobile phone, but she did move to hold it down at her thigh.

This seemed to please the man holding the cards enough. At least he stopped looking at her with his thunder features and returned to perusing his cards.

Jenny wondered just when this card game was going to resume, given that the man's opponent looked pretty much out for the count. Then again, she guessed that, wherever the hell she was, time wasn't all that important of a commodity.

"Pull up a chair, if ya like," the man with the cards said.

Jenny considered this offer. What was really on the table for her right at the moment? Sure, she could wander on a little longer, follow this river to wherever it ended up, or maybe cut away from it and stumble into the darkness a while.

She glanced back at her mobile phone screen, saw that the battery was still full.

Not only full, but it hadn't even twitched down so much as one per cent of its life.

Whatever this place was, it did wonders for mobile phone batteries.

"Make ya mind up then, ya stayin' or ya goin'?" the man said, still staring at his cards.

Jenny thought things over another second, and then, seeing the floored man was still . . . well, pretty much *floored*, she took up the offer, and sat herself down in the chair at the head of the table.

She placed her mobile phone down beside her, the screen still shining its dim glow over the table top. And she saw, to her left, where the floored man had sat, that his cards remained there, fanned and face-down. She glanced to the man sitting with his cards, and said, "Uh, do you have any idea what place this is?" She paused a second, then said, "Where are we?"

The man continued to look over his cards, took another swig of his ale, and then glanced at her briefly. "Damned if I know."

She knew that she had to ask, if she didn't she'd be thinking about it for ages after she got out of this place, annoyed at herself for not having asked . . . if she even ever did manage to get out of here. "Why're you wearing that dress?" she said.

The man finished the last of his ale, and then set the flagon down on the table with a slightly woody *thud*.

It made Jenny flinch a little. But she retained her composure.

He stared at his cards, still fiddling with their positions as he went. "In the airport on our way to a stag do, innit?"

She caught a whiff of musk, that sour, sweaty, man smell. It sent a slight, involuntary thrill through her, and then she got herself back under control. "Is that right?"

"Uh huh."

And that seemed to be the end of the conversation. If Jenny wished to leave it here, she was sure that she could continue stumbling onwards deeper into the darkness. But now she'd come this far, found *someone* to speak to, she couldn't pass up the opportunity. It might mean the difference between her finding her way out of this place or getting herself trapped here for all eternity . . . which was what seemed to have happened to these two men.

The floored man made a slobbering sound and turned over onto his side. But he remained unconscious.

"Do you have any idea of where the river leads to?" she said.

The man grunted something incomprehensible.

"Sorry?"

The man looked up at her, over his cards, irritated. "Nah."

"Oh," she said, then stared down at the table, to the hardened wood grain there, and she observed the . . . well, there must've been several thousand rings from ale flagons, and she didn't spend much time wondering just how long it'd taken to get all those branded there.

She sucked up some more courage to continue her inquisition. "And you've never thought to follow it at all?"

The man snorted. "Nah, why should I?"

"Don't know, don't you want to get out of here?"

The man slammed his cards down on the table, face up.

A shred of fear passed through Jenny's stomach, and she stared down at those cards, at the cards the man had laid out there. Four of them.

Ace of hearts.

Ace of spades.

Ace of diamonds.

Ace of clubs.

When she looked up at the man, she saw that he pressed his lips tightly together, and his forehead had knitted into about a dozen frown lines. And then, just as she was on the point of asking another question, she saw a tear glisten in his eye, and then break free and roll down his cheek. Before Jenny could say anything to console the man, he dropped his head down onto the table, cradling his head in his folded arms.

His shoulders shook with his sobs.

As if in response to this outburst she noted, out of the corner of her eye, the floored man twitch in his sleep.

Jenny guessed now was as good a time as any for her to move on.

5

J ENNY WANDERED on her way again for what felt like several hours. She stuck to the stream, although she wasn't sure why. She would've said that she didn't want to get lost . . . if she hadn't been lost already.

She heard the splashes over her shoulder, and she turned back, phone in hand, glow emanating out into the darkness.

Her breath hitched in her throat as she waited for whatever was coming. And her mind flurried with ideas, thinking of anything from a porpoise, to a submarine, to that man in the blue-and-white checked dress doing butterfly stroke to catch up with her.

But it was something much more fathomable.

A boat.

A *canoe*, in fact.

Sitting inside the canoe was a young girl, perhaps seventeen or eighteen years old. She wore a flappy-eared, knitted hat, and she made great big strides with the paddle, jerking the canoe along, following the torrent of water.

Jenny was undecided whether or not she'd speak to the girl, when the girl made up Jenny's mind for her, calling out.

"Hey!" the girl said. "You there!"

Jenny stood rooted to the spot and waited.

The girl paddled her canoe up to the bank of the river, right up beside Jenny. She was panting a little, and her sweaty skin sparkled in the light from Jenny's mobile phone screen. Jenny caught a whiff of tuna on the air, and noticed that the girl had a sandwich on her lap.

That made Jenny's mouth water a little.

Whatever it was about eternity, or whatever place this was

where she found herself, it didn't mean that she could get away from her hunger pangs.

The girl held the canoe to the side of the river, using her paddle to keep it in place.

Jenny looked over the canoe.

It was a pretty sad-looking vessel, kind of that same olive-green as the service doors to the metro—the *normal* service doors, anyway. And it had been patched up several times with white and black stuff. The technical name for that *stuff* escaped Jenny.

Blond hair jagged down from beneath the girl's foppy-earred hat, and she looked up at Jenny with deep, azure eyes. Her features were delicate, her nose obscenely breakable, and her lips fragile and a light—almost bloodless—shade of pink.

Jenny realised that the girl was taking her in, while Jenny took her in.

The girl stared at Jenny then said, "So, you getting in, or what?"

Jenny looked down at the canoe.

There was no doubt that there was room for the two of them there. She peered in over the side of the canoe, and saw that there was a light splash of water in the base of it, but it didn't look too dramatic. From the little she knew about boats, she guessed that anything short of a raging torrent gushing in through a hole in the side wasn't much of a problem.

Then she looked back along the bank of the river, back in the direction she'd come. She tried to peel back the darkness beyond the glow of her mobile phone screen but could not. When she turned back to the canoe her mind was more or less made up. But she still needed that final shove.

"Where're you headed?" Jenny said.

The girl shrugged, pouted a little, in a very little girl sort of way. "Dunno, just gonna follow the stream, I guess."

"You don't know where it goes either?"

"Nah, I was just bumming about in my grandparents' house, down in the basement, when I found this door—"

"And, don't tell me, it had this strange, out of place, blue-and-white checked design to it?"

The girl smiled, showing off her pearl-white teeth, and a dab of her pink tongue. "Yeah, how d'you know that?"

"Just instinct," Jenny said, glancing back over her shoulder.

"You're the first person I've met down here, uh," she closed one eye and her brow wrinkled, "well, other than those two guys playing cards a way back." She pursed her lips and frowned. "They were both wearing summer dresses. That same design as the door I came through to get into this place."

"You didn't stop to speak to them, did you?"

The girl shrugged. "Just for a second or so, but one of them was knocked out on the floor, or something, and the one sitting at the table just seemed busy with the playing cards in his hand."

"Yeah, that's just how it was like when I was back there."

The girl nodded to Jenny's hand. "You brought your phone, that was smart."

Jenny looked down at her phone, she was sure, with an expression that suggested she'd completely forgotten it was there at all. Then she said, "I wouldn't say that it was much of a choice, I was on my way to work, you see."

The girl cracked another smile. "So you coming along with me, or what?"

Jenny looked round her again, trying to see whether there might be some other options forthcoming, but seeing that there weren't, she hoisted herself over the side of the boat, and took up her place behind the girl.

Hardly had she sat down when the girl thrust her hand in her direction, and dialled up her smile a couple of notches. "Name's Hannah," she says.

"Jenny," Jenny replied.

And then they pushed off from the concrete bank.

6

JENNY FOUND another paddle in the bottom of the boat, resting against her leg. She lifted it up and was surprised by how much it weighed. It was metal, and slippery in her grip. The metal was cold against her skin, and slightly wet. She guessed that it'd been resting in the bottom of the boat for quite a while, getting soaked.

For some reason it occurred to her to sniff the water on the paddle. She wasn't quite sure what she'd expected, perhaps that it would stink of sewage, or sea water, like the salty smell that filled the air of this place. But, no, it smelled fresh. So fresh, in fact, that she trusted it enough to give her paddle a surreptitious lick. And right then, inevitably, Hannah turned round and looked at her.

They exchanged a glance, and Jenny let her paddle fall back down into her lap.

Hannah frowned at her. "If you're thirsty you can use this," she said, ducking down to her side, before producing a plastic camping mug and then handing it over to Jenny.

Jenny took it from her. "It is all right to drink this water, then?"

Hannah shrugged. "Hasn't done me any harm." Then she turned her back to Jenny, and picked something up from her lap, and Jenny saw that it was the wrapped tuna sandwich. Hannah got busy unfurling it from its wrapper, and then, with a clean tear, she parted it in two and handed one half over to Jenny. "There you go," she said. "Almost forgot about the sandwich. I had it in my pocket when I went through the door."

Jenny thought about refusing the sandwich, and then those hunger pangs returned, and she knew that she was physically, and emotionally, incapable. So she took the sandwich from her.

The business of tuna-sandwich eating done, they paddled on

hard along the stream. Hannah managed to convince Jenny that they were better off paddling into the centre of the stream, that its current would carry them more quickly where it was deepest. And although Jenny didn't quite like the idea of being over a deeper portion of this unfathomable river, she decided that they might as well get wherever they were going a touch quicker.

And, after all, she'd only a little while ago shucked the idea of doing herself in by throwing herself into the river. So maybe she'd get a chance to test her hypothesis for escaping this place if a particularly fierce wave or current happened to strike them.

Earlier on Hannah had been sticking to the river bank, not having a light herself she hadn't wanted to get herself lost in the swirling torrents of water. But now that she had Jenny with her, and her mobile phone, they could afford to be a touch more adventurous.

Soon enough, though, the light from Jenny's mobile phone became unnecessary.

From up ahead a strong light shone, and Jenny's first thought was that it was the sun, shining in through the tunnel . . . or wherever they were.

In fact, it grew from being a great help in lighting up the water, to becoming nothing short of a great nuisance, almost blinding Jenny as she paddled on, now feeling the sweat dampening the back of her shirt.

But they paddled on, regardless, heading for the light.

Jenny noticed it while Hannah ducked her head down to give them a few hefty strokes, to propel them on a little harder. She saw, up ahead of them, a wooden dock, sticking out into the water. And, up on top of it, a figure silhouetted by the shining light behind.

Jenny nudged Hannah, and showed her just what they were headed for, and together they paddled harder, incentivised now that they had a solid location, somewhere to actually aim for.

Someone to aim for.

As they got closer and closer, and Jenny allowed herself to rest up a little from the frantic pace of the paddling, she took in more details.

The dock there was cobbled together out of various pieces of wood, much like the table back with the men in dresses. Jenny could see the nails sticking out from it now, at all angles. And, up on top of the dock, the figure there came a little clearer too.

And for a second Jenny couldn't believe her eyes.

It was the man in the dress from earlier.

7

JENNY WASN'T SURE why she should be frightened, but she was. She recalled how the man back at the table, with the cards, had slammed his flagon down hard. That had been what had startled her, but he'd never actually taken a swing at her . . . not *directly* threatened her in any way.

But that didn't mean she wasn't going to be cautious.

Their momentum was so great that, even when she delivered the warning to Hannah, it was too late for them to slow down. The current, too, had picked up around them, and they were now driven relentlessly towards the dock.

Jenny kept her eyes fixed on the figure sitting up on the dock, on his large, muscular frame, and that summer dress with the blue-and-white check design flowing off him. And as they grew closer she came to the realisation that it *wasn't* the same man from earlier.

Looking harder at his features she realised that he wasn't the floored man either.

This was another man.

Another man in a summer dress.

As they slipped over the water, Jenny lost herself in the rush of water along the side of the canoe, and her heart beating gently in her ears. She felt herself slick with sweat. A cool breeze blew in from the opening to the tunnel. She shuddered a little, and felt for a couple of morsels remaining from that tuna sandwich with her tongue, explored round her teeth.

Got that fishy, salty taste again.

The man sitting up on the dock made no movement towards them, he just followed them with dopey eyes, his chin resting on his fist, his elbow resting on his knee.

If Jenny had had to guess as to his current mental state, she would've said he was bored. Nonetheless, she refused to take her eyes off him as the canoe butted up against the wooden dock.

Hannah caught the dock and pulled them into it.

Jenny saw a soiled rope coiled up on the dock, and she hauled herself out of the canoe, grabbed hold of it, and then tied it up to the iron ring at the front of the vessel.

There was no telling whether or not this was a dead end.

Even with that bright sunlight—?—flowing ahead of them.

They might need the canoe again to get back out onto that water.

When they'd got themselves up onto the dock, Jenny noted that the man in the dress had made no movement towards them. He wasn't even looking at them now. He was just resting his head on his fist and looking out across the endless water, out into the gloom, to the final point where the light coming into the tunnel faded out, mixed into darkness.

Jenny's eyes had grown accustomed to the bright light now, and she no longer needed to squint or hold her hand over her eyes to shield them. She looked to Hannah, and Hannah looked back to her. Then Jenny looked off into the distance, into the source of the light.

It was certainly an opening, an escape from this place, and she was almost decided to head for it when she got caught by the suckers' disease.

She found herself feeling sorry for this dopey-looking man in a dress.

With a quick glance to Hannah, Jenny moved towards the man, stopping when she was half a dozen paces away from him. She drew a breath, enjoying the fresh air which blew in through the opening to the tunnel. "Do you know what's outside?" she said.

The man remained facing away from her, still staring out across the water, and then, slowly, as if his neck was fixed on top of some kind of a cogwheel, he turned round to face her. He remained grim-faced, that same expression the other man had worn. "I'm the groom," he said.

"Oh," Jenny said, feeling something inside her chest twitch slightly. "Then you must be looking for your friends."

The man gave her a murmur and then turned off to face back off into the gloom.

Jenny felt Hannah nudge her in the small of her back. She could tell that Hannah was growing anxious, that she wanted them to get on with it, for her to get back to her grandparents.

But Jenny felt a last shred of charity within her.

She spoke to the back of the man's head now. "We ran into your friends, they're a way back, off in the darkness. If you like you can take our canoe, down there"—she nodded to the canoe, still teth-ered to the dock—"if you just follow the bank of the river you'll get to them."

The man looked back to her again, his movements still as slow as ever. For a few moments she was certain that he hadn't under-stood her words, and was about to repeat herself, when he gave her a tired, almost indistinct, "Thank you," and then, with weary and exaggerated movement, got up off his haunches and lugged himself off down the dock, in the direction of the canoe.

Jenny watched as he got into the canoe, and untethered himself. And then, just as sombre as he'd always looked sitting up on the dock, he pushed himself off with the paddle, and then drifted off into the water—apparently the current didn't provide any opposi-tion to his gentle thrusts of the paddle.

But Jenny guessed that was just what you got in a 'magical' place like this.

Together with Hannah, Jenny watched the man disappear, canoe and all, into the all-consuming gloom, and listened to the splashes of the paddle disappear.

"Can we go now?" Hannah said, sounding a little impatient.

8

THE WAY into the light at the end of the tunnel was somewhat rocky. Which was to say, as they headed up on their way, up the steep incline of the slope, there were boulders, and loose pebbles beneath their feet.

That put paid to any lingering wish Jenny might've had to save her work shoes from too much undue strain. But, she guessed, she'd just be happy to get out of this place now.

It was just *weird*.

Although it felt like they'd been walking hours and hours into that unrelenting bright light, Jenny knew that if she had bothered to check her mobile phone then she would've seen that no time at all had passed.

So she just didn't bother.

The slope got steeper still, and Jenny lost her footing a few times, finding herself stumbling over the rocks, listening to the pebbles skittering off behind her. But she stayed upright, and focussed on her goal.

And before she knew it, the land beneath her feet flattened out, and they were getting towards the exit to the tunnel.

It was funny, the way the adrenalin kicked in all of a sudden, the way that her heart skipped harder, and her breathing got shallower. The light bathed her in its effervescent glow, and she could hear Hannah stomping along beside her.

Having someone else here just made it seem real.

More real, anyway.

They kept on their way, and soon Jenny observed the concrete of the tunnel enveloping them slink back and a bright blue sky emerge above their heads. And then the bright sun sitting pretty up in the sky.

Jenny glanced over at Hannah, saw that she was smiling, and only then realised that she, too, was grinning.

They emerged from the tunnel and onto a beach. Sand sprung up all around them, light-coloured, *sandy* sand. And Jenny felt her heart flutter up to her throat.

In the near distance she could see palm trees, and a little further off a twinkling blue sea. A gentle breeze blew, the same one, she supposed, that she'd felt back inside the tunnel. She heard a bird—a parrot?—let loose a *screech* from somewhere.

And then she tasted the salty sea air, felt it cling to her nostrils, wiping away whatever memories she'd had of the metro, of all those crammed-up people all bustling to catch their train. Then, as they walked on a little way further, she felt the sun warming her skin, crisping her up in its glow.

She glanced over to Hannah, but Hannah was fixated on some point in the distance, on something that Jenny couldn't immediately see. And then, following Hannah's gaze, looking to just where those blue eyes of hers looked, she saw the rock face.

It was a granite-grey rock face, with birds ebbing out of it, from the nests they'd built into the crevices. And then, as Jenny allowed her eyes to stray further south, down the rock face, she saw, nestled right at the bottom, at ground level, a single door.

A door with a blue-and-white checked design.

The same door that she'd gone through to escape the metro?

As Jenny turned to look at Hannah, she knew just what was playing out in her mind. Over there, that door, that was the way back to their real world—to their real life. And just as Hannah parted her lips, ready to say just what Jenny expected her to, Jenny interrupted her, beat her back just for a second.

"How about we spend a little time here," Jenny said, "You know, just a little while?"

Hannah's eyes sparkled in the dazzling, cloudless day all round them, and then she pressed her lips together and nodded vigorously.

"Come on," Jenny said, hearing the smile in her voice, and she reached for Hannah's hand and they went dancing down the sand, headed for the crisp, clear, waveless water.

WHAT A DEGREE IN CLEMENCY TAUGHT ME

*I n compliance with the policy of our prospectus, we open the door for
alumni to share their personal experiences at Polisbrudge University in
the hope that it might help to shine a light on the path into magic which*
—hopefully!—*awaits you.*

What a Degree in Clemency Taught Me
Shaun A Hypersgrithe

Most prospective students reading this will, no doubt, have been
struck dumb by the Open Day displays they have recently experienced. They will have been struck by the bright lights and the
transforming of people into objects, and vice versa; the steaming
concoctions of this potion, or that one; the taming of these magical
creatures, and those magical creatures. However, what is much
harder to communicate to prospective students is that which does
not make a neat and tidy five-minute song-and-dance.

Yes, prospective student.

I speak to you of clemency.

If you have managed to get past that last line, as few do, then
congratulations, perhaps you do have what it takes. Because it is
certainly one thing to flourish a magic wand about the place—
setting fire to this, and that—but it is quite another to be able to
demonstrate restraint.

To be able to say no to those little urges that drive us magical
folk into such barbarities as those which, I am sure, you have
observed in both the mortal and magical news mediums.

Although perhaps there is something to say for turning an

entire technology firm into an ant farm, as we all witnessed in this past year . . .

Those who deride clemency often mark it down as being 'one of those sixties fads'. They decry that it is a 'dumbed-down version of magical philosophy' which offers even worse career prospects . . . outside of our *dear* Academia, of course.

But clemency is neither of those things. And I hope to be able to explain why.

So, when you write 'clemency' along that dotted line, what is it that you can expect from the course? Well, unlike such rough-and-ready courses as alchemy or enchantments, classes in clemency consist mainly of restraint. With your tutor you shall discuss various situations one might come across in day-to-day life. And how you should handle them considering that you have—*one should hope!*—magical blood flowing through your veins.

To give such an example, let us imagine that you are running late for a train, and that you find yourself in the queue for a ticket. The queue is long and winding. Nobody pushing or shoving, just an awful lot of tutting and shaking of the head behind backs, in that very peculiar British way.

In such a situation, you would have many options open to you.

Why, you ask, are there no automatic ticket-dispensing machines?

Well, in this theoretical example all such machines have been rendered inoperable. They won't turn on, let alone dispense a valid ticket for your required journey.

The queue is the only option.

So then, how about magicking all those people away—wouldn't that do?

Of course it would, to the bog-standard graduate of enchantments.

Perhaps a potions graduate would be packing some sort of a

stop-time vial within the inside pocket of his jacket for such occasions. And just a light sprinkle in the air would be enough to halt the Earth on its axis for a matter of moments. For the time it would take such a specimen to reach the front of the queue. It would be so easy, wouldn't it?

But might we ask what strength it would take for us to slither along with the queue?

For us to stand up alongside the mortals, and to wait in line just as patiently as they do, as if we had no magical abilities at all?

Restraint.

Responsible wizardry.

Clemency is nothing less than a mind-set—a device, if you will —which offers the graduating magic practitioner the skills to survive in the real world—in the mortal world. It teaches them the skills to live alongside, to live in peace, and to tread lightly despite the majestic powers we possess.

Could anything instil better values in a person than a degree in clemency?

I think not!

It is all very well to ask what clemency might be able to offer you, prospective student, but, in reality, the question you should be asking yourself is:

What can I offer clemency?

AUTHOR'S NOTE

Thank you for taking the time to read one of my books. If you would like to hear about my latest releases you can sign up for my newsletter here: www.raymondsflex.com

Thanks for reading!

Raymond S Flex

Only The Moon
A Short Story Collection

www.ingramcontent.com/pod-product-compliance
Lightning Source LLC
Chambersburg PA
CBHW020941260626
47169CB00006B/1764